COCO CHANEL

&

IGOR STRAVINSKY

COCO CHANEL
&
IGOR STRAVINSKY

Chris Greenhalgh

RIVERHEAD BOOKS
New York

RIVERHEAD BOOKS
Published by the Penguin Group
Penguin Group (USA) Inc.
375 Hudson Street, New York, New York 10014, USA
Penguin Group (Canada), 90 Eglinton Avenue East, Suite 700, Toronto, Ontario M4P 2Y3,
Canada (a division of Pearson Penguin Canada Inc.)
Penguin Books Ltd., 80 Strand, London WC2R 0RL, England
Penguin Group Ireland, 25 St. Stephen's Green, Dublin 2, Ireland
(a division of Penguin Books Ltd.)
Penguin Group (Australia), 250 Camberwell Road, Camberwell, Victoria 3124, Australia (a
division of Pearson Australia Group Pty. Ltd.)
Penguin Books India Pvt. Ltd., 11 Community Centre, Panchsheel Park,
New Delhi—110 017, India
Penguin Group (NZ), 67 Apollo Drive, Rosedale, North Shore 0632, New Zealand
(a division of Pearson New Zealand Ltd.)
Penguin Books (South Africa) (Pty.) Ltd., 24 Sturdee Avenue, Rosebank, Johannesburg 2196,
South Africa

Penguin Books Ltd., Registered Offices: 80 Strand, London WC2R 0RL, England

The publisher does not have any control over and does not assume any responsibility for author or
third-party websites or their content.

The epigraph from "Dedicatory Poems" is from *Poem Without a Hero* from *You Will Hear Thunder*
by Anna Akhmatova, translation by D M Thomas, published by Secker & Warburg. Reprinted by
permission of The Random House Group Ltd.

Previously published in the UK as *Coco and Igor* by Review Books in 2003
First Riverhead trade paperback edition: December 2009

Library of Congress Cataloging-in-Publication Data

Greenhalgh, Chris, 1963–
[Coco and Igor]
Coco Chanel & Igor Stravinsky / Chris Greenhalgh.— 1st Riverhead trade
paperback ed.
p. cm.
Originally publsihed: London : Review, 2003, under title: Coco and Igor.
ISBN 978-1-59448-455-1
1. Chanel, Coco, 1883–1971—Fiction. 2. Stravinsky, Igor, 1882–1971—
Fiction. I. Title. II. Title: Coco Chanel and Igor Stravinsky.
PR6057.R372C63 2010
823'.914—dc22
2009037875

PRINTED IN THE UNITED STATES OF AMERICA

10 9 8 7 6 5 4 3 2 1

For Ruth, Saul, and Ethan

And behind it will come a man
Who won't become my husband, yet together
We shall deserve such things
That the twentieth century shall stand agape.
> from *Dedicatory Poems*, Anna Akhmatova

CHAPTER ONE

On the morning of her death, a Sunday, Coco went for a drive.

It was the one day of the week she allowed herself off from the shop. Wrapped in a woolen tweed overcoat against the January cold, she sat by the window behind the chauffeur. The face revealed in the driver's mirror belonged to a woman in her late eighties. Her eyes were scribbled with blood and her lashes long as an ostrich's. Deeply wrinkled, her skin had a swarthy toughness from too much sun and too many cigarettes.

"Where to, Mademoiselle?"

"I don't care. Around."

Picking up speed, the car achieved an even hum on the cobbles. Dwarfed in the backseat, Coco was conscious of the empty space around her. A smell of leather rose from the seats. She felt their coldness penetrate her bones.

"Disgusting, isn't it?" the driver said.

"What?"

He gestured with both hands: "This."

Coco muttered as she put her glasses on. Outside, she registered an untypical stillness. Trees hovered remote as ghosts. Bells rang flatly from the Madeleine, answering in widening circles of sympathy the damp sound of church bells around the center of Paris.

Slowly she noticed something shocking. The streets were strewn with the bodies of dead birds. Pigeons, mostly. With alert, nervous movements, she glanced first through one side window and then the other. Her face broadened like a shadow as she spoke. "Stop! I want to get out."

The chauffeur pulled over. His peaked hat slid against the ceiling as he hurried to help her from the car. Though sprightly for her age, she was still frail enough to require the support of the young man's arm in stepping onto the pavement.

Her eyes blinked quickly as she gazed around. The avenue was littered with the stiffening, horny-toed corpses of birds. Limp-winged, predominantly gray, with dabs of lilac and rhythms of iridescence in bands around the necks, there they lay—their heads to one side and their beaks slightly open. Feathers from the wings of one bird flapped slackly close to Coco's foot.

"My God!" A ripple of disgust ran through her. For an instant, she felt faint.

Beyond she witnessed a scene of even greater carnage. The dried-up bowl of a fountain was choked with the ragged bodies of dead birds. More mute lumps of feathers asterisked the sandy paths.

"What happened?" she asked, both puzzled and upset.

"The mayor ordered a cull. They were filthying the city, flying into windscreens, spreading disease . . . ," the young man answered matter-of-factly. "It was in the newspapers," he offered, careful not to imply any rebuke.

"But how . . . ?" Her arm attempted to include the scale of the massacre in its sweep.

"They put poison in the basins of the parks overnight," the driver went on. "Just strong enough to kill the pigeons." He rubbed his black-gloved hands together. Wearing a thin liveried suit from the Ritz, he was beginning himself to feel the chill. Seeing her hungry for more information, he added, "They chose Saturday night so the streets could be cleaned up easily on the Sunday."

Coco noticed for the first time the small army of street-cleaning vehicles already humming about the empty city center. She watched men in pale blue overalls going about the grisly business of sweeping up the dead birds. They looked, she thought as they raked them in, like gruesome croupiers.

Her limbs went watery, and she clung to a railing to steady herself. Little flecks of rust rubbed off on her gloves. A voice spilled from inside her head, a self-directed chatter, a high insistent hum like tinnitus in her ears.

"Mademoiselle?" The driver tilted his head to listen, but guessed correctly that the words were not for him.

Her thoughts had bent elsewhere—toward Igor and his collection of birds. How he'd grieve to see such destruction, how he'd be appalled.

She was startled to discover how much she missed him, even now. She had seen her partners die off one by one to leave her old and unaccompanied. But he was still alive.

Odd, she pondered, how they had both survived when almost everyone else had gone. She remembered with tenderness that summer they spent together in her villa, Bel Respiro. Fifty years ago now.

She was surprised to experience an acute sense of loss. A feeling of emptiness possessed her. For a second everything around her seemed so hollow she guessed that, tapped, the world might ring.

The driver stood there patiently, awaiting her next whim. "Mademoiselle?"

Absently, "What?"

Recalled to the present, she saw the trees withdrawn to a twiggy thinness and heard the silence now that the bells had ceased. She grimaced as the odor of decay reached her nostrils. "I'm cold," she said with a sudden shiver. Her fingers were numb inside her gloves. Pulling her coat close about her, she indicated with a quick movement her wish to return to the car.

As they raced away from the curb, she struggled to fix her jiggling image in the mirror of her compact. "Slow down!" she muttered. "What's the hurry?" That buzz again inside her head like a wasp inside a jar.

On a day that seemed robbed of it, she felt an urgent need for color. Even the normally gaudy advertisements seemed bleached of their high gloss. Shakily she maneuvered her lipstick across the taut line of her mouth. Painted a vivid red, her lips made a small bright space in the morning. As she peeled off her gloves, though, she saw her fingers, stringy and distinctly gnarled. Repulsed, she looked at them as though they were claws, as though the liver spots that afflicted them were a kind of leprosy.

Coco loathed being old. It was the inevitability of it she hated, the sheer relentlessness—like the leaves turning brown, or the cold coming. Effortlessly feminine all her life, she felt at this instant less like a woman and more like just another parcel of skin and bone poised to rejoin the earth. It had all happened so rapidly. Her life was a blur, and had rushed by like the city now pouring past the window of her car.

They returned swiftly to the Ritz, where Coco kept her own suite of rooms. The chauffeur escorted her through the broad revolving doors.

"I can manage from here," she said, dismissing him. "I'm not a cripple."

With a look of contending tolerance and respect, the young man touched his cap and returned to the car outside. Coco felt the change of temperature as the warm air touched her face. She walked on through the foyer, where a vacuum cleaner moved in giant arcs across the floor. She took care not to snag her feet in its wire.

"Good morning, Mademoiselle Chanel," declared the receptionist above the din. Warily, and without looking around, she raised a hand in acknowledgment. The wire, she knew, was all part of a conspiracy to trip her—like the slippery beeswax and the rugs they kept adjusting in her room. They were all out to get her, she was convinced. She smiled at the thought that she had thwarted them again. Another attempt to kill her hindered.

As she walked on toward the elevator, the stench of the

Grill Room hit her. Asparagus, this time. And if it wasn't asparagus, then it might be tarragon, or garlic. It always reeked of something. She blamed the maître d. He did it deliberately, she was certain. She'd told him several times how dreadful it was having to smell other people's food. He never listened. It was his way of assaulting her, she decided; his strategy for forcing her out.

Like an avid mouth, the lift doors slid open. Behind her they sucked shut.

By this time Coco's maid, Céline, had arrived and was busy making her mistress's bed. The key scratched in the lock and Coco opened the door to her room. Standing to attention, the maid wished her good morning. Without stopping, Coco looked her up and down.

"Your hair's too long, girl, and your skirt's too short."

Céline smiled, half apologetically touching her Alice band and tugging the hem of her miniskirt down. She knew she was being teased. "It's the fashion," the girl answered.

"What do *you* know?" Coco snapped.

Stung, Céline resumed making the bed. But Coco, placing a restraining hand upon her arm, and in a gentler, almost beseeching tone, said, "I'm very tired now." She leaned for support upon one of the brass balls at the corners of her bed and saw herself drastically foreshortened in its orb. She felt dizzy. "I want to lie down," she said.

The maid nodded in response. Her lips leaped into a smile. Coco removed her coat and glasses and, with a kneading effort of her feet, her shoes. Then, sitting on the edge of the bed, she allowed her head to be set back on the pillow. She flinched a little in bringing her legs around.

She had never felt so exhausted. Seeing the dead birds had depressed her. Her stomach churned. Why did she have to confront this on her one day off? She needed rest before returning to work tomorrow. And there were a hundred things she had to do. She'd barely completed the spring collection, and already she was being pressed to submit designs for the summer. The pressure was on. Every year it seemed to get worse. Her mind busied itself with the following week's schedule, the details merging in an impossible knot. Her head began to throb, and a tension entered her shoulders. She felt the blood run sluggishly to her fingers and her toes.

She closed her eyes and allowed herself to recollect those months she spent with Stravinsky in her villa. The century's greatest composer living with its most celebrated couturiere and perfumer. Who would have guessed it back then? Who would believe it now?

Slowly the tendrilous threads of her current worries unraveled, giving way to memories of sunlight and birdsong, and the re-created spasms of a piano. Its rhythms melted imperceptibly into the rhythms of her breathing as she slid into a dream-filled unconsciousness and succumbed to a deeper sleep.

An hour later, she awoke feeling a sharp star of pain in the center of her chest. The pain spread rapidly to crowd her arms. It pressed down from above upon her skull. Fear seized her body. Her mind filled with alarm. She glanced about. She saw first the white walls of her room, then the table by her bed. A glass of water rested there next to a white-shaded lamp and a triple icon — a present given to her by Stravinsky half a century before.

The white walls. The bedside table. The icon. In panic, Coco tried to orient herself from these reference points. Still she felt displaced.

Abruptly something tilted within her. Her eyes took on a wild expression. A surge of panic filled her head.

"Lift me up quick!" she called to the maid, who came running through from the adjoining room. A feeling of suffocation rose in her throat. "I can't breathe!" Her eyes were wide with fright. Her voice in her own ears sounded disembodied. As though they were responsible for choking her, she pulled at the white pearls strung around her neck. Then unpreventably the room began to spin, whirling in a vertiginous blur. Suddenly covered in sweat, her skin gave off a sharp scent of agitation. The spokes of her irises seemed to form wheels.

Céline grabbed a syringe and with difficulty broke open a vial of Sedol. "It's all right, I'm here now. Everything will be fine."

Coco's eyes were drawn to a corner of the room. Her body drained of color. Her fingers lost their responsiveness. A high note penetrated her ears. "They're killing me!" she managed, with a half-silent scream.

At that instant, she felt something irrevocable fit itself around her. And in the split second before the shape of her death took hold, as the last swatches of oxygen escaped around her brain, a million images processed themselves on a palpitating membrane at the back of her eye.

It all came with the vividness of a mirror, the diffused brilliance of a dream. And in this final clarity she recalled how he looked as he bent to kiss her, remembered sharply his dark eyes.

She mumbled, "So this is it!"

Then she fell through into silence. Her face lost its shape. Around her, all she could see was darkness. Everything went blank.

Too late, Céline held the syringe fast against Coco's arm. Gently she set it down. With a calmness that surprised her, she closed Coco's eyes.

CHAPTER TWO

·1913·

Coco is at home in the rue Cambon, dancing spiritedly to some inner music. She sings to herself in front of a full-length mirror.

> *Qui qu'a vu Coco*
> *Dans l'Trocadéro . . .*

Her lips are red, her eyes sable, and her white dress cut with ravishing simplicity.

Several times she turns around, admiring her slim silhouette. She relishes the crackly sound her petticoat makes as it rubs against the silk of her gown.

All week she has labored over that gown, fussing over the collar and fretting at the hem. Now at last she is happy. It looks stunning, and she knows it. Daringly the tiered white silk hangs well above the ankle. Straight and fluted at the bottom, the dress flows like a liquid down her body.

She has slaved away, too, at the hat: a broad brim of black silk and a close-fitting crown. She pulls it on, and tucks away a lick of hair, adjusting the brim until it hangs at a sly angle. A shadow falls across one side of her face.

Où? Quand? Combien?
Ici. Maintenant. Pour rien!

She laughs. Then tilting her head back amorously, she dabs with a single finger a smidgen of perfume along her throat.

Tonight she is excited. She has never been to a proper concert before. Several works are to be performed, including the premiere of a piece by Stravinsky. Everyone will be there. It should be an event. She feels a little apprehensive, but experiences, too, a heady intensification of her senses. Each whisper of her dress, each spore of her perfume, every texture that answers the touch of her hands seems to sharpen her awareness of the world around her.

The telephone rings, startling her. She chooses to ignore it. The driver is already waiting, and she doesn't want to be late. She checks she has her purse, her parasol. The ringing stops. She hopes it wasn't Caryathis saying she couldn't come. Too bad, she thinks, thrusting her hands into her gloves.

Descending the stairs, she's conscious of the mannequins in the shop below. Cold torsos. Plaster heads. Stiffly angled hats and gowns. She feels the heat they are cheated of. Everything seems so quiet and still here compared to the agitation she feels inside. As she opens the door, the smells and noises of a raw spring evening greet her. She takes several head-clearing breaths, inhaling deeply as if receiving a new draft of life. Then with a quick movement, she steps into the back of the waiting car.

It is dusk. Lighting-up time. All around her the city's lamps are coming on. A garish splendor spreads across the capital, extending up the avenues' spurs. Trams thunder along the boulevards. Omnibuses bully up the streets. The car moves slowly past the bar at the back of the Ritz and turns sharply right into the rue St. Honoré. Idling for a moment in the traffic, the driver swings left down the rue Royale toward the Place de la Concorde. Crossing one of the tram tracks at an angle, the wheels protest with a high-pitched squeal. The car jolts from the impact. Coco's hat bumps against the roof.

"Careful!" she scolds the driver.

"Sorry."

"Pfff," she says, waving him away.

She has been working hard all afternoon. Her stomach feels empty. She has not eaten now for several hours. She wouldn't feel comfortable in that dress otherwise. And she's keen to meet her escort. It's all been arranged by a friend.

Her nervousness and the motion of the car mix together to make her giddy. The sensation of weightlessness stretches to her limbs. It's odd, but as the car swerves lightly this way then that, she has the sensation of being drawn toward something by invisible lines of force. For a moment, she sees herself from above. She feels as if she's floating.

Finally, after picking its way through the crowds in the avenue Montaigne, the car comes to a stop. Glued to a Morris column is a poster advertising Stravinsky's *Rite of Spring*. The theater doors have opened. The flower sellers are out in force. Hundreds of people are milling around.

Coco slides out into the humming darkness. The air

seems warmer here, as though charged. Something sappy in the atmosphere attracts her. The magnolia and horse-chestnut blossoms are brighter almost than the lamps.

She straightens her dress and retilts her hat to an even perkier angle. Something in the energy and press of the people here tells her this is going to be a good evening. She can sense the attention of men's eyes upon her. Her feet seem scarcely to touch the floor.

Feeling almost bridal, she glides toward the theater's lights.

Igor sits in his dressing room at the theater, cutting his toenails.

A scatter of crisp little moons has gathered on the carpet, the color of old piano keys. Snip. Bending low, he examines the horn of his big toe. He has cut too deeply with the cuticle scissors. A tender ridge of skin has been exposed, leaving a raw pink crescent around the nail.

"Shit!"

Worse, his new shoes pinch him, and he winces as he stands. As he pulls on his shirt, it snags around his head. The buttons are fastened too high. For a split second he experiences the panic of being smothered. His vision whites out. He hates it when that happens. It reminds him of the time as a child he fell under the ice. Headless, he wrestles his arms into the sleeves. Then he reaches up to release a button, and surfaces with a gasp.

Looking in the mirror, he's half startled as always by this extension of himself, this twin who appears with features tweaked, and with left and right queerly reversed. Testingly he raises a hand to his face. The motion agrees with a feeling in his cheek. He feels relieved, but when he coughs the noise seems to come from somewhere outside him.

Agitated, he paces around. His fingers perform complex phrases against his trouser legs. He worries that the first violin and flute parts are ill-balanced. He worries that the score is too difficult and that the dancers aren't fully prepared. The choreography is too intricate, he thinks. It doesn't correspond to the tempo. He's told Nijinsky over and over, but he doesn't listen. He seems incapable of counting properly and has trouble even clapping in time. Meanwhile Diaghilev just indulges him; his lover, of course, can do no wrong.

Igor has a premonition of terrible notices and humiliating reviews. His mouth feels scratchy; his throat is dry. He realizes he needs a drink and reaches for his glass. His spectacles catch the wine's vibration as it rises to his lips.

Simultaneously the muffled sound of tuning instruments insinuates into the room: scales being played, little runs undertaken, complex passages rehearsed. Unperformed, the music seems not to have left him yet. Its jerky rhythms twitch inside him, pulling invisibly at his limbs. Something fluttery in his stomach responds to the woodwinds warming up. He hears the stepwise descending minor chords against a rising sequence of sevenths in the bass and experiences that queasiness again. His hands, he sees, are mottled. He feels almost sick with fear.

In his mind, he pictures members of the orchestra crowding the stage, thickening like knots of crotchets. He tries not to think about the audience. A restless spectator himself, it unsettles him to conjure the image of hundreds of people filing in.

In truth, he's not quite sure they're ready for this. He almost pities them, sitting there. Little do they suspect what's going to hit them. God knows how they'll react.

His thoughts turn toward his wife, Catherine: his ideal listener. He half wishes she were here. She's pregnant with their fourth child. And sick with it. Instinctively he feels for the small studded crucifix she has given him as a good-luck charm for tonight. It's in the left breast pocket of his jacket: the side where his heart is. Detecting its shape through thicknesses of cloth, he smiles, uplifted. He wants that new baby. And yes, let it be another girl as Catherine wishes. Two of each would be good, he thinks; the symmetry appeals. He wants tonight to be a triumph for her. He takes out the cross and kisses it.

In a couple of hours it will all be over, he reminds himself. But the success or otherwise of tonight's performance could determine his whole future. His career as a composer may well depend upon it. In the last few years he's done some good things; he's been noticed. It's said that he's promising, that he has potential. And now, at thirty-one, he knows it's time for him to realize it. He needs a big success to secure his reputation, to establish himself; to arrive. If tonight goes well, it could be the turning point.

A boy knocks. "Five minutes, sir."

As he drains the last of the wine, slivers of red flicker across his face. He worries at his cuffs. For the hundredth time, he looks at the clock. He waits until the spasms of the minute hand reach twelve.

He takes one final reassuring look full in the mirror and brushes some imagined fluff from his lapels. He crosses himself. "Please, God, let it go well!"

Then, breathing in deeply, he opens the door. The music grows louder. His heartbeat quickens. He strides toward the hall.

Inside the new white marbled splendor of the Théâtre des Champs-Élysées, a line of gilt runs around the walls, connecting the boxes with a golden thread.

The whole of fashionable Paris is here. Everywhere there are perfunctory introductions and enthusiastic reunions between the coolest of friends. Laughter swells and ebbs locally. Fans ventilate the flames of gossip. Rumor and counter-rumor run along the aisles.

Coco has dreamed many times of taking part in such a spectacle, but now she's anxious that she might not fit in. She feels ill at ease among these strange rich people. The opulence has a corrupt whiff to it. She looks closely at the men in their dress-suits tweaking their ringed fingers, and at the women swathed in turbans or strangled by ostrich boas.

They regard her, these women, with disapproval, without quite knowing why. It's not as if she's more decorative. Quite the opposite. If anything, the cut of her clothes is austere. The simplicity of her gown, its restrained elegance, makes them seem almost gaudy by comparison. And her silhouette is intimidatingly slim. It is this quality of understatement, this *nonchalance de luxe*, they find disrespectful. The impression she gives is that she's not even trying. It seems so effortless, they feel undermined.

To Coco, conscious of the disdainful glances she's attracting, these others seem ridiculous in their plumes and feathers, their taffeta gowns and heavy velvet dresses. If they want to look like chocolate boxes, then that's their affair, she reasons. As for her, she prefers to look like a woman.

The place reeks of privilege. Diamonds glitter and pearls scintillate under the chandeliers. For a moment she feels like an imposter. Memories of her upbringing crowd her brain: a dilapidated farmhouse, a tiny allotment, mother sick and father absent, her brothers and sisters squabbling like so many hens in the yard. A dim recollection comes to her of carrying armfuls of carrots back from the fields. Now, though, surrounded by the supremely rich and casually amused, it is as if she has imagined it.

Believing in her own blessed destiny, she has closed her mind to that part of her life and reinvented herself, conceived herself anew. She has used men, and been used by them. She has learned how to operate in business and succeed. Everything she's achieved, she has worked hard for—and no one works harder, she is sure of that. And here she is; she's made it happen. Her shop is thriving. There's a trail of men all besotted with her. And among her clients she can count some of the richest women in France. Not bad, she reflects, for an orphan girl. She will *be* someone; she knows it. She will cast a shadow. These women will see.

Her nervousness evaporates, to be succeeded by a sense of exhilaration. As programs are consulted and small talk pursued, she feels her confidence grow. She even begins to cultivate a slightly absent air, meeting several people with whom she shakes hands coolly, responding indifferently to their eager smiles.

The odd thing is, she had not meant to go. She is acting as an escort for Charles Dullin, who refuses to be a gooseberry in the company of her dance teacher, Caryathis, and her rich German lover, von Recklinghausen. So she is making up numbers. She has to start somewhere and is glad of the opportunity to be involved. For Coco then, tonight is a kind of debut.

Seated next to her, Charles is gentle and attentive. He's an actor, and she has long enjoyed his performances and admired him from afar. Meeting him up close, though, he's not as spontaneous as she'd supposed. She finds him quite ordinary, in fact. Without a script, he has little of brilliance to say. And if he intends to make an impact, it's too late. He's been upstaged.

Already tonight, Coco has felt herself on the edge of a sensation. For Caryathis has arrived hatless, and with her hair severely cropped. Scarcely able to contain her delight, Coco asks, "My dear, what have you done?"

Caryathis explains. A few days previously, rejected by a man to whom she was rashly attracted, she had attacked her hair with a pair of scissors. Then, feeling compelled to make a gesture, she'd tied the tresses in a ribbon, and hung them from a nail on the man's front door.

"It was too long anyway. It just got in the way."

Coco says, "But you look like Joan of Arc!"

"I know, and I'm going to play the part to the full."

Coco is thrilled by the reaction Caryathis elicits from the gathering throng. The trajectories of most opera glasses confirm her as the focus of a thousand eyes. Sitting next to her, Coco glories in the attention. There's something about the two of them together that invites scandal, she knows. She's quick to grasp the impact they have on those around them.

On her other side, Dullin already feels superfluous: a bit-part player, an extra. She was meant to be *his* escort. Now it's beginning to seem like the other way around.

Coco asks him to hold her program. She knows she is being watched. And while Caryathis whispers into her ear, she fans herself languorously, training her lorgnette on the company below.

Eventually the buzz of conversation distills into a hush. Coco sees Serge Diaghilev, impresario of the Ballets Russes, seat himself in the front row to applause. The conductor and principal violin are greeted warmly. Soon the lights are dimmed.

From the darkness float the haunting tones of a bassoon. Six high notes reiterate a simple motif. The notes dissolve quickly into birdlike twitterings, thin scratches and scrapes. Blind flurries come from the woodwind, followed by scurryings on the strings, and then the entry of thumping brass. Great swerves of sound.

The transitions are so abrupt that Coco jumps. The instruments come together in choppy, dissonant chords. The spastic rhythms alarm her. She's heard nothing like it before. The notes collide at odd angles and set the air vibrating strangely. Warned to expect something different, she has not prepared for this.

Then, against a painted backdrop of rolling steppes and sky, twelve flaxen-haired nymphs in black disport themselves and resolve into a provocative tableau. Adopting primitive positions—knees touching and elbows clamped to their sides—the dancers lurch awkwardly in time to the beat.

One of them makes an obscene gesture. Coco is shocked. Other spectators let out howls and shrieks. People stamp their feet. As the nymphs join in the crude movements, many in the audience begin to hiss. Not far from Coco, an old lady stands, her tiara almost slipping from her head. "This is a disgrace!"

Onstage the dancers continue, whirling around and coming together in startlingly ardent friezes. They leap about in splendid abandonment. The music harshly accents the movement of their hands.

"All very Slavic!" Caryathis remarks.

One of the foreign ambassadors, seated in a box to their right, begins to laugh out loud at the spectacle. Coco takes a mischievous delight in watching the scene unfold.

A man rises to his feet and appeals for silence. A lady in a nearby box slaps a neighbor, who is hissing, across the face. Enraged, another man shouts, "Shut up, you bitches!" aiming his abuse at some of the most refined and beautiful women in France.

"That's Florent Schmitt," Caryathis whispers. "I've seen photographs he has of the composer—pictures of him in the nude!" In the dance teacher's mind flashes the image of Stravinsky naked, hands on hips, on a small wooden jetty— wedding tackle in profile, buttocks pert and muscular—a scrawny white horse incurious in the background.

Coco laughs, amazed that this kind of thing goes on in the upper echelons. The more one advances socially, it seems, the more depraved one is allowed—even expected—to be.

The audience is becoming more restive, she notices. Chords clash, and the rhythms seem ugly, foreign. To the Parisian elite, an impression of crudeness persists: of Mongolian brutishness and Tartar savagery, of herrings and bad tobacco.

And while Coco laughs along with the rest of them, something experimental and impulsive in the music chimes with her sense of novelty in being here. Like her, the rhythms seem driven. Her body feels beaten by the hammers of the piano, her skin abraded by the horsehair of the bows. The raw energy of it all feeds through her as if she's a lightning rod in a storm.

Amid the conflicting rhythms, she senses Charles looking at her from the side of her vision.

Abruptly the pace of the choreography quickens. And so does the furious energy of the dancers, who twist themselves into all manner of agonized and erotic postures. The temperature rises detectably, setting fans flapping and generating an impression in Coco's mind of trapped birds all over the theater.

The demonstrations reach such a pitch that it becomes almost impossible to hear the music. Some women in front of her are so upset—or so moved to hilarity—that tears thicken their lashes, where they mix with mascara and run in black lines down their cheeks. Of course, Coco has seen much worse in the taverns of Moulins and Vichy, where she used to sing and dance. But that was entertainment for the troops. Here, instead, it's the costive calm of the upper orders she sees being broken—spectacularly.

Charles leans so close, his whiskers brush her cheek. He wears too much cologne, she notices. He whispers something, but she doesn't quite catch it, such is the tumult of the music and the continuing uproar. She feels his hand take hers. Without looking at him, she extricates her fingers skillfully from his grip.

Where there is standing room only, the more impecunious enthusiasts are creating their own din. There is chanting and clapping; obscenities are hurled. And still the ballet carries on. To her astonishment, it is not long before fights break out around her. A few dozen people even begin to strip. Coco delights in the anarchy. The house lights, which have been flickering intermittently, go up while arrests are made.

Onstage, the prima ballerina enacts her sacrificial dance. Head tilted on her hands to begin with, soon her whole body is wracked with spasms. She jerks fiercely to the rhythms, ending in an ecstasy of trembling as she collapses on the floor.

Distracted by police whistles and startled by the sudden illumination, the conductor—a plump man with a walrus mustache—glances around at the turbulent scene behind him. Having reassured himself that at least no one is about to invade the stage or storm the orchestra pit, he keeps going, aware that dancers in the wings are desperately clapping time.

The lights go down again. Without warning, Coco feels Charles's hand upon her knee. She looks across at him. He's staring at her. Once she might have responded, but not now, not here. She recrosses her legs away from him, causing his hand to slide from her dress. Still, his touch sets off a tingle inside her, a tiny thrill.

Then, just as the indignant protests and peals of laughter rise to their climax, Coco sees a jaunty balding man, looking dapper in his dress-suit, stand up at the front. Small, five feet one perhaps, he marches down the center aisle in full view of everyone. His face shines whitely under the house lights. The dab of a bald spot glints. Hunch-shouldered and slightly bandy-legged, he strides on. Row after row, pairs of eyes turn to watch him as he sweeps heroically out of the hall. In a fury, he slams the door shut behind him. The action corresponds with a thud on the drums.

"Who's that?" Coco asks Caryathis.

"Stravinsky."

"The man with the nude pictures of himself?"

"That's right."

"Ha!"

"You wouldn't think it, would you?"

"And is he married, this Stravinsky?"

"He certainly is." Her head moves closer to Coco's as she adopts a scandalized tone. "To his cousin!"

"I didn't think that was allowed."

"It isn't," Caryathis whispers, settling back behind her fan.

The two women look at one another and begin giggling wickedly.

The orchestra and dancers battle on until the farce comes to an end. With a grave sense of duty, the principals take their bows. Members of the orchestra solemnly file out. Still buzzing, the audience swarms from the auditorium, spilling onto the streets and into the May night.

Coco emerges from the scrim. Sweating, she is glad to be out in the cool evening air. But she feels exhilarated, too, having experienced the same volatility within her that agitated the theater's tight space. A spark still lingers, lighting her eyes.

Caryathis asks, "So what do you think?"

"Astonishing."

"No, not the ballet. Dullin!"

"Oh, Charles! I'd almost forgotten." She allows her lips to sink with indifference.

Actually she did quite like him until he began feeling her knee. He's charming company, and handsome. But he's too forward, she decides; she doesn't like that. Besides, he's an actor. Actors are poor and, well, she's rich. Success has raised her expectations.

"I feel faint. I want to eat," she says. Her ears still ring with the music. Her body still hums with the vibration from the floor.

Caryathis gestures to the men. "Let's go."

Then Coco exclaims, "Hey, look!"

She directs her friend's gaze toward the magnolias. As though shaken down by the force of an explosion, she sees that everywhere the pavement is suddenly scattered with white blossoms. For an instant, struck by the theater's lights, the petals almost dazzle her.

Feeling again the excitement of a bride, she throws back her shoulders and presents her profile, poised as on a coin.

"Yes, come on," she says, "let's go."

Linking arms, Coco and Caryathis lead the way. The men follow. A chastened Charles plants his hat on his head. He pokes disconsolately at the blossoms with the steel tip of his cane.

Signaling for them to hurry, Coco adds, "There's a table waiting at Maxim's."

CHAPTER THREE

·1920·

Frustrated by his lack of access to a piano, Igor fingers a dummy keyboard in his hotel room in Paris. Reduced to silence, he sits on the floor with the keyboard ranged across his lap. His feet press at nonexistent pedals. His youngest son, the ten-year-old Soulima, sits next to him, fascinated by the odd bridges his father's hands make as they noiselessly span the keys.

"Can I have a go now?"

"Not yet. I haven't finished."

"When will you finish?"

"Why don't you watch and try to get the pitch?"

Soulima accepts the challenge. He hums along, his voice approximating the modulations in tone signaled by Igor's fingers. His voice cracks as he reaches the upper notes.

Igor laughs. "That's pretty good."

"*Now* can I have a go?"

Igor ruffles his son's hair. "All right."

He loves the boy, his big guileless eyes and little upturned nose. Motioning him to sit on his lap, he supports the keyboard with his knees. He notices how Soulima has inherited his long fingers, delicate and fine; not stubby like his brother's. His hair is thicker and his eyes darker than Theodore's, and he is, Igor recognizes, by far the more handsome boy.

"Try leaving your right hand in the same place and changing the harmonies with your left. That's it."

Watching him practice, Igor imagines the sounds generated by the pressure on the keys. That pattern of black and white.

He has felt, in his three years of exile following the Revolution — and in the two years since the end of the war — a quickening sympathy for the black keys in particular. They exist at an angle to the white notes, giving them a healthful tweak. Like these black notes, he, too, has experienced a kind of otherness. They feel like he does, slightly off center, as though the world has tilted ten degrees.

Russia has been violently tilted and he has been displaced, together with thousands of fellow refugees, by the inexorable slide westward. Now he and his family are crammed into two small bedrooms of a modest Parisian hotel. And they manage thanks only to the generosity of patrons and the meager receipts from occasional concerts and published scores.

In Switzerland when hostilities broke out, Igor had lost everything: his money, his land, and — most precious of all — his language. Denied the dignity of saying good-bye to friends, refused the opportunity of gathering personal belongings, he has yet to come to terms with his loss in any meaningful way. With the ground so cruelly pulled from under him, it still feels as if he's falling.

Catherine, his wife, has been unwell since their enforced

exile. Their two sons and two daughters are growing up stateless. But while it is true that their lives are unstable, Igor consoles himself with the thought that the family is now more close-knit than ever before. They've learned to be self-reliant, to trust each other utterly. Never in one place long enough to establish roots or make new friends, the brothers and sisters have quickly become one another's best friends. And, stripped of the support of an extended family, their parents' marriage has become the one fixed star in an uncertain universe.

"How long are we going to stay here, Papa?"

"Until we find something better."

"How long will that be?"

"I don't know yet. Not that long probably."

"I don't like it here. I want my own room."

"Well, we all have to share. You know that."

"I don't like being in the same room as Milène. She talks in her sleep and keeps me awake, and she's always pinching me!"

"Well, it's hard for her, too."

"Would we be killed if we went back?"

"I don't think so. We've done nothing wrong."

"They killed the czar and his children, didn't they?"

"It'll be summer soon. Things will be easier then. You'll see." It is a statement made more out of hope than conviction. Guilt seizes him. He senses Soulima's fingers press more strenuously upon the keys.

Igor adores his children. He admires their resilience, the way they've coped with everything that has been thrown at them, the way they just get on. For him, though, the need to escape has taken on the quality of a contagion. Having fled his homeland, he feels impelled to keep moving. He experiences it as an itch. There's a momentum now within his bones that wants to fling him on. And because there's no longer a place he thinks of as home, he relishes that sense of elsewhere, however remote and obscure. To remain in one place too long generates an acute sense of restlessness within him. He longs for the perpetual motion of the truly free—the frictionless existence.

Flight.

He feels imprisoned here. Living in such cramped conditions has strained as well as strengthened family relations. He longs for more time and space in which to compose. He's done some fine things in recent years. *The Nightingale* was well received, and *The Soldier's Tale*, but he's lacked financial backing. He needs a structure to his life, some kind of support. At the moment, he finds the two givens of his existence—his family and his work—slide against each other like continental plates. Inevitably fault lines have appeared, causing the odd division between the children and their parents and local eruptions between the parents themselves. Quick-tempered, he recognizes that he can get upset for no reason. And then he feels angry with himself for taking it out on the ones he loves.

He prays each night for a change in their fortunes, for a new turn in their luck. Meanwhile, he awaits news from Diaghilev on future funding for his projects. A couple of new commissions would do the trick, would bring in some revenue and allow them to live more comfortably. Now, though, pressing soundlessly at the keys, he guides Soulima's trusting hands in runs along the board.

This, he reflects, could be the way he'll spend the rest of his life. A faint shudder runs through him at the prospect of teaching counterpoint to bored housewives and adolescent boys.

Soulima ceases playing. They both stop to listen as the room is wrapped in a high-pitched hum. The rain that has been falling all day has suddenly become torrential. They can hear it drumming in the gutters. With his son, he moves close to the open window. Stray droplets leak through, touching their hands and faces, spotting the marble floor. He places first his palms then his brow against the cool of the glass.

He remembers as a young boy blowing on a five-kopeck piece and holding it to the frost-covered window until the heat of the coin melted through to a view of the world outside. And for a moment in his head a vanished world revives. As if glimpsed through a peephole, his childhood is revealed: promenades down the Nevsky Prospekt, sleighs drawn by elks, and light from a porcelain stove in a corner of his old room. As if on a miniature stage, there is St. Petersburg, the city of his birth: the Admiralty's spire and the Maryinsky Theater with its dome and perfumed interior. It all comes back to him. Fragments catch and gain a shape, like the bits of scenery he used to see transported to the theater down the Krukov Canal. And with these privileged glimpses drift the smell of tar, the odor of wet fur from his hood, and the distinctive fragrance of Mahorka tobacco lingering on the streets. Accompanying these smells, and overwhelming them, are the city's sounds: the clangor of streetcars, the cry of vendors, the awkward rhythms of hooped wheels on cobbles, and the sudden crack of a whip.

Abruptly thunder shakes the room. Igor feels the window shudder against his forehead. In an instant the peephole closes over. The odors fade, the rhythms recede, and with a start he remembers where he is: in a cheap hotel, in exile with his family, his breath in this cold room clouding the glass.

Catherine emerges from the bedroom and hands Igor a musical manuscript, heavily annotated.

"How was it?"

"I've written it all down."

He looks at her quizzically.

"It was good."

"Just good?"

"It's too controlled," she concedes. "It needs more energy. Passion."

He flicks through the pages, reading some of her comments and looks up, a little hurt.

"You want me to be honest, don't you?"

"Nothing gets past you, does it?"

"I'm hun-gry," Soulima complains.

Rain falls like the long train of a mauve gown over Paris and its environs. The city is infused with an odor of damp. Streetlights shed vague halos on the pavement. Into one of these pools of light steps Igor, shaking out the wings of his umbrella.

He arrives with customary precision on the dot of eight o'clock. He apologizes to Diaghilev on behalf of his wife, who cannot attend owing to ill health. The damp weather is doing her no good, he says, and the little one, Milène, is sick at the moment, too.

By contrast, Igor feels galvanized by the downpour. The spring rain always does this to him—that sense of renewal and the impression, irresistible amid fresh blossoms and the scent of lengthening grass, of things simmering away. He wipes spots of rain from his spectacles and pushes his hair back with his hand.

"To take away the chill . . . ," Diaghilev offers, pouring him a glass of wine.

"Thank you," he says, putting his handkerchief away.

The guests tonight are mostly émigré artists associated with the Ballets Russes. Also present are José-Maria Sert, a Catalan painter, and his French wife, Misia. A man of seignorial charms and passions, Sert comes over and pumps Igor's hand. "Good to see you again." His mouth opens a gap within his beard.

"Likewise," Igor says.

Misia approaches. An inveterate socialite, her combination of wealth and beauty has made her as influential as she is distrusted in artistic circles. Despised by many as a treacherous meddler, she has always been good to Igor, helping him through the lean months following his exile. They greet each other with respect as well as a faint wariness. She receives his kiss with a little hint of the proprietorial. He bestows it with the courtesy of a subject introduced to his queen.

"I see your husband is here," Igor says.

"Which one?" she asks, laughing.

Coco arrives an hour late, just as they are about to eat. Her tardiness is compounded by the fact that, of all the guests, she has the least distance to travel. The rue Cambon, where she lives, runs parallel to the rue Castiglione, where Diaghilev is staying. She apologizes with a flourish and in rapid French that Igor has trouble following. She dismissed the driver early, she says, intending to walk, but then the weather was terrible, so she waited for it to let up, but of course it never did. She shrugs winningly and is forgiven. A maid takes her hat and coat. Her hair matches the blackness of the dress she has on.

Old friends, Coco and Misia exchange sisterly kisses. Diaghilev gives her a hug. They met the previous summer in Venice through the Serts.

"Delighted you could make it." For a stout man, his voice, Coco is reminded, is pitched surprisingly high.

He has put on weight, she notices, since she saw him last. His fingers are plump around his several rings. A lush double chin rests on his necktie, which is fastened at the throat with a fat black pearl. As he bends low to kiss her fingers, she sees again the white streak that runs like a flaw through his dark hair.

He proposes they postpone the meal while Coco dries herself. But she will have none of it.

"At least accept a towel for your face and hands."

Blinking, she dabs at her pinkened face and rubs her hands vigorously. While she does so, Diaghilev introduces her to the rest of the guests. "I'd like those of you who don't know her already to meet Gabrielle Chanel. She designs the most exquisite clothes."

"You're too kind."

She feels nervous among this gathering of talent. A certain entrepreneurial verve, though, makes her seem animated and vibrant.

"And what can you tell us of the latest fashions?" Diaghilev asks, offering her an entrée into the conversation.

"Hemlines are going up, and waistlines coming down," she says, hitching up her knitted skirt.

"Let's hope the two soon meet," says José, winning a dig in the ribs from Misia and drawing a chorus of laughter from everyone else.

Coco is seated opposite Igor, who rises to shake hands over the table. She's an attractive black-haired woman, he notices, with carbon-dark eyebrows, a wide mouth, and a little tipped-up nose. He feels, as their palms make contact, a low current shoot through his body. His fingers tingle, having experienced a mild electric shock. He gazes first at his charged hand and then at Coco in astonishment. It's from rubbing her hands on that towel, he thinks.

Coco sees him recoil a little and wonders if he's fooling. She regards him quizzically. Her first impression is of a man trying too hard to appear bohemian. She finds his neckerchief comically debonair. The cigarette holder seems a dandyish accessory, as does the monocle he has just put on.

"I see your name everywhere," he says, reestablishing his grip on her hand.

"And I never stop hearing yours."

He's as short as she remembers him from seven years earlier, though a little balder perhaps. Close up, she notices his teeth are bad, and his smile is tight-lipped to conceal the fact. But she notes with admiration his large hands and broad knuckles, his long clean manicured fingers. He has the scrubbed white hands of a clinician — in contrast to her own, which have been coarsened by years of sewing.

With perfect courtesy, Igor presses her fingers to his lips. They stare at one another for a moment, the way strangers do on the Métro. Her smile chases him around the table. She senses his reluctance to release her hand. Embarrassed, she gasps, "This looks fabulous."

Between them, the table is prepared for a feast. Each place is laid deep in silver cutlery. At both ends of the table huddle flasks of vodka and carafes of wine. Whiskey decanters in the shape of the Kremlin make their own bronze square in the center of the table.

Two maids bring in the food. Glistening hams, salads, salvers of caviar, Black Sea oysters, mushrooms, and swordfish are unveiled. Igor cracks his fingers, stretching them as though about to launch into a demanding piano solo.

Candlelight fills the tables. Conversations are struck up. The talk is of music, opera, ballet, and the day-to-day gossip concerning the arts. Diaghilev reminds the company how Igor was arrested recently for urinating against a wall.

"Well, it *was* Naples!" Igor says, in his defense.

Diaghilev adds, "And what about the time you were arrested on the Italian border during the war?"

Coco asks, "You were arrested again?"

"The man's a common criminal!"

"Really, Serge, your guests will form a very dim opinion of me."

But he tells the story. While searching his luggage, the guards had found a strange drawing. Igor claimed it was a portrait by Picasso, but the guards refused to believe it. All those squiggly lines—they'd never seen anything like it before. Instead they concluded the sketch must be a secret military blueprint or a coded invasion plan.

"You're obviously very dangerous," Coco says.

"They let me go eventually, and the portrait was sent on later." He takes a long swallow of wine.

"It must be worth a lot now," she says.

Igor purses his lips and makes a so-so gesture with his hand. All this, he knows, is a prelude to the real reason Diaghilev has assembled his guests tonight: his wish to revive *The Rite* again early next year—eight years after its initial *succès de scandale*. The plan is revealed between courses. Diaghilev expresses a hope that the ballet might enjoy a longer run this time. But there is a desperate lack of funding, he says, and the prospects do not look good. They need sponsors badly, he goes on. There seems something urgent now about the evening and his hospitality.

Coco notices Igor grow suddenly despondent. Discussion of *The Rite* provides an overture to his woes. He's thinking back with a shudder to that riotous first night. Some critics have since declared his music emptily avant-garde. As a victim of Bolshevism, he has a horror of being called revolutionary, even in the arts. The epithet leaves a bitter taste in his mouth. Others, meanwhile, already consider his music reactionary and bourgeois. He can't win. No one seems willing to back a revival. Worse, his wife is ill, his children growing up in exile, and his mother languishing in Russia having been refused a visa. Moreover, the Communists have confiscated his property, and all his savings have been seized.

Watching him and knowing something of his predicament from Misia, Coco realizes his dandyism is an act. It masks a deep sense of insecurity and a profound sense of loss. Loss of state and selfhood. The man is clinging on, she thinks.

It is Coco who proposes the toast. Extending her glass with casual vehemence to Igor, she says, "To *The Rite!*"

Solemnly they all raise their glasses: "*The Rite.*"

For a second, Coco dominates the space around her. The glasses, chinked, vibrate like the drawn-out note of a tuning fork, slow in dying and returning infinitely to the same true ringing note.

There's a moment's silence after they drink. Then Igor becomes conscious of voices recombining around him, conversations rushing in to fill the void. He puts a few stripped fish bones onto a separate plate.

"I was there, you know," Coco says.

"Where?"

Almost whispering, "In the audience, the first night of *The Rite.*" Suddenly the candle between them seems the only light there is.

She recalls that explosive night in the theater seven years before, and the savage rhythms that made her feel as if her insides were being pulled out. It's hard to believe she's sitting here now with the man responsible for all that.

"Really? That's extraordinary." Igor winces. A wave of self-loathing sweeps over him. Another witness to his shame.

"I remember it vividly."

Bitterly, "Me, too."

Overhearing, Diaghilev adds, "Come on, it was the best thing that could have happened."

"It didn't seem so at the time."

Coco says, "We both survived, at least."

"Yes."

There's more than a touch of the gamine about this woman, Igor decides. The insolence with which she shoots oysters into her mouth. He's reminded of the heroines in Charlie Chaplin's films. She has that southern temperament, loquacious and fiery. And there's a residual coarseness about her, too, that a late effort of breeding has softened into something fine and vital. Her mouth is wide and expressive. Her skin sparkles, vibrantly alive.

He can't keep his eyes off her, and she knows it. Yet he barely registers what she says. It's partly that he's drunk too much. But there's something else besides. They are both aware that something subtle and wonderful is going on. There's a warping of the air between them, a distortion of the usual boundaries that outline figures and make them distinct. They share a rare attentiveness, a depth of connection, a complementary reaching out. It lasts only a few seconds, but both are sensitive to a strange pull within them. At its simplest, it's a longing to be happy, and in the sympathetic tilt of their heads they each seek an answering happiness.

"To *The Rite*," Coco says again, this time only to Igor. She feels the champagne ripple deliciously like a melted icicle down her throat.

She does not address him again directly throughout the rest of the meal. Or even afterward as they relax at the table with cigarettes. She does not need to. For every incidental remark, every gesture she makes, each gleam of her eyes is meant for him alone. Her whole being dances silently in front of him in a language beyond words.

Looking at her shining hair, her dark eyes and vivid lips, Igor feels something rise from within as if to swallow him. The pearls around her neck glimmer milkily. And there's a wickedness in her that twists her whole face sideways when she smiles.

He feels a heat in being near her. A taste of something burned enters his mouth.

"The clay was warm the day God made *her*," Igor says.

Alone with Diaghilev after dinner, he experiences that familiar sense of light-headedness he gets whenever he is drunk or inspired. The image of Coco smolders in his memory. Its heat generates the softness of a mold, merging with the warmth of alcohol in his stomach.

Diaghilev pours two brandies and draws two fat cigars from a tin. He hands one of each to Igor. "She may not be from the best stock, but she's rich, Igor. Rich," he confides with a smile. "Can't you just smell the money?" He runs his nose luxuriously along one side of his cigar.

"What do you mean, not from the best stock?" Choosing

to stand, Igor twists his brandy in slow circles below his waist.

"Well, she was born illegitimate—though she'll never admit it. Her father was an itinerant peddler . . ."

"I'm sure I heard her say he owned horses. I presumed he ran a stable."

"And she went to an orphanage run by nuns after her mother's death—though the word 'orphanage' never passes her lips . . ."

"Goodness."

"Rumor has it"—Diaghilev's voice lowers as he goes on— "she even pays off her brothers to pretend they don't exist."

"No." Igor feels the brandy burn a hole in his solar plexus. With a shrug: "She's a seamstress. She likes to embroider."

"That's incredible."

Cigar in hand, Diaghilev strokes with a bent forefinger the furrow below his nose. "I suppose she's needed to be ruthless to succeed."

"I still don't understand how she became so wealthy, though."

"She had men who kept her for a while, I think—most of them, I believe, in the Tenth Light Cavalry! Then she started making her own hats and clothes, gathering a few clients. Eventually she opened a small shop. And when the war came along, all the male designers were drafted into the army and most of them were killed."

"So she was able to mop up?"

"Exactly."

Cigar smoke issues in a cloud from Igor's mouth. "She was lucky, then."

"She's talented. She works hard, too. And now she has clients like the Duchess of York and the Princesse de Polignac and employs upwards of three hundred staff in Paris, Biarritz, Deauville . . ." Rubbing the thumb and index finger of his right hand together, Diaghilev continues, "She's loaded, with no one to spend it on. And she's desperate to be accepted." He looks for Igor to complete the logic of his thoughts.

"You think she'd finance the revival?"

Satisfied, Diaghilev relaxes. He sits back and draws deeply on his cigar. "She might. She just might." He removes a bit of tobacco from his lip. "She can certainly afford it. The whole of society is clamoring for her clothes."

"So I gather."

"Half of her staff these days are émigrés. You might know some of them."

Suddenly wary, Igor says, "I'm not willing to humiliate myself."

"My dear boy, nobody's asking you to." Diaghilev gives him a trusting look.

Reassured: "She's a remarkable woman."

"Indeed she is."

"And she's not married, you say?"

"She's a modern woman in every respect."

"I'm not sure I approve."

"Oh?"

"I'm not even sure I know what it means."

"It means she's rich and single, for a start."

"What are you suggesting?"

Diaghilev holds his hands up. "Nothing, old boy. I swear it."

With a decisive movement they both finish their drinks and stab the last of their cigars into an ashtray.

"Another brandy?"

Igor shakes his head. "I must go," he says, straightening. "Thanks for a marvelous evening."

"Well, let's hope it's not been wasted."

As he pulls on his coat and scarf, Igor adds, serious for a moment, "As always, I appreciate your help."

Diaghilev nods and says, "Give my love to Catherine and the children."

"I will."

"And I'll let you know if there's any news."

"Yes, do." Embracing, they pat each other warmly on the back.

After closing the door, Diaghilev sighs and shakes his head, then pours himself another drink.

Outside it has stopped raining. The streets are damp from the departed shower. Igor pulls his collar up close around his neck. The fresh air seems to revive him. He feels as if he could walk for miles. Tapping his umbrella on the pavement, he walks back smartly toward his hotel. The sound echoes on the cobbled streets, beating time.

Half an hour later, Igor slips into bed next to his wife. In the humidity of sleep, Catherine's body smells faintly rank. Her face has taken on wrinkles from the pillow. Squiggles of hair are plastered to her brow. She's in the throes of another night sweat. And he knows, if touched, she would feel hot. But he does not touch her; nor does he wish to particularly. His body is still vibrating with the charge from Coco's hand.

Lying there, he feels as if he could stay awake forever. His eyes remain open, staring upward. The heat of the brandy still lingers on his tongue. Around him the temperature seems to have risen.

Something deep within him sways.

CHAPTER FOUR

For a few days following the meal, Coco is unable to banish the thought of Igor from her mind. She makes inquiries and discovers the parlous state of his finances. Then, on an impulse, she rings and asks to meet him. There is something important she wants to discuss, she says, but not over the telephone. They arrange to meet at the city's zoo.

Struck in an obscure way by their encounter the other evening, Igor is keen to see her again. He remembers the odd response of his molecules to her touch. Arriving punctually at ten o'clock, he clutches behind his back a bunch of yellow jonquils. In order to meet her, he has sacrificed a morning's work—something, ordinarily, he is extremely reluctant to do. But here he is at the entrance to the zoo. Coco is late and his frustration is mounting.

Restless, he displaces bits of gravel with his foot, then tamps them down again. He's not sure what to expect from this meeting. If she wants to offer the ballet financial support, why doesn't she just approach Diaghilev directly? It would be proper to go through him. What is it she has to speak to him so urgently about anyway? He's flattered, of course, but hopes he doesn't have to humble himself. Yes, he'd welcome patronage, though not at any price. He'll make it clear to her that he can't be bought. Sober, he'll show her he's not so easily won.

She arrives more than half an hour after the time arranged and offers no apology. He has prepared an admonitory speech, and is ready to deliver it, but his anger evaporates the moment he spies her gliding toward him. They smile to see each other from a distance. The chief emotion he feels now is relief. She greets him, holding out a white-gloved hand. He kisses her solicitously on both cheeks.

The other night, he gained the impression that she was much younger than him. But he knows from Diaghilev that they are roughly the same age. She's maybe a year or two younger. Thirty-six? Thirty-seven? He recognizes, though, why he was tricked into thinking this. Her figure retains the tautness of a woman still in her midtwenties. Her arms are slender, her bosom high, and she steps with a girlish lightness.

Igor conjures the jonquils from behind his back. "For you." He sees how tight her skin is around the temples, how tense and muscular are the little dents that appear at the corners of her mouth when she smiles.

As she looks down, her chin borrows a yellowish tint from the petals. She holds them in front of her with one hand like a torch. "Thank you, they're lovely." Then, chastened, she says, "I *am* sorry I'm late." A few grains of pollen adhere to her white gloves.

As if to make amends, she insists on paying the entrance

fee. They visit first the aquarium. Inside, a bluish gloom plays about the walls and their faces. The flowers turn green in the light.

Bending low in front of the tanks, they see the fishes' hearts beating visibly through their bodies. A silence ensues as they watch them and their own reflections in the glass.

Then straightening, and with the air of someone coming to the point, she says, "You know what I thought the other night, at dinner?"

"No, what?" Igor straightens, too.

"I thought, why isn't he talking to me?"

"Really? I thought I did."

"You didn't speak to me after the first half hour."

Defensive. "You could have spoken to *me*."

"True, but I chose to wait and hear what you said first."

"And?"

"I'm still waiting."

Igor is rarely scared of women, other than his mother, but he is beginning to be afraid of Coco. His mouth goes dry; he feels tongue-tied and clumsy. A tightness enters the base of his throat.

As they move outdoors, Coco sees that he's perplexed. Her joke has misfired. She knows she's spoken out of turn, and now she's worried that he'll think her disrespectful. She watches as he walks on, hands behind his back. But she needn't worry—he doesn't feel slighted: outmaneuvered, rather.

Before them, two lions describe tight circles as they pace around their cage. The bars are reproduced in shadow on the floor. Igor seizes his opportunity. Perhaps inspired by a sympathetic impulse, he begins bitterly to complain about his straitened circumstances and the cramped conditions in which he works.

He grumbles about the lack of privacy he has to endure, with him, his wife, and their four children all squeezed into a small apartment in Brittany—miles away from Paris. They are in the capital now only for a short time to rehearse his new ballet, *Pulcinella*. He feels frustrated and finds it difficult to concentrate. His creativity is being stifled. All he wants is more space to compose, and to be at the center of things. And yet the rents are so expensive.

"Everything costs so much more here," he complains.

"Do you have to be in Paris?"

"Everyone is here. Satie, Ravel, Poulenc." He seeks to flatter her by association. "It's where the twentieth century is."

"Well, you might just be in luck."

"What do you mean?" He wonders guiltily if he's exaggerated his plight.

"Would it bother you if I were to help financially?"

"It would have years ago."

"And now?"

"It bothers me even more."

The remark hits her at the right angle, making her smile.

They walk on and begin circling an ornamental lake where two besotted swans float in state across the water.

"Business has been going well recently, and my accountant has advised me to invest in some property. I've just completed the purchase of a villa in Garches. It's quiet, in the suburbs, with a large garden. Not a palace exactly, but it's not bad. I intend to spend a couple of months there in the summer—but otherwise it'll be empty most of the year. I was thinking . . ." She comes to a halt and turns to look at him. "You might like to take advantage and move in."

Fingering his necktie irresolutely: "I couldn't possibly . . ."

"If you move in by the beginning of June we could spend a few weeks there together. You'd get to know the place, enjoy a bit of a holiday, and have the space you need to work. Then for the rest of the year it would be yours." One of the swans elongates its neck luxuriously. Beads of water drip from its beak.

He looks at her to see if she means it. "That's a fabulous offer, and very tempting. I don't know that I could leave my family, though . . ."

Startled: "My dear, of course not. The villa is very big. They could move in, too. I don't suggest for a moment that you leave them behind."

Embarrassed that he has misunderstood the nature of the offer, Igor is quick to laugh it off. "It's very kind of you, but you don't realize what you're letting yourself in for. You haven't met the children yet. They're terribly noisy."

"At their age, they *should* be noisy. Besides, I won't be there much for them to disturb me. Apart from July and August, I usually stay in rue Cambon above the shop. It's up to you, but you're—all of you—welcome."

Igor is stunned. He doesn't know what to say. Of course it is a stupendous offer, and he'd be a fool to refuse. But he feels humiliated at having to rely on charity such as this. He sees the swans poised between the promise of the bank and the security of the island. Then he remembers what Diaghilev said. She's fabulously rich. Financially this is nothing to her. If she's doing it for the kudos, well, so what? It doesn't alter his integrity as an artist. She won't own him. It'll merely provide him with the wherewithal he needs to pursue his work. Besides, he's intrigued by her. He feels a sense of challenge rise within his chest. She needn't insist. He thanks her.

"It's decided, then. You'll come and stay." And again: "All of you." Her eyes are birdily alert. "Provided, of course, your wife agrees."

Rightly or wrongly, he sees this as a jibe. "She'll be delighted, I'm sure." In fact, it will be marvelous for her, he thinks, to live in comfort and feel secure. And there's a garden, too. That will be fantastic for the children.

She goes on, "How long have you been married, to . . ." After a false hesitation: ". . . Catherine, isn't it?"

A strand of hair, briefly iridescent, blows across her cheek and makes her blink. Coolly she lifts it off with her fingers.

"Fourteen years."

With a faint suggestion of condescension: "You must have married young."

"We'd known each other for ages."

"That's always the best way."

He finds it difficult to gauge her tone, but it's interesting, he thinks, the way she fences with him. He's beginning to enjoy it. She's nimble-witted, and there's an intentness about her that demands his total concentration.

She regards again his gift of flowers. With a renewed effort at sincerity, she says, "And there's no time limit. You're welcome to stay as long as you like."

The point she wants to make, of course, is that she could just as easily have chosen someone else. He should be flattered she's asking him. It's not about status or prestige, she wants him to realize. Or, at least, it's more complicated than that. She likes him, for God's sake. Ever since that night seven years ago, she's felt their destinies to be connected in a mysterious way.

He, too, feels a rare sense of affinity exists between them, a remote and unspoken bond. Someone once said it, and the idea has always appealed to him: as two people approach a street corner from different directions, what are the chances of them both humming the same tune and, as they meet, of each reaching the exact same phrase? What are the chances of that happening, and what would it mean if it did? He can't explain it, but here with Coco he senses the same dim rhythms of chance establish themselves around him, and feels invited to supply one half of that shared melody.

"Now, if you'll excuse me, I *must* get back to the shop. Baroness Rothschild is waiting for me, and I'm already late. I'll telephone again soon to confirm the details. Okay?"

It is not so much a question as a directive. Igor feels bewildered at the way she seems already to be shaping his life. He is mesmerized by her energy and charm.

They shake hands in parting. A milky stain, he sees, has leaked from the flowers onto her gloves.

Bowing gravely, "Thank you," he says.

As an afterthought, she offers him a peck on both cheeks. Then, pleased with the way things have gone, she is off. She likes being in control. And she's struck again by the immense power her money seems to wield. She finds it grants her in-

stant authority, an immediate influence. She's secretly delighted, too, at his misunderstanding of her offer.

She has come a long way in the last seven years. She recalls being in awe of him that first night of *The Rite*. Yet now
he seems within her reach. It's funny, but each time she
thinks someone is beyond her, she finds herself quickly rising
above them. She's become a snob because of it. The trajec-
tory of her ascent is so steep, she thinks, soon nothing short
of royalty will satisfy her. The thought makes her feel con-
ceited, she knows, but it makes her feel lonely, too.

Igor watches her walk slowly, and with exaggerated grace,
to where her chauffeur is waiting. He notices she does not
look back.

Deciding to stay a little longer, he sees some of the animals
being fed. The cage of a panda is unlocked for a moment as
food is taken inside. Two zebras bolt at his approach. Then he
is caught in a brief shower. Sheltering under the trees, he sees
the gentle event of the rain occur around him.

The cloudburst over, light strains through the leaves. The
earth opens up, and he breathes the odor of the lilac trees as
they release a heady scent. He feels anointed, blessed, as
though touched from above. And as the wetness leaks through
his clothes, slowly he senses the native restraint of his nature
drain away. He starts to walk more jauntily and even breaks
into a run. He has never felt the air so fresh, never felt so free.
He lifts his head to breathe in fully.

Then suddenly aware of the time that has passed, he hur-
ries to catch the Métro. Feeling energetic, he stands up all
the way. Reemerging into the light, the city seems newly
painted. Wet, the railings flash and gleam, and the tram

tracks glisten like the threads of an enormous web. He races back home, only stopping at the door of his hotel to think for a moment.

He needs to consider before rushing in to tell his wife the excellent news.

CHAPTER FIVE

Three weeks later. The first Saturday in June. The hottest day of the year so far.

Coco's villa, Bel Respiro, is nestled in woodland to the west of Paris. The house is screened by a variety of trees: elms and beeches, apple and cherry, and a flowering plum that yields a soft and oversweet yellow fruit. Asters and marigolds star the garden, contending in their scents with lilies and narcissi. Shutters lacquered in black punctuate the villa's cream stucco. A bleached gray roof adds to the pallor of the house.

In the distance along the lane, the noise of a motorized van grows louder, until suddenly it is spraying gravel as it trundles up the drive. Two large Alsatians bark and are quickly joined by five small puppies. They snap at the vehicle as it halts outside the house.

"Hey! Hush now!" Coco cries. The dogs are instantly and impressively obedient.

First to emerge are the children, made restless by the journey and excited at the new house. Then Igor alights, helping down his wife.

She wears a broad white hat to keep off the sun and is slow

to look up. When she does, the first thing Coco notices is that Catherine is not beautiful. There is something frankly mannish about her features and prim about her lips. A squareness about her jaw gives her a gruff and clumsy look. Her limbs are long and gangling, and Coco registers with surprise that Catherine is some inches taller than her husband. Coco feels for a second intensely feminine. Something kittenish enters her gestures without her willing it. "Delighted to meet you at last," she says.

When the two women shake hands, it is a strong, weight-testing handshake. Coco notes the hotness of Catherine's fingers. And though she feels her own small palm eclipsed in Catherine's grip, it is hers that is by far the firmer. She senses within herself an underlying toughness, and she wants Catherine to feel it, too.

For her part, Catherine feels alarmed at Coco's attractiveness. Not only is she rich, she is also beautiful. She fights an instinctive contempt for her as a parvenu. And there is something incongruous, it occurs to her, about Coco's smallness and the size of her house. It seems gross, vainglorious. A swollen folly.

While she has to admit that the overall effect of the villa and the garden is tasteful and restrained, nevertheless there's something about the place that makes her feel immediately uneasy. She decides she doesn't like the funereal chic of the shutters. Black! She all but recoils. And the lawn has that manufactured look like the nap of a snooker table. Such a difference from the lush and unkempt grass of her own Russian home. She misses that. It had life, a thickness to it, a texture. By contrast, the garden here appears sterile.

But there's something more about the house. Then it strikes her: it seems godless. Color for her has always been a clear sign of His presence, a symbol of His brilliance leaking through. She thinks of the stained-glass windows of the church and the tints of the living world. In its stubborn monochrome, the villa seems stripped of divinity, robbed of God. It fills her instantly with a sense of foreboding. Feeling she needs a shield, she unfurls her white parasol. Raising it against the sun, she twirls it nervously around.

Then she checks herself. It is not like her to be unkind. She may think differently when she sees inside. She must be gracious. The woman is offering them a home, after all. And anyway, these first impressions, she tells herself, may be blurred by her fatigue. The journey has exhausted her.

"I want to thank you for allowing us to stay," she says to Coco. "I can't tell you what a relief it is finally to have some stability in our lives. Especially for the children."

"It's a privilege to have you here. Everyone, welcome!" Coco declares, in a grand gesture of largesse that includes Catherine and the children in its sweep.

The politenesses have a rehearsed air about them and, despite the warm words, a wariness establishes itself in the looks between the two women. Coco immediately sees in Catherine a woman destined to suffer. She's met the type before. It's as if, she thinks, her kind sees something noble in misery and self-denial. If she's a victim, then it's likely she invites it, Coco thinks. She tries to imagine this other woman's tall, skinny body in bed with Igor, and finds she can't.

Sensitive to the tensions in this first meeting between the two women, Igor has prepared Catherine as best he can, enthusing about Coco's generosity, but setting his wife's mind at rest with unflattering references to her lack of pedigree. His wife understands that a well-bred woman would never run a business. A little charity work, perhaps, but certainly nothing commercial. That would be vulgar, both agree.

Igor asks if his wife might sit down. The jostling motion of the vehicle on the roads has unsettled her. Beneath her hat brim her eyes seem pale and washed-out, and upon her cheeks are these dark crimps as if the skin there has been pinched. Coco gestures at a bench. As he looks at her, together they cannot resist a smile. Then they turn, disturbed by a growl.

The Stravinskys have a cat, Vassily. Seeing him, the Alsatians have bristled, their tails thumping on the grass. A low growl smolders in one dog's throat. The cat arches its back, and its mouth lifts in a snarl. But they needn't be concerned, for Vassily lords it over the dogs as they sniff inquisitively around him. His miniature fierceness interests them. The threat of violence evaporates. Typical, Igor thinks.

Joseph—the majordomo—and his wife, Marie, emerge from the house. They worked previously for Misia Sert, until she changed husbands three years ago—and with them her domestics. Coco introduces them to the Stravinskys. Igor recognizes Joseph as a man of rectitude and gentleness. Marie wears an expression that is slightly more severe. But she smiles as she takes Catherine's jacket and leads her inside. Joseph follows them in, leaving Igor and Coco together with the children.

Watching them as they run and chase the dogs in ever-tighter circles, Igor says, "They're very lucky."

The two boys, Coco notices, have their mother's fair hair and her lashless eyes, while the girls have inherited Igor's darker features. Theodore shies away when Coco tries to speak with him. But after a little stiffness he, along with the others, responds energetically to her invitation to play.

"They'll be all right," she says.

The driver is unfastening the hasp at the back and is climbing onto the wagon. Appointed to help unload, Joseph comes back out.

Turning to Igor, Coco says, "Come on, I'll show you around."

The villa has several bedrooms and bathrooms. The ceilings are high and the windows deep. The walls are beige with black lintels. White floral displays accent every room. And though there are surprisingly few paintings on the walls, there is a superabundance of ornaments and books.

Coco steers him upstairs to his bedroom. Already sitting on the large square bed, Catherine mops her brow.

"How are you feeling?" Igor asks.

Catherine looks up without smiling. "Awful."

The inside of the villa is as austere as she had feared. The walls are bare as a hospital or prison. Even the furniture seems primitive. A headache slices like a thin knife through her skull. She hasn't removed her hat yet and feels a barely suppressed impulse to get up and leave.

Igor touches her shoulder lightly. Meant to be a comforting gesture, in the circumstances it seems perfunctory. But he's impatient to see the rest of the house. "Joseph is bringing up the cases. I'm just having a quick tour." He feels the need to add, "Don't worry, I won't be long."

Listening with an amused look, Coco waits outside the room. When he emerges, she points the way back down. The stairs unwind into a corridor, halfway along which she stops to open a door.

"And this is your study."

It is spacious, with a chaise longue, and two big shuttered windows at one end. He is openmouthed in admiration.

"It's south-facing," she says.

Unfastening the shutters, she flings the windows open, leaning her elbows on the sill. Birdsong floods the room, together with the noise of the children playing. Leaves flutter minutely, throwing spidery shadows across her arms.

There's a pause while he takes it in. Rooms are important to Igor. Some he feels instantly comfortable in, and his work flourishes as a result. Others he finds oddly hostile. This one has light; it has air and space. Immediately it gives him a good feeling. "It's superb!" he says.

"I hope you'll do a lot of work here."

"If I don't, I'll only have myself to blame."

There is, in their tentativeness, a reaching out, a seeking after warmth and understanding, a tone on the verge of intimacy.

In the corridor behind them, Joseph and the driver begin ferrying in the luggage. The first things they bring in are half a dozen cages containing lovebirds and parrots.

Joseph stands there, unsure exactly who to address. "Where shall I put these . . . ?"

"Goodness! Did you bring the zoo with you?" Coco asks, a little abashed.

"I hope you don't mind."

Silence hovers for a moment. He has made no mention of the birds; still less sought permission to bring them. She senses his awkwardness.

"I'm sorry, I should have said . . ."

Her first thought concerns his presumption. It's a bit cheeky to say the least. Isn't it enough that she's housing him, his wife, and four children, without bringing an aviary along? As she stands there regarding them, something seems to catch in the skull of one pistachio-colored parrot. It angles its head and squawks.

"In the outhouse for now, I think," Coco says.

She looks to Igor, who nods in rapid approbation. She's astonished by her own tolerance and tact. Given other circumstances she might have erupted. She wonders why she doesn't insist that he make alternative arrangements. But then she feels that a sense of wonder somehow accompanies the birds. A promise of the exotic.

The parrots are followed by packing cases, hatboxes, and several heavy crates. Finally, and most awkwardly for the driver and Joseph, comes the piano. Sensible of the need to deliver the instrument unharmed to the composer's study, they take great care in bringing it in. Several attempts are made to jockey it into the room before, with a measured heave and an adroit twist, it is managed. Joseph feels the small of his back and stretches himself tentatively. The driver wipes his brow as he retires.

Coco sees Igor's fingers twitch. "Don't you want to play, then?"

He looks afresh at the instrument. Without sitting he lifts the lid and rests his hands on the keys, then presses down.

Behind the piano's ashwood cabinetry and ebony veneer, he feels the hammers begin to hit the strings and set the sound-board vibrating. The room brims with music, a series of ice-bright major chords. The notes, as they mingle with the sunlight and Coco's presence, create in him a transcendent joy, a delicious sense of freedom. It is, he feels, as if he has been given back his voice.

Coco smiles, marveling at the ease with which he plays. As he continues it seems to her that something takes over and his hands enjoy suddenly a life of their own. The sinews and bones of his fingers become in her eyes one with the wood, wire, and hammers of the piano. The keys seem liquid under his fingers.

Upstairs, Catherine hears it, too. Her stomach feels hollowed out. She understands from the glad sounds that they will be staying for some time.

Late into the evening, the crates are painstakingly unpacked. The Stravinskys have become accustomed to life in transit. Wrapping paper gathers in heaps across their suite of rooms. Objects accumulate: cups, spoons, samovars, paper-weights, apothecary jars, and Catherine's prized collection of icons; plus all manner of gadgets including pocket watches, a barometer, and a gramophone with a detachable handle and folding trumpet. A large framed portrait of Emperor Nicholas II takes pride of place on Igor's study wall.

He sets the metronome going on top of the piano. It swings on a pivot in its pyramidal case. Listening to its rhythm, he feels something obscure revive within him. There's something vital in the act. A new start. A fresh beginning. For a moment, he feels marvelously enlarged.

That night, as Igor helps put the children to bed, he hears his older daughter Ludmilla whisper, "Coco," to her sister. He closes the door behind him and listens briefly as they giggle, elevating the name into a soft chant that echoes after him down the stairs. He, too, finds himself repeating her name inside his head, discovering as he does so in the hollow of those strong vowels a sweet roundness as of holes or suns.

New routines establish themselves inside the house.

Igor rises, as he does every morning, on the stroke of eight o'clock. He executes fifty sit-ups and as many push-ups until he feels the veins in his arms bulge from the strain. More stretching exercises ensue. It is a daily ritual. He prides himself on his fitness, and there's a sense of military discipline in his approach.

Breakfast comprises two raw eggs, each swallowed in a single gulp; a cigarette; and a cup of tarry coffee. The exhilaration of the day's first cigarette mixes with the coffee to create a bitter taste that lingers on his tongue.

It is his habit to work in the mornings until lunch. He works punishingly hard and can concentrate for long periods. He likes his life to be regulated by routine, and the rage for order in him is strong. The door to his study is always closed. He cannot stand extraneous noise and is not to be disturbed on any account. Only Vassily, the cat, is permitted to enter. There is a strict prohibition on anyone else.

Laid out like a surgeon's instruments on his study desk are

penknives, letter openers, rulers, india rubbers of various sizes, a monogrammed cigarette case, a pot of pencils, and a roulette instrument he has designed for drawing staves.

Surrounding Coco on her work desk are pincushions, different-sized thimbles, packets of needles, spools, and ribbons of cotton thread. On the floor lie stacks of tracing paper, balls of wool, and masses of material: silk, cambric, crêpe de chine, linen, muslin, chiffon, satin, jersey, cotton, velvet, and tulle. Everything is highly organized and has its rightful place.

While the piano sounds in one room, the snip of scissors undoes the stitching of a dress in the other. While a pencil dangles sideways from Igor's lips, Coco toils away down the corridor with pins between her teeth. While Igor presses the pedals of the piano, Coco works the treadle of her sewing machine. Both mutter to themselves inaudibly as they go on.

The third night of their stay in Bel Respiro, Igor and Catherine sit with Coco in the living room drinking tea. Outdoors, cicadas charge the darkness. An owl floats its long mournful notes across the woods.

Igor is particular about his tea. He likes it very weak and very hot. An antidote to his usual vodka. He is explaining to Coco the battles fought with successive neighbors over his playing the piano.

"One man used to beat the ceiling with a stick until the landlord complained about his damaging the plaster. Another threw pinecones at my windows, and even smashed one of them."

"It *can* be unsociable, dear," Catherine says. The couple exchange a look, hinting at the tolerance that obtains in their relationship.

Coco says, "Well, here you can play as loudly as you want!"

Suddenly the door swings open and in walks Milène. She has awoken in a strange room, terrified, not remembering where she is. Worse, in her fright, the bedroom furniture has taken on a nightmarish presence: a chair in silhouette has swollen into an ogre; a lamp shade has become a giant spider; and a nightgown on the back of the door has assumed the proportions of a headless ghost. Bravely she has made her way along the unfamiliar corridor, heard the voices of her mother and father downstairs, and come into the room. As she enters and sees her parents, she flashes them a look full of hurt, mixed with relief at having found them.

"Oh, darling!" Catherine stands up, opening her arms wide for Milène to run into. "What's wrong?"

Coco says, "The poor thing! She's obviously disoriented."

Milène says nothing. She's too frightened even to cry. Her face is frozen in a mute appeal for love and reassurance.

Igor walks over to his daughter. He bends down to address her at her own eye level. Stroking her hair gently, he says, "Don't worry, sweetheart. Mama and Papa are here. And Coco, too."

"There's no need to be afraid," offers Coco. "This is your home now for a while."

The little girl's expression softens. Her eyes glimmer with light from a nearby lamp. Leaning toward her, Igor says, "Everything will be all right."

Catherine whispers, "I'll put her back to bed now."

"No," the child says.

"Come on, we'll read a book."

Milène pleads, "Can't I stay down here for a while?"

With gentle firmness: "No. It's very late now. It's time for bed."

"Yes, and you'll need your sleep because tomorrow is going to be very exciting. We're going to play lots of new games in the garden, and you'll need plenty of energy if you want to keep up." Coco pumps her arms up and down athletically to illustrate.

Milène recognizes this for the sop that it is, but seems happy to go along with it.

"Now kiss Papa good night."

Milène hugs her father. Squeezing her tight, Igor administers a tender kiss on her forehead. "Good night," he says. "And give Coco a kiss, too, and say thank you for letting us stay here."

"Thank you, Coco," chants the child.

"That's quite all right."

"Now, young lady, up to bed. Come on." As Milène opens the door to leave, Catherine pauses at the doorway. "I'll retire now, too, if you don't mind," she says. "I'm very tired. Good night."

She hasn't felt well the last couple of days. She trusts her husband will follow. Though she's not jealous by nature, she doesn't like leaving the two of them alone.

Igor says, "I'll be up soon."

"Good night," echoes Coco musically.

Catherine leaves the room, clutching her reluctant daughter's hand. She still has her doubts about the situation here. There's something not quite right about the place. She feels it instinctively. All the carpets are new, the furniture is modern, and everything is spotless. The smell of fresh paint is everywhere; even the grass looks immaculate. Yet it doesn't feel real somehow. It seems to her as if she's living in a stage set, and she half expects at any moment the audience to reveal itself. Still, it has always been her habit to reserve judgment, so she agrees with herself to give it time.

Igor and Coco remain, listening to the pattering footsteps of the child and the more solemn steps of her mother as they drift up the stairs. Between them, the cat stretches its rough tongue in a yawn.

"She's a lovely girl."

He looks up. "She is."

"You must be very proud."

In the silence that follows, the note of the cicadas seems to rise a semitone. Having returned to his chair, Igor adjusts the newspaper's slippery leaves across his lap. The print in front of him starts to swim. He is conscious of Coco's presence like a massy object on the other side of the room. She seems closer than she was before, as though his chair has been tugged toward her. He feels suddenly uncomfortable and is aware of his wife now waiting upstairs. He sets the newspaper down and folds it with unnecessary neatness. Then with equal formality he finishes his tea and announces that he, too, is going to bed.

"Good night," he says. A sense of challenge informs his voice. A muscle twitches on the right side of his face.

Her eyes tilt up toward him, catching the lamplight shallowly. She leans her head sideways, shifting her weight in the chair. Something about her look unnerves him. Boldly he meets her gaze.

"Good night," she says.

Her voice is husky, rough-textured, like velvet brushed the wrong way. The pitch of it sticks with him as he goes on up to bed; as his head hits the pillow; as his mind begins to generate the nonsense of his dreams.

CHAPTER SIX

Igor sits at the piano, penciling in corrections. Sheets of music are propped high on a board above the keys. With head held intently and glasses pushed up onto his brow, he resembles a cardsharp or racing driver: a man who might take risks.

Constantly he juggles combinations of notes and plays with their durations. He's after that arresting coincidence of sounds, that correspondence of tones that's so thrilling it's like someone piercing you with a needle between the ribs. He tries out different chord sequences, adjusting the position of his fingers until there's a density of texture that seems sweet and difficult all at the same time. He finds the answers lie rarely in straightforward harmonies. The solutions are more slanted. They come at an angle and surprise you, so that what can sound at first discordant turns out to be penetratingly complex and superb.

There is a knock on the door of his study. He presumes it is Marie come to tidy. But no, it is Coco. Hurriedly he stands up. His glasses slip down his face, almost falling off his nose.

"Coco," he says, resettling his spectacles.

"Just to let you know, I've arranged for a doctor to call upon your wife."

"You're very kind." A respiratory ailment has laid her low in recent days. She wasn't even well enough to go to church on Sunday.

"And don't worry about the expense. I'll attend to it."

"No. You mustn't."

"Don't be silly. You are my guests here. I can't stand to see people ill under my roof."

"It's my responsibility. I'd feel insulted if you were to pay."

"Nonsense. Consider the matter closed. He'll be here this afternoon around three o'clock." Igor makes to remonstrate, but Coco insists.

They both laugh uneasily. She's aware that her tone is a bit schoolmistressy. At the same time, he knows how expensive doctors can be. He knows, too, that he could never afford to pay for any lengthy course of treatment. He feels the weight of Coco's money tilt the balance of authority between them. Humbled, he looks down. As he does so, he notices a hole in his shirt gape open, exposing the skin of his stomach beneath. A few dark hairs crinkle finely in the light.

She follows his gaze. "You've lost a button."

He colors slightly and closes over his shirt.

"There it is!" Her eyes seem to bend around the piano in seeking it out. Reaching low, she picks up the button. "I'll sew it back on for you."

He can't bring himself to argue again. "Thank you. I'll leave it with Marie this afternoon."

"I'm going out this afternoon. It'll only take an instant. Come on, I'll do it now."

Slightly thrown by her urge to do things promptly, he blurts, "Well, give me a minute and I'll go up and change."

Startled by his formality, Coco is even more abrupt. "No need." That toughness in her voice again. "You don't even have to take off your shirt. Sit still, I'll be back in a second." Her dress whispers deliciously to him as she leaves the room.

Discomposed, Igor feels the need to assert himself more. But each time he speaks to her, his resolution melts. He finds himself constantly disarmed by her frankness. He removes his glasses and wipes them clean with the tail of his shirt. It is then he realizes his hands are trembling.

Coco returns, bearing a small tan packet of needles and some thread. "Face the light," she says. She wets the thread with the tip of her tongue and pokes it through the needle's eye.

Obediently he turns to the window. The light crowds his white shirt, making it transparent. Igor stands, shyly immobile as she attends to the button at his waist. With his arms lifted and his head raised high, he feels the ceiling close above him.

Coco senses the squat musculature stiffen beneath his shirt. For a small man, he is impressively athletic. It is her turn to hesitate. She plies her needle with quick hands, drawing the thread out tightly and working the point in briskly through the seam. A little too briskly, for she pricks her finger. Pain blooms inside her. She curses as the room turns red beneath her lids.

Igor recoils, dropping his arms and looking down. "What's wrong?"

She shoots her finger between her lips. Flared, her eyes reflect the whiteness of his shirt.

A sudden tenderness wells within him. He has to suppress an impulse to take that vulnerable finger and heal it inside his mouth. Then, with a spasm of courtesy, he remembers himself. He says, "Here, take this handkerchief."

"It's nothing." A bubble of blood oozes up. Further proof for him, if proof were needed, of how full of life she is. She tamps it with the handkerchief, covered now with a pattern of small red stars. "I'm sorry. That was careless of me."

"Are you all right?"

An attraction flashes between them. Unspoken and remote, perhaps, but as real and clear as the button she sews back on to his shirt. Igor feels an obscure queasiness in his belly, as though he has just eaten seafood. An undertow of longing pulls at him. The sting of the needle in her finger has quickened the heat in his blood.

"Of course. Let me finish off."

Before he can protest, she's back at work. The button hangs limply by its crimped string from the hole. Raising his arms again, he looks down. Her hair is tied in a bun above a white turndown collar. He can smell the lye soap, ubiquitous in the bathrooms, rise from the back of her neck. He can feel the pressure of her hand against his chest.

She says, "Here, hold this."

He puts his finger against the button as she ties a knot around it.

"Now let go."

He releases his finger and the button is secured. Unthinkingly she snaps the thread with her teeth. She leans back, inspecting the finished article.

"There!" Coco's mouth broadens into a smile, forcing a dimple into her left cheek, a puckered shape almost like the beginnings of a second mouth. She gathers up her needle and thread and makes to leave then turns around, recalling why she came in the first place. "So he'll be here around three. I'll be out having my hair cut. Joseph will show him in."

Conscious of having thanked her enough already, he merely nods. He remains standing, listening to her steps grow fainter down the hall. Cut again! Her hair is boyishly short as it is, he thinks.

Then he sits down. He places his glasses back on his forehead, picks up his pencil, and returns to work. His hands, widely spaced, make different shapes on the piano. There's a sudden roundness to the sounds, a richness to the tones, a fatness to the harmonies. Reaching up to the board above the keys, he changes a minim into a crotchet by filling it in.

With his thick index finger and thumb, the doctor draws the skin of Catherine's eyelids up. Her corneas roll, revealing a filigree of broken blood vessels across the whites of her eyes.

As she breathes deeply in and out, he listens with a stethoscope to her chest. Then she sits up from her bank of pillows while he taps and listens from the back. She submits in silence to his repertory of tests, conscious of the labored operation of her lungs. She feels them wheeze like a squeeze box as the air snags before being expelled and wonders for a moment what *he* must hear. She watches for his reaction, but he gives little away. In fact, he barely looks at her. He removes the stethoscope from around his neck and winds the tube around his hand. Stout, with an olive complexion and an abundance of dark hair, he is himself radiantly healthy. Who'd trust a doctor that was anything but?

No deep furrows mark his forehead, Catherine notices. Nothing has worked to disturb the smoothness of his brow. He has never suffered any life-unsettling wrench, she thinks. Indeed, he has shrewdly restricted his constituency to that rim of the city where only the wealthy can afford to live. His practice has fattened happily with clients such as Chanel entrusting their medical welfare and expenses to him. Catherine's own father was a country doctor. She knows the strains he had to endure in serving the poor of the town.

"Well?" Igor says. He moves toward a corner of the room to confer. Impatience colors his voice.

The doctor presses the stethoscope into his case. His look promises nothing. "The right lung is very weak," he says, with an effort at frankness and loud enough for Catherine to hear. Her face falls exhaustedly back against the pillows. She resents these two dark-suited men talking about her health, as though she is not a real person with feelings and a certain purchase on her own life.

She is more alarmed than she cares to admit at the move to Bel Respiro. True, the fresh air and sunlight are undoubtedly good for her health, as Igor—and Coco—persuasively maintain. But what is she to make of the captivating Mademoiselle Chanel? Does she not have other, darker motives for inviting them here?

The exile from Russia has affected her more than it has Igor. He, at least, has his work to go on with. She has abandoned everything: her friends, her property, her sense of belonging. And the constant traveling has eroded her health. All that sustains her is a deep religious faith. That, and the love of her husband.

Turned to one side her eyes hold a reflection of the window and the sill tricked out with lilies. They seem suddenly malignant to her, these flowers: snake-tongued and venomous. And they stink. She doesn't quite know why, but she feels contaminated in this room, in this godforsaken house. A sympathetic taste of acid coats her tongue. Watching a wedge of shadow darken the bed, she feels she wants to vomit.

Sensing his wife's resentment, but fearful of what the doctor might have to say, Igor ushers him from the room. The two men descend the staircase and pause in the corridor at the bottom. Two bluebottles orbit a light fixture, buzzing dementedly in repeated squares.

The doctor's tone is solemn. "Has she coughed up any blood?"

"Not recently."

"Any history of that happening before?"

"She was mildly tubercular in her youth," Igor concedes. "It came back after our youngest was born."

"When was that?"

"Six years ago . . ."

This seems to confirm a suspicion. The doctor nods while biting his lip. "Well, she might be showing signs of that again."

The angle of Igor's shoulders communicates distress. "Is it serious?"

"She needs to be looked after."

"Is there anything she should be doing?" He lifts a hand to his cheek, where his fingers begin stroking.

"Getting plenty of bed rest and fresh air. A little walking might be a good idea. Nothing too strenuous, you understand. Gentle but regular exercise. Also, she's a bit on the thin side. She should eat a little more. She needs to build up her strength."

"Of course." Igor continues needlessly to stroke his cheek.

"I've prescribed something that should calm her down. It'll allow her to get the rest she needs and make her breathe more easily. It may make her sleepy, though."

After fizzing inside the lamp shade, the two bluebottles alight on the ceiling. Both men notice the silence.

"I appreciate your coming over at such short notice."

The children cluster. "Is Mama going to be all right?"

Igor feels love surge within him for these young things. The doctor touches their heads as if healing them. "She'll be just fine," he says. For the first time, he breaks into a smile. Igor wishes his wife could see this.

Joseph appears out of nowhere. He returns the man's hat and opens the door. A square of light frames them sharply, making them squint for an instant.

"Be sure to give my regards to Mademoiselle Chanel."

"I will."

Deferentially, the doctor has parked outside the gates. His feet shuck the small stones in the drive. The sound in Igor's ears is louder than it should be. The sharpness of the light and shadows seems to extend to the air and its ability to carry sound. It extends, too, to his conscience, where it amplifies a pang of guilt.

He experiences mixed feelings at the news of Catherine's illness. Pain at her renewed suffering mingles with excitement at the thought that her convalescence might afford him more time with Coco. Then, remembering his children's instinctive loyalty, he feels wretched entertaining such thoughts. But they ripen within him darkly and will not go away.

He thinks of the six years he has spent looking after his wife; the difficulties he's had squaring the demands of his work with the need, pressingly vivid, to watch over her. The sacrifice has been great. But, he reminds himself, he's not a saint. He loves her, of course, and can't imagine ever being without her. She's the mother of his children. Yet here he is, he reflects, thrust into a world bristling with possibilities, alive with new hopes. Now thirty-eight, and still smarting from the injustice of his exile, he feels the need to be affirmed not only as a musician but as a man.

Coco pushes her sleeves midway up her arms and sits down to dinner. She has on an open-necked blouse with a sailor collar, and a long knitted skirt. A black bandeau echoes the dark arc of her eyebrows.

Shaking out a napkin, she asks, "No Catherine this evening?" She can't conceal the fact that she thinks Catherine a malingerer—the way she carps the whole time, and that insipid way she has of calling downstairs for Marie. Coco can't fathom why Igor puts up with her. She seems to do nothing for him.

"I'm afraid not," Igor says. He gives a summary of the doctor's visit.

"Well, I'm glad to hear it's not *too* grave."

Picking up his cutlery, Igor says nothing. He allows her to pour him some wine.

"With Catherine not here, do we still need to say grace?" Coco has been startled recently by the ritual of a prayer before each meal.

Igor becomes complicit. "Fine by me." But he feels treacherous as he says it, both to Catherine and to his own deep-rooted sense of faith. A primitive loyalty stirs within him, an infant possessiveness. Something wooden in his grin alerts Coco to his discomfort.

She glances at the children. It means little to them. They speak Russian mostly, except when rehearsing their courtesies in a highly trained fashion to Mademoiselle Chanel. Igor chivvies them into delivering their pleases and thank-yous and insists they hold their knives and forks in the proper way. If only it were the same during the day, Coco reflects. Without any discipline from their mother they just run wild, bickering and squabbling and making a racket. Meanwhile Igor seems largely oblivious of their needs. So they constantly come to her, interrupting *her* work. And she's just as busy, if not more so, than him.

Generously, though not without regard for herself, she has engaged a local governess to tutor them for the summer. The truth is, someone has to control and look after them. And it's not going to be her!

She tucks into her starter of chicory and Gruyère. There is a silence before she throws at Igor, "So, you like it here?"

Shuffling off his discomfort: "I do, yes. Very much."

"But you prefer St. Petersburg."

There she is, at him again. There's no letup with her. "Not necessarily. I'm fonder of it now, though, than I've ever been."

"Now that you can't go there?"

The delay occasioned by his sipping the wine adds emphasis to his response. "Exactly."

"But your wife misses it terribly, doesn't she?"

Setting down his glass, he composes his fingers about the stem. Since arriving at Bel Respiro he realizes how, intimidated by Coco's sociability, Catherine has withdrawn into her own shy world. He can't blame her, though. He feels intimidated himself.

"It must be hard for her here."

"Yes." He looks down at his plate.

"And the children?"

"Children adapt. They always do." His gaze switches to the four of them. Seeking out the innocent spaces behind their eyes, he experiences another reflex of guilt. As he looks, bits of Catherine leap out from their features like strands of color in a rug.

But slowly, like his children, Igor grows more relaxed and animated, more comfortable with himself again. Coco responds. They both talk of their ambitions and warm to their themes. She wants to democratize women's fashion. He wants to redefine musical taste. They speak with vigor and conviction, finding a common loathing of fussiness and luxuriance. She hates frills and furbelows, ruches and puffing. He pours scorn on the empty decorativeness of recent music, its syrupy rhythms and glutinous tunes.

She's determined not to be outdone. Her work is just as much an art form as his, she considers. And if God didn't clothe us the first time around, she thinks, then it takes a second act of creation to put that right.

She tells him how she likes working with jersey. Given the unavailability of most fabrics after the war, the thing about jersey is, it's cheap, stretchy, and practical to wear. You can be simple and chic at the same time, she says. If you can't walk and dance in a dress then what's the point of wearing it? And if the textile seems inferior, then you can always embellish it with embroidery or beads, with films of lace or tassels. All you need do is add a neckerchief to see how the simplest of outfits might be transformed.

Igor recalls what Diaghilev said about her, but she's convincing him. She's making sense. He listens to her intently. It's not only what she's saying, though, it's her manner he finds compelling. That wide mouth, the inflection of her gestures, the dark sweetness of her eyes.

She's looking for a new simplicity in her designs, she says. Unadorned clean lines, a more masculine cut. She wants to know why it is that men get all the comfortable clothes. "Isn't it time that women had clothes designed for them by other women, instead of being packaged like Easter eggs?" Women aren't ornaments, she reasons; they are human beings. "They need to be free to move, and at the moment that means taking away. It's a matter of subtracting and subtracting until you've pared a dress down to the fit of a woman's body. Is that so hard to understand?"

He admires the passion of her arguments. He's never met a woman like her before. There's something absolutely feminine about her, yet with a new confidence, a new sense of independence. He likes that, though it frightens him slightly. It's as if her sexuality surrounds her like a shape he can almost see.

Having stuffed themselves with meat and cheeses, the children are excused. Coco and Igor talk on about their work.

"I rarely begin on paper," Igor says. "I almost always compose at the piano. I need to touch the music, to feel it rise between my hands."

"The same with me. I find it hard to work from sketches. I'd far rather start on a model directly. And I always begin with the material handy. I have to shape and feel it first."

This need for direct contact in their work establishes a braid in their relationship and knits their conversation together. There is a shared commitment and dedication that allows them to connect. To connect, but also to compete.

Igor drinks almost a whole bottle of burgundy, while Coco consumes several glasses herself. They argue about who works hardest. Igor contends that he starts much earlier, while some days she's not even up until noon. She counters that she works until the early evening, whereas he frequently stops in midafternoon. They become eager to outdo one another in the hours that they put in.

As he drinks, he hears her voice bubble up warmly toward him. The overlapping sensation of the wine and her buoyant talk makes him feel heady. A thought strikes him. He hears some inner prompt. The sentence escapes his lips before he's fully conscious of delivering it.

"Misia told me about Arthur Capel." Immediately he feels he's overreached.

There's a catch in her voice as she answers. "She did?" She seems stunned, disbelieving. "She told you about him, really?" Her face becomes a mask, her voice suddenly small. "Everyone called him *Boy*."

"You must have loved him." He surprises himself again.

She gathers herself. "He betrayed me."

"Oh?"

Shot through with bitterness, her voice nevertheless remains calm. "Without telling me, he married an aristocrat. English. Someone with better credentials," she adds acidly. "And then he died." As though reexperiencing the grief in accelerated time, her mood is propelled through desolation, numbness, and anger within a few seconds. A tear starts in the corner of her eye.

"I'm sorry."

"A car crash." Her eyes darken as if dipped in shadow. "He was always in too much of a hurry."

Her heart falls through the silence that follows. She feels the wine go flat inside her. Something drags at the corners of her mouth. As if in a trance, she volunteers, "When he died, I had my bedroom painted all in black, with black sheets and black curtains. I wanted to put the whole world into mourning for him." She looks up at him stonily. "He was the beat of my heart for nine years, and now he's gone. I can't stand it."

He reaches across and puts his hand on hers. A gesture of consolation, heartfelt and humane.

Her fingers respond minutely. She feels the hairs on his fingers brush her palm. The metal of his ring surprises her with its coolness. "I was nothing before him. He made me. But you know something? I paid him back, every penny. I built the business by myself."

There is a softness and depth to their glances that melts the space between them.

Her free hand plays with a napkin ring.

Joseph enters to ask if they want coffee. Shocked to find someone else present in the room, their hands spring apart. Igor rapidly finds his glass. Until this instant, they've been unaware of how well they are getting on. With this recognition, each seems to withdraw a little. The previous uneasiness renews itself. Some dim impulse tells them both, simultaneously, to take out a cigarette. And no, they don't want coffee, thank you.

Joseph retires. Igor snaps a match from a packet given as a souvenir in some Swiss hotel. He has to strike it twice before it lights. Coco moves her head forward. With the cigarette in her mouth, her face presses into his vision. The tobacco flares. She leans back. Smoke rises over the table in simple loops and threads.

She says, "It would just keep me awake all night."

A rim of lipstick appears like a wound at the end of her cigarette.

Igor says, "Me, too."

CHAPTER SEVEN

Coco knocks softly on Catherine's bedroom door. After a
short pause, a weak "Come in" issues from inside. She enters,
wary of transgression, holding the door as she peeps in.

The room is stuffy. The curtains are half closed. The air
has an odor of stale sweat and sickness. Prolonged notes from
the piano lap about the house from downstairs. "It's only me,"
Coco says.

Raising her head from the pillow, Catherine says, "Yes,
come in." Music manuscripts are spread about the bed, filled
with her careful annotations.

Coco draws a chair close to the bed. She looks at Catherine. Her face, she notices, is thin and sallow. Her cheeks are
wastingly pale and drawn. Her eyes have a swollen look, lend-
ing her a permanently startled expression. Shadows of ema-
ciation darken the skin beneath. No sooner has her head
sunk back than she needs to sit up again to suppress a fit of
coughing. The hard, dry rattling sound makes Coco shiver.
It reminds her of the shuttles in a textile mill.

Catherine recovers sufficiently to be dismayed by her appearance. She makes an attempt to straighten her hair, which

is wheat-pale and damp on one side where she has been sleeping.

Coco asks, "Can I get you a glass of water?"

"I have one here already."

Automatically she reaches across the table for her glass. The water is tepid and flat with few bubbles. She takes several ineffectual sips then sets it down.

"I'm sorry you haven't been well recently."

Catherine detects a laziness, an air of duty about Coco's visit. She says, "I'm sorry, too."

There is a sharpness to the response that makes Coco sit up and concentrate. She quickly revises an impression of her as pathetic. Catherine doesn't suffer fools gladly, she can see. She's a serious woman, and learned. Books surround her bed: poetry and novels, and volumes of theology. Her French is better than Igor's, too, Coco notices — more fluent and less affected. As a student, she spent three years in Paris. But Coco can't shake the impression that her intellect has been won at the expense of vitality and life. Coco hates sickness in people and is slow to tolerate their ills. If she's honest with herself, it's also got something to do with class. Coco sees in Catherine the anemia of the upper orders, the thinness of blue blood, the weakness of an aristocracy that has had its arrogance exposed.

Her attitude is complicated, too, by the fact that, when she was eleven, she watched her own mother succumb agonizingly to consumption. Now part of her feels resentful that Catherine is so pampered, while her mother died with a quickness reserved for the lonely and impoverished.

An uneasiness exists between the two women, punctuated by the piano's experimental chords down below. This uneasiness is quickened by the friendship Coco so obviously enjoys with Igor. Catherine doesn't believe in friendships between members of the opposite sex. In the end, they're either fraudulent or erotic, she thinks. Aside from Igor, whom she likes to think of as her best friend, she's never enjoyed a meaningful friendship with another man. She likes Diaghilev, of course, but that's different. He prefers men, anyway.

The two women's eyes slide over one another. Oil on water.

"The doctor did say, remember, that you must get some fresh air."

"I know."

"Do you want me to open the window?"

Catherine hesitates. This is the first time they have been alone together. And there is something about the act, she feels, that grants Coco a kind of power. Instinctively she distrusts her, finding her sly. Yet, despite herself, she wants to like her—and be liked. There's a charisma about the woman that's undeniable. She recognizes that. Again, she tries to fluff out her thin hair.

"Yes," she says.

Coco rises from her chair. She pulls back the curtains fully and pushes at the window. It is sticky with humidity. Catherine was unable to open it earlier. But with a firm shove it gives, and the window opens wide. A warm breath of air enters and diffuses through the room. The curtains flutter gauzily, the manuscripts stir on the bed, and the edge of Catherine's hair lifts. She winces at the light.

Coco declares, "That's better."

"Yes," Catherine says, intimidated all the more by the note of decision in Coco's voice.

"The sun gives you energy."

But the sun mocks Catherine in the goodness and health it administers. Coco sits down, uncrosses then recrosses her legs. During an awkward silence, the piano repeats a difficult phrase.

Catherine stares at the bedclothes. Her throat is dry, but she resists reaching for her water again. She knows it will communicate weakness.

She is aware of Coco's origins—her illegitimacy, her orphan status—and admires the ferocious energy she must have drawn upon to claw her way up. But she also fears that energy and how it might be used against her. She feels, in her presence, as though she's in the path of a tornado.

On an impulse, Coco rises again and moves toward the wardrobe. "Do you mind if I look at some of your clothes?"

The request surprises Catherine. It seems presumptuous. But Coco moves with such fleetness, she feels overwhelmed. It comes as another reminder that they are living here thanks to her charity. This is her house. It is she who pays the doctor, she who pays the bills. What can she, Catherine, do? Refuse? A sense of obligation weighs upon her chest and constricts her airways even more. Her voice is thin as she says, "Of course."

Coco tugs open the wardrobe doors. A sweet, musty smell escapes. For Catherine any sense of privacy melts away. Revealed are all her things. She feels almost violated, so intimate is the act.

Most of her clothes are fussy formal gowns and dresses: heavy, old-fashioned things. Mostly winter wear, and not too much that is appropriate for summer. There are a few gypsy-type shirts with flounces; a series of fur outfits, including shirts with fur collars; and a large number of skirts.

"Most of them are too big for me now."

"I like this," Coco says, pulling out one of the simpler skirts with a bell-trumpet design. She inspects the embroidery around the hem.

"Oh," is all Catherine can manage. "It's just some peasant thing." She thinks for a moment that Coco is teasing, but her interest seems sincere. "I got it in St. Petersburg before we left."

"I like it," Coco repeats, removing it from the hanger and holding it against herself.

Catherine watches as she flourishes the skirt around the waist of her blue dress. "I'm glad," she says.

Coco, though, doesn't seem to listen. Deaf to any condescension, she picks out something else. "And this is wonderful, too," she says, holding up a long belted blouse in wool with embroidered bands on collar and cuffs.

"That's a *roubachka*," Catherine says.

"A *roubachka*," echoes Coco, determined to pronounce it right.

Catherine understands now Coco's championing of inferior materials like jersey: in effect she's promoting herself. "You can borrow it if you like," she says.

This shocks Coco back into the present. "No, no. I didn't mean . . ." Hastily she replaces the blouse, but continues to rummage undeterred. She takes out a few more things and holds them up. Each time, she elicits comments about their purchase and when and where Catherine has worn them.

Eventually Coco's fingers, reaching deep, feel a quantity of tissue paper. She tugs the hanger along the rail until it is possible to squeeze it out. Catherine says nothing. Disturbed, a cream-colored moth staggers tipsily from the cupboard. Its lightness seems to infect Coco's mood. She lifts out the hanger. The shape of a gown is concealed beneath opaque layers of paper.

Intrigued, she asks, "What have we here?" She peels off the tissue until the last couple of sere sheets reveal the crisp white silk of a wedding dress. Coco lifts it up for a moment. She sees what it is and stops. Of course, a wedding dress. She blanches.

Catherine says, "I haven't seen it for years."

Coco is stunned into wordlessness by the sight of the dress. It is as if some fugitive outfit has been conjured from the cupboard, something that doesn't belong.

Levelly, Catherine asks, "You never married?"

A vision of bridal whiteness knits itself in front of Coco, white like a scream. The power she feels she has established evaporates in an instant. Thirty-seven, unmarried, and with no children to her name, she realizes she must appear a failure. She fights an impulse to justify, to explain. Then, in reaction, she feels a sudden hardness. The truth is that, since Boy, men have been dispensable to her. Looking at Catherine now, she recognizes the softness of her loyalty, the weakness of a wife.

"No," she says, more contemptuously than she intended.

She rearranges the paper hastily over the dress, replacing

it deep within the cupboard. Then, drawing the hanger back evenly across the rail, she closes over the walnut-colored doors. One of the jackets snags. She has to tuck it back in and reclose the cupboard. The delay frustrates her.

"If you ever want to borrow the skirt, just say so," reiterates Catherine. She is dimly aware of Coco's discomfort and keen for them to end on a positive note. Charitably, for the moment, she assumes that Coco has balked at her own brashness in fingering the wedding dress.

"What?" Coco asks, preoccupied. The words filter slowly into her consciousness. "No. No. Thank you." Perplexed by the strength of her reaction, she sits down, subdued, then abruptly stands again. She becomes hard-eyed. "What time is it?"

Catherine glances at a timepiece on the bedside table and starts to answer. But before the information can be conveyed, Coco decides she must leave. She has urgent business that must be attended to. Right away, she says.

"Well, thanks for coming to see me," Catherine says. Her tone is polite, but also detectable is a fear, which leaks through into her voice, a growing fear that, with her bedridden, Coco and Igor might become more closely involved. She feels threatened by this woman's vitality, her determined energy and strength.

The presence of both her and Coco under one roof inevitably begs comparison. It is a comparison that Catherine does not enjoy making, even to herself. In addition, she feels compromised as Coco insists on paying her medical bills. At once indebted and resentful, her sympathies oscillate between two opposing poles.

"Sorry?" Coco is already on her way out.

"Thank you for coming to see me." Her tone is sincere. She understands she can't afford to make an enemy of this woman.

"Oh, yes. Not at all. 'Bye," Coco manages, with candid disregard. She halts, then quickens, leaving the room filled with light and air.

Catherine begins coughing hard again. Coco hears her muffled convulsions as she steps unsteadily down the stairs.

CHAPTER EIGHT

Clouds gather tumultuously throughout the afternoon. Plum-colored, the thunderheads churn into a premature dusk. The elms sway, and shutters flap in a rattling staccato. Fat spasms of rain begin to fall.

At the first pulse of lightning, the children move inside. The dogs bark fiercely, sensing a chemical event. In a superstitious reflex, Marie hides away the silver. Coco watches as rain spatters the windows. One flash fills the glass like the filament in an electric bulb.

The storm continues after dinner when Igor hears his study door click open. It is Coco. He sees her reflection in the window. Oily shadows course down her face. He turns. She seems exhilarated.

"Beautiful, isn't it?"

Storms always thrill her—the more spectacular the better. She loves their power, their ability to pulverize the earth. She feels animated suddenly and experiences an urgent need to participate, to draw like a galvanic battery on the fury of the storm. Yet having entered Igor's study, she feels unusually tentative. She's there for no other reason than she wants to see him. It seems odd that within her home there are areas that feel out-of-bounds. But with a stern sense of privacy, Igor has already made this space his own. Her energy converts into an itch to quit the room. But she can't just leave. Her visit would appear purposeless. Another vivid flash outside is enough to spark a decision. "Let's *do* something," she blurts.

"What?" Magnified by his glasses, his eyes hold a reflection of the last lightning flash.

On previous evenings, Igor has played chess with his children. Tonight, however, Coco decides it is too sedate an occupation for the whole entourage. Instead, she proposes the children have some fun performing songs and dances.

As he looks at her, her weight shifts one way and her head tilts the other. An angle is established between her upper and lower body, as though on the keyboard he had struck adjacent chords.

She walks over and takes his hand. "Come on."

He enjoys this sudden contact of her palm, relishing the pressure of her skin against his. His fingers tingle, remembering the shared electricity of their first meeting. Standing up, he seems to float toward the door.

The piano is moved into the living room to accompany the songs. Catherine, though too ill to participate, is persuaded to come downstairs to watch. Installed in a chair with blankets around her, she readies herself to be entertained.

They begin with Russian folk songs. Coco joins in as best she can, humming along once she gets the melody. Then the children sing some songs in French that Coco taught them earlier in the day. They are joined by Joseph and Marie's daughter, the fourteen-year-old Suzanne. She helps lead the singing, filling in the lyrics when the children are uncertain. Igor strikes up jauntily on the piano. Then, together with Coco and Suzanne, the children start to dance.

The music hits the walls and bounces back. Coco pushes her hair up with both hands. Then, while the children dance with one another, she peels off, describing a wider circle around them. She responds to the accents of the music, feeling them chime with her insides. The high notes seem to express a sharp passion. The low notes set off a deeper sympathy. It's as if a dialogue is being articulated between his music and her movements. In the lightning that irradiates the room, for a moment she looks goatish.

Catherine registers with increasing alarm the intimacy that has grown between Coco and her husband. It is obvious they share an unspoken rapport. Shocked that this has happened so fast, she feels hurt and excluded. The two women have hardened against each other since their encounter the other day. She wishes now she had not been inveigled down. She feels the music and the thunder combine to drum inside her skull.

One of the dances ends. The children rush to their mother, expecting encouragement. Instead, she tuts and turns her head. But, as she does so, the children leave her side again. They run to Coco, who beckons them back onto the floor.

At the children's insistence, the music begins to quicken. Suzanne and Ludmilla whirl ever more swiftly around the room. Seen from above, they form a wobbly revolving wheel. Coco holds herself very straight, maintaining an erect posture—the result of years of ballet lessons from her friend

Caryathis. Her figure is given an eerie symmetry in the long French windows at the end of the room.

The chords build; the music bubbles up. Lightning flashes thrillingly in glittering ribbons, shocking the trees into relief. Shapeless rumbles of thunder follow. Torn pieces of sky hurry overhead. Igor begins to play louder and more urgently. Coco feels an ache in her neck. And there's the sensation in her head of something spilling over. The feeling takes seed and widens within her circle by circle until the chairs, tables, lamps, and piano begin to blur together in a vertiginous wheel. The ceiling spins around. The chandelier at its center flakes light. Rising in redoubled fortes, the music and the dance accelerate until Coco collapses in a climax of calculated abandon, and Igor jumps from the piano to catch her in his arms.

Catherine can scarcely believe her eyes. A flush of anger spreads across her face. Her mouth twitches nervously. This is too much.

Igor looks bewildered. Coco still plays faint. Coming in with some tea, Marie is shocked by the scene that now confronts her. An impulse of sympathy toward Catherine contends with another that prompts her to check that Coco is all right. These feelings war within her. Before she can decide, she is summoned to bring a washcloth and some water.

Supporting the back of her head with his hand, Igor administers the water in careful sips to Coco's mouth. The children, including Suzanne, gather around. The sense of an audience makes him all the more solicitous in performing these healing rites.

Opening her eyes, Coco looks up groggily. Igor sees a

glazed film pass across her pupils. He loosens the kerchief at her throat. A sweet odor steals across his face as he inhales.

"Come on, now. Bed!" Catherine corrals the children prior to marching them upstairs.

Soulima asks, "Is Mademoiselle Chanel all right?"

"She's perfectly all right," his mother answers curtly. "Believe me!"

"She doesn't look so well," the boy insists.

Supporting herself against a chair, Catherine feels her own infirmity mocked. "I can assure you, she's very well." Each syllable is hurt into being. Her words are spoken clearly enough for Coco to hear.

"Thank you, Soulima. I'm all right," Coco manages, sitting up. Though Catherine might find it hard to credit, this is not something she has planned. The truth is, she did feel faint; the dancing did for an instant make her dizzy. But now something opportunistic in her nature takes over. She exploits the moment for all it is worth.

Soulima makes to speak again but, recognizing the strength of his mother's indignation, he says nothing and leaves the room. Reluctantly the other children follow on up to bed.

Catherine herself turns to go. With barely suppressed rage, she says, "Good night, Igor. I'll see you upstairs shortly."

He looks up at his wife, miming a gesture of helplessness. But Catherine is unimpressed. Her look tells him she thinks he is pathetic. He has been taken in, consciously or unconsciously. Surely he can see that. If he's acting involuntarily, he's a fool. If he's acting willfully, then he's cruel and dishonorable. Abruptly she feels the need to revise everything she knows about her husband. In leaving the room, she slams the door.

Joseph and Marie withdraw into the kitchen while Igor dabs at Coco's brow.

"She's got a nerve," snaps Marie to her husband.

"Careful. She might hear you."

"Honestly," continues Marie, without lowering her tone. "What on earth does she think she's doing? She invites these people to stay and then insults them. Her problem is, she's got too much money and doesn't know what to do with it."

"Shhh!"

"She sees herself as some great patron but hasn't the grace to carry it off. Actually she's no better than you or I. And does she pay us any more for all this extra work? Like hell she does!"

Suzanne has come into the kitchen in the middle of this. She listens to her mother, trying to unpick the complex weave of what is going on. Anxious that she shouldn't understand too much, Joseph makes a quieting gesture to his wife. He doesn't want to get involved. Seeing Marie subdued, he backs toward the door, his finger to his lips.

Reentering the living room, he asks, "What about the piano, sir?" Igor is distracted. He needs to repeat the question.

"We'll leave it until the morning, I think."

"You can go now, Joseph." Coco waves him off with a motion evoking helpless fatigue. "Thank you," she volunteers softly to Igor when they are alone. She blinks rapidly. Her small breasts heave.

The echo of melodies continues inside the room, making its space seem all the more vacant now. Igor glances at her neckline and its ellipse of pearls. His mouth feels parched and he tries not to swallow. There is a loaded silence between them. Her eyes seem black as lakes.

Then, seeing her cheeks suddenly flushed and her lips open florally, he shocks himself with the thought of kissing her full on the mouth. The image surprises him in its vividness; and he is surprised, too, to find himself thinking there is nothing improper in this. The impulse comes from somewhere deep within him and seems natural and good.

Holding his arm, Coco manages to stand. She walks the short distance to a chair and sits down heavily. "I'm all right now," she says.

"Are you sure?" Remaining close in case she swoons again, he feels overattentive suddenly.

Sensing his awkwardness, she fails to answer. She shakes off her headband, tucking her hair behind each ear.

At a loss, Igor says, "We were worried about you there for a minute." His remark ends with an attempt at a laugh.

Her self-possession recovered, without lifting her head, Coco raises her eyes to look at him directly. Again, he resists a fierce impulse to kiss her.

After a long pause that seems to dilate in time, she says, "You'd better go upstairs. Your wife is waiting."

Having acted out of an instinctive urge, her expression now closes over. Gone is any sense of recklessness. It's as if a seal has set across her face. And it is he who feels suddenly vulnerable and exposed. He senses her renewed coolness and is at pains to understand this capriciousness in her. He finds her opacity maddening. It's hard to know what she thinks sometimes. Hard to know what he thinks himself, come to that.

Above them the rain continues, picking its way along the tiles of the roof.

In leaving the room, he feels himself move through an invisible curtain. The air seems cooler in the hallway, the light harsher. Sheepishly he heads upstairs to confront another storm.

When Igor gains the top of the stairs, he finds the door to his bedroom closed. Pushing it open, in the corner of his vision he sees his wife sitting up in bed. Daringly he whistles the tune he was playing when Coco fainted.

She perceives this as a taunt. "Stop that awful noise!"

He elects not to respond. But something cussed in his nature breaks through. He feels angry. He acted in good faith back there. It was Catherine who in her joylessness turned it into a scene. He moves toward the bathroom. In locking the door, he shuts her out. When he emerges a few minutes later, he knows he has made things worse.

"What do you think you were doing down there?"

"What do you mean?" he says, removing his shoes and unbuckling the belt of his trousers.

"I mean, what do you think you were doing staring at Coco all night and then taking her in your arms?"

"Don't talk nonsense! And stop being so possessive and jealous. You've spoiled a perfectly good evening."

"Am I supposed to watch as another woman flirts with my husband right in front of my face?"

"And am *I* supposed to let her fall back and crack her head?"

As though talking to a child: "She didn't fall, Igor. She leaped!"

"You're being ridiculous." Quickly he adds, "And you haven't had the grace to ask if she's all right."

"Ask if she's all right? I think I know the answer to that one."

"Good for you!"

After a pause, and in a quieter voice: "What's going on, Igor?"

"Nothing's going on, I can assure you."

"Oh, no?"

"No."

He tries to laugh the suggestion off. The laugh sounds hollow in his own ears. Although nothing has happened, a feeling of guilt thrills hotly through his body. This surprises him. He has yet to admit it consciously, but it is true: in his heart he harbors a desire for Coco. An obscure longing has ached within him since he arrived at Bel Respiro. But he must maintain a sense of perspective. As long as they remain abstract, such thoughts are harmless, he tells himself. It's natural for men and women to flirt, and it's a commonplace for them to be attracted to each other. That doesn't mean, though, that anything needs to happen. He's a responsible husband and father. Doesn't Catherine realize that? He can understand that she might feel threatened, but he feels she should trust him, and is hurt that she doesn't.

"I'm waiting for an explanation." The vibration of anger still rings within her. It is an anger that masks a larger fear.

Anxious not to prolong the argument, he prefers to be dismissive. He knows the more he talks, the more he'll implicate himself. "You're going on about nothing," he says, continuing to undress and folding his clothes with obsessive neatness.

"Look at me," she says.

"What?"

"Look at me!"

Reluctantly he submits to her stare.

"You're guilty." Her features harden. A perceptible tremor passes across her face.

"What are you talking about?"

"Guilty!" she shouts, with shrill vehemence. Her voice contains within it her profound belief in the existence of sin. Her cheeks are flushed with religious fervor. Her look of bashful piety has become for the moment a vengeful glow. Agitated, she tugs at the sheet on the bed. "I can tell."

"Oh, for God's sake!"

"I'm not as naïve as you think, you know, Igor."

"Can we stop this now? Please? You're making yourself ill."

"It's you who's making me ill." She makes an effort to be rational and calm. "I can't believe you behaved like that—in front of the children as well. What must they think? A grown man abandoning himself so easily."

He seizes with relief this shift of attention away from himself. His anger quickens into righteousness. "They think nothing of it. And they're right to think nothing of it. Remember, we are guests here. If anyone behaved appallingly this evening, it was you."

"Why did she invite us here anyway? What's she after?"

"Has it ever occurred to you that some people are just good? That they're not *after* anything?"

"She's only interested in you because she wants to show you off. The great composer! Ha! Another rung advanced on the social ladder."

He slips into bed. "She's more complicated than you think."

Insulted. "Why isn't she married? A nice lady like that?" Following a pause, which Igor refuses to fill, Catherine goes on, "I'll tell you why. Because no rich man would lower himself to her level."

"Well, *I'm* certainly not rich enough, if that's what you're concerned about."

His humor is misjudged. "I'm warning you, Igor . . ."

Catherine's voice trails off. In the quiet created by his wife's sharp remark, he switches off the bedside lamp. The sudden darkness puts an end to the argument. An accusatory silence establishes itself between them, sustained like the moonlight slung across their bed. They lie parallel and untouching and rehearse unanswerable speeches inside their heads. But the lectures go undelivered; the inner applause for their eloquence fades. Each becomes conscious of the other's quickened breathing. Anger gnaws at them. For the rest of the night, they face away from each other, like two opposing letter Cs.

In the next bedroom Theodore, their eldest, is still awake. Though nothing his parents said was distinct, it was clear to him they were rowing. Not used to hearing them argue, he feels upset. His mother, especially, has always been so tranquil. He doesn't understand but guesses it must have something to do with Coco. A notion of defiance takes shape inside his head. He decides he doesn't like her. He decides he doesn't like living here either. The villa is too big. He's become used to living in small apartments. Though they were cramped, they were also intimate, and the family felt together. Here he feels alone and obscurely under threat. He flinches at the indignity of exile and longs to be free. Keeping his eyes open in the darkness, he listens intently. But it's all gone suddenly quiet now.

Downstairs, Coco has also heard raised voices coming from the Stravinskys' room. She listens, too, as silence folds its wings about the house. She is, she realizes suddenly, the only one in the house not part of a family. For God's sake, even the servants are married and have a child.

She needs some air. Opening a window, she smells the odor of damp grasses. A scent of rich greenness mingles with that of the lilies on the sill. The thunderheads have cleared, she sees, to reveal stars so big they seem to shout.

Staring out, she traces with the quick of her finger the shape of her own mouth. She takes several deep breaths. Then on an impulse, moving to the hall, she picks up the telephone and dials.

"Misia?"

"Coco? Is that you?"

"Yes."

"It's almost midnight. What's wrong?"

"Listen, what do you know about Catherine?"

"Life there getting complicated, is it?"

Shoving her hand on her hip: "Not yet. I just need to know a couple of things."

"Has he kissed you yet?"

Indignant. "What? No!"

"Does he want to?"

She twists the cord around her finger. "He might."

"Do you want to kiss him?"

"He's not handsome."

"No, but he has greatness."

"You think?"

"Everyone says so."

"That doesn't make me want to seduce him."

"It's your house, dear. You can do whatever you like."

"There are limits."

"Who says?"

Sternly. "I do!"

"Sometimes I feel the urge just to go to a hotel and ask the first man I see to sleep with me."

"Have you told José?"

"You think I tell him everything?"

"Shouldn't you?"

"One thing you learn, Coco—women want grand passion; all men feel is a little lust."

There's a silence.

"Believe me," Misia goes on, "a double bed can seem awfully small if you're sharing it with someone you don't love."

Before going to bed, Coco closes the lid of the piano solemnly, like the way she set the telephone back on its hook. She switches the lights off one by one and tugs the window shut.

CHAPTER NINE

The chauffeur polishes the bodywork of Coco's new Rolls-Royce. He has been waiting over an hour for her to emerge from the house. Stepping out eventually, she takes a look at her new purchase. She likes its straight lines, its simple assembly of squares, and she likes the color: black.

Hot air warps around the car. Its dark metal gleams. The engine sets up a powerful hum. On opening the door, she's immediately besieged by the heat trapped inside. She removes her hat and fans herself rapidly. A prickling sweat spreads across her skin.

The traffic in the capital is motorized and noisy. The avenues are dense with people, the air thick with stirred-up dust. Coco smiles. It's good to be back, she thinks. Her inner space craves the bigness of the city. This is where she belongs.

She plants her hat back on as the car draws up outside her shop in the rue Cambon—a narrow but affluent street backing on to the Ritz Hotel. The name CHANEL is stenciled in thick black letters above number 31.

She glances at the outfits displayed in the window: a sleeveless evening dress, a gray silk jacket edged with fur, and wool jerseys with broad pockets. A brooch on one catches the light and glitters.

Though she has been working hard at home, she has not visited the shop in over a week now. Usually her arrival is well telegraphed. On this occasion it is unannounced. There is a measure of disquiet and flustered activity among the girls in the shop. She has heard from Adrienne that they are demanding a pay raise. God! The minute she turns her back, there is unrest. Ungrateful bitches! Why, she considers, should she pay them more? Don't they realize that working for *Chanel* gives them unprecedented opportunities to meet rich lovers? Can't they see that some of them might even get a husband out of it? What more do they want?

Only Adrienne is unequivocally pleased to see her. Although almost the same age and often mistaken for her sister, Adrienne is in fact Coco's aunt. They have supported one another loyally for the last twenty years. Of the two, Adrienne is the more matronly and straitlaced. Coco has always been the leader. Together they ascend the helix of white stairs to the apartment on the third floor. Coco smiles to see again the Venetian mirrors and smoked crystal chandeliers, the white flowers and satin drapes of her home. She picks up one of the carved wooden animals from a table and examines it for dust. It is spotless.

She reapplies her lipstick after the journey, then bites on a handkerchief, leaving a red kiss. Adrienne quizzes her about the last two weeks. But she finds Coco strangely reticent about life back in Bel Respiro and particularly reluctant to talk at any length about Stravinsky.

"He's a cold fish," remarks Coco. Her right hand cups her chin. She hooks the little finger into her mouth and toys with the nail between her two front teeth.

"Yes, but he's a big fish."

She looks accusingly at Adrienne, resisting her suggestion that she might be out to catch him. Her features soften. "Actually, he's quite small," Coco says, with a winning smile. They both laugh.

She lets slip how difficult Madame Stravinsky is, detailing her persistent illness. She thus avoids having to disclose very much about Igor. She'd find it hard, anyway, to articulate what she thinks about him. She's not sure herself. It's like the snags that happen in their conversation, the opacities that slide between Russian and French. She has yet to find the key to decode exactly how she feels. Maybe nothing at all. Who knows?

Briskly she moves on to talk about the shop. She asks to look at the accounts. Scanning the columns, her eyes register the usual July torpor of sales. Coco sighs. "About as good as could be expected."

Eager to raise Coco's spirits, and keen to prove her own managerial acumen, Adrienne tells her how hard everybody has worked in her absence and how diligent they have been.

"What's all this about them wanting higher wages, then?"

"That's the French. The others don't complain at all. *They'd* be happy to work longer hours for less pay!"

"So it's the natives causing all the trouble, eh?"

"Don't worry, they're not going to revolt!"

"Mm."

"I can handle things. Trust me."

Slowly Coco breaks into a smile. She closes the ledger, clapping her two hands on the top. "I'm sorry. You're doing a great job."

Returning downstairs, Coco pauses for a moment. Unseen, she leans over the mezzanine rail and scans the scene below. There are her designs made flesh: crêpe de chine belted blouses, sleeveless evening dresses in black tulle, and cropped tweed jackets with patch pockets and turned-back cuffs.

She watches clients run their hands across the textures of the dresses. She loves that. The touch of the stuff. The friction of the material as it slides between the fingers. It gives her a thrill just thinking about it. She can't wait to return to work.

A generalized chatter percolates upward, from which she can discern as much Russian spoken as French. She has to smile. Here she is, it occurs to her, an uppity Frenchwoman of humble stock, lording it over these dispossessed princesses and countesses. The flotsam of the Revolution. The cream of the Moscow and St. Petersburg drawing rooms, all modeling and selling for her!

Coco has an idea for a dress she wants to try out.

One of her dark-haired models is on hand to oblige. They work in the room above the shop, surrounded by several mirrors. The model stands as near stock-still as she is able. Coco shuffles around her, first on her knees, then on all fours, then standing up, then sitting down. All the time she mutters incomprehensibly to herself. A pair of scissors dangles from a ribbon tied around her neck. Consulting a blueprint on a muslin toile, she works on the fabric directly.

It is a beige silk dress with an uneven hemline and a collar like a crossed scarf. Adjusting a ruche here, straightening a pleat there, she simplifies the line of the dress inch by inch, allowing it to flare softly at the bottom. Then she attends to the arms. "I can never get the damn sleeves right!" she moans.

Bits of material clutter the floor. Coco holds the pins in her mouth, sideways as you might a rose or a knife. When the model moves slightly or shifts her weight, Coco screams, "Can't you keep still even for one minute? What am I paying you for?"

The model is new and unaccustomed to these tantrums. Chastened, she freezes into a stiff pose until she can stand the weariness no longer. And when inevitably she loses balance or alters her stance, she is subjected to another faintly hysterical round of abuse.

"Stand straight, girl!" The need to keep the pins between her lips stretches Coco's mouth wide as she shouts.

It is hot above the shop, and she works furiously. Already afternoon, they have not stopped for lunch. Worrying obsessively at the sleeves, she nimbly pins and tucks until eventually she is content. The dress is dispatched downstairs to be made up for a customer. A magnet is passed over the floor to pick up any stray needles and pins.

Coco relaxes with a cigarette on one of the square suede sofas. Her body makes the shape of a Z. Idly she wonders what Igor is doing back in Garches. She's surprised to catch herself thinking like this. The intuition hits her: she misses him.

He is just such a presence, she finds. At the moment, he acts as a kind of ballast in her life. This is terrible! She went back to work partly to see how she'd feel being away from him for a couple of days. Earlier, she found herself writing his name over and over on a napkin, like a young girl practicing her signature. Afterward, she felt pathetic.

She's fond of Igor, and he *is* different from other men: more serious, more mature. She admires his independence of mind, his musical genius. She recognizes something of herself, too, in his dedication to work. He's not dashing, perhaps, but he's no dullard either. She finds him stimulating.

She orders a present for him. Knowing he loves gadgets, she has bought him a mechanical bird. It's an intricate little windup thing and comes complete with its own cage. Its head tilts as it claps its beak, and its wings twitch into life. It even whistles shrilly. If he ever lets them play with it, the children might like it, too.

From downstairs the clangor of the shop bell restores her focus on the afternoon. She finishes her cigarette and descends, affecting an almost regal air. She knows the rest of the staff will have heard her berating the model. This is good. It will help keep them on their toes. Such strictness is necessary if standards are to be maintained.

With Coco away at the shop for two days, the villa seems suddenly still.

In her absence, a numbness spreads through Igor's body. A warp appears in the shape of his day. He finds he cannot concentrate. His thoughts continually bend toward her, and his mind slides from his work. He sets down his pen, leans back in his chair, and shoves his glasses up onto his forehead. An insect wanders across his manuscript like a demisemiquaver with its multiple legs.

On an impulse, he rises. The house is silent. The children are with their governess. With a new sense of decision he steps out into the corridor and advances in long strides up the stairs. Moving quietly so as not to disturb his wife—relations have been strained since their fight the other night—he creeps toward Coco's room.

The door is unlocked. Trembling, he enters. A sense of daring pushes him on, as well as a need, a longing, to be close to her and her things. Inside, sunlight projects shadows sharp enough to cut against the walls. Noticing photographs of Coco, he moves closer to inspect. One captures her at a stable, a touch of the equestrienne about her, a hint of cavalry braid on the sleeve. Another has her reading on a terrace, her hair tumbled loose. A third frames her relaxing in a sailor jacket at the beach.

Turning, he sees her bed: the cool of pillows, the intimacy of silk sheets. He notices some clothes draped over a screen. Resisting an impulse to touch them, he has a superstitious fear that something of her still inhabits these fabrics: a ghostly presence that, if touched, might ripple into life. The air around him thickens as he imagines her nearness.

He catches a glimpse of himself in the dresser mirror. A flaw in the glass generates a blurred patch by the door. For an instant he thinks someone is coming in. Fear seizes his body. His heart races. His image ricochets off the mirror, burning holes into the wall. But the moment passes; everything is still.

Slowly his blood recovers. Something in him screams to leave, but the impulse to remain and root around is overwhelming, almost criminal in force.

He spies the door leading off to Coco's bathroom. Intrigued, he walks inside. Immediately he hears the different pitch of his shoes as they move from carpet to cold hard tiles. A flattened sound. A minor third.

The fixtures gleam so whitely, they almost hurt his eyes. This is the bath she must lie in, he thinks, and these the taps that she must touch. He imagines her emerging all rosy and self-forgetful from the tub, her chin tilted upward as if in an advertisement, her limbs slick with oil, and her breasts prinked like paradisal flowers. A shiver of longing runs through him. His palms grow moist. Something catches in his nose: a powdery scent. He turns.

Above the sink, he sees shelves brimful with colognes and spices, fragrant pomades and scented soaps, bath oils and dye pots, shampoos and aromatic balms. Rarely has he seen these things in such profusion, and never so artfully arranged. It reminds him of a fabled Arabian store. Warring with one another slightly, the odors fight off a collective rot to yield an overpowering sweetness.

He lifts an atomizer of perfume, inhaling the fragrance in a couple of drafts. Something occurs to him. And with a thrill which seems illicit, he undoes two buttons of his shirt and dabs the liquid experimentally upon his chest.

He realizes how swollen with goodness he feels here in Garches. He seems able to breathe more easily. It could be the climate, the open spaces, but there is also an aura that

Coco exudes. The air becomes richer in the exhilaration she gives off. He has found new reserves of oxygen to draw upon, a delicious renewal of energy to affirm the certainty that he is alive. And he knows it is Coco who has given him this.

Returning furtively to his study, he sniffs at his wrist where a scribble of veins runs just beneath his skin. He smells the echo of the odor on his fingers. Then he slinks back with delicious indolence into his music and the middle of the afternoon.

That evening, Coco and Adrienne make the short walk to a restaurant. The two women are soon joined by their friend Misia Sert.

"I don't want to make this a late night," Coco says. "There are things I have to do tomorrow, and I want to be back in Garches before it's dark."

Adrienne remarks, "That makes a change."

"You normally get up late and work until late," adds Misia.

"Can't I change my work habits even for one day?"

"No need to get tetchy," Misia says, with a wink at Adrienne.

Coco is not amused. They both see that. Adrienne attempts to cajole her, telling her everything is taken care of, but Coco throws her a determined look. She's not to be contradicted. Adrienne relents. In a mute gesture of surrender, she taps the ash from her cigarette.

Over dinner, Coco eats less and drinks more than usual. She watches the waitresses glide by like low-grade ministering angels. "Why can't *my* girls work like this?"

"Oh, come on! What's the matter?"

Pressed by Adrienne after several glasses of wine, Coco confesses she feels drawn to Igor. "But he's married," she complains.

"So?" Misia says. "I've been married three times already. It needn't be an obstacle, believe me."

Coco has seen Misia distraught often enough to know her flippancy is hard-won. "He has children, for God's sake!"

"That will keep Madame preoccupied, then, won't it?" Adrienne says.

Coco wonders why she's attracted to him, anyway. He isn't handsome, exactly. He certainly isn't wealthy. He's married, with four children. And she knows that, if she wanted, she could easily get other men. She'd be crazy to get involved with him, she reflects. And she cannot stand to be hurt again. Not after Boy. She shudders again to think of his death.

Fortified by wine, Adrienne blurts, "To hell with marriage. There are few enough men left after the war without worrying about that." She's half joking, but Coco doesn't smile.

"Oh, this *is* serious!" says Misia, in a moment of revelation.

Coco sips a little water and blinks quickly. Then something within her trips. "I don't want to talk about it any more. I don't propose to humiliate myself. He cares too much for his work even to think of getting mixed up with me." Suddenly sitting up: "And frankly I care too much for my own business, too."

Offered more wine, Coco, newly resolute, clamps her hand on top of her glass. She's already drunk too much. "Anyway, I have other things to think about."

"Such as?"

The redirection of her attention seems to energize her. She talks about introducing an in-house perfume into the store. Misia is enthusiastic. Adrienne is cooler about the project, fearing it will compromise the design side of the business. She is worried they might overreach themselves.

Coco says, "A new fragrance."

"Most people don't even wash," Adrienne says.

"A woman should smell like a woman, not a rose."

"I need a new scent. Something less floral," Misia says. "I've been bitten *twice* in the last few days." As evidence she offers two small lumps on the back of her arm.

Adrienne winces in sympathy but is quick to counter. "People won't care so long as it masks the stench of their bodies."

"People will change," Coco says.

One thing the nuns taught her: to be clean, to wash properly. If women want to smell nice with her fragrance, then they'll have to rinse themselves first. It's that simple.

"You stand to lose hugely if a venture of this sort fails."

Coco twists her glass in a ring of moisture, casting hoops of light on the tabletop. "You have to take risks in life."

"I'll drink to that," Misia says.

Adrienne speaks with exasperated emphasis. "You've taken enough risks already to last a lifetime."

"It's worked for Poiret, hasn't it?"

There's a silence.

"The business will expand massively if it proves a success. It's simply a question of manufacturing the stuff. Once it's developed, the hard part is over. It's not like clothes where

you have to design something new every season. You just
churn the perfume out."

"But why jeopardize everything you have for this . . ."
Adrienne casts around for a more contemptuous word but
fails to find one. ". . . scent?"

"It will give us a bit of distinction, enhance our standing.
Think of it as an exercise in style."

What she has in mind is not just another toiletry; it's something totally new, something unprecedented, something
enchanting and sublime. She wants a perfume so splendid
that, at the merest whiff, a man will be intoxicated. It will be
glorious, she thinks. Along with love, she feels perfume is
what makes a woman complete. And if one inspires the other,
then so much the better.

Sensing the wine at work within her, Adrienne says,
"Don't you have to research it first?"

"Darling, I already have. I've chosen my perfumer."

"Who?"

"Ernest Beaux."

"He's French, then."

"He's from St. Petersburg. But he works in Grasse."

"Another Russian!" Adrienne exclaims.

"His father was perfumer to the czar."

Misia says, "You really go for these Slavs, don't you?"

"Oh, stop it, you two!" She clenches then unclenches her
hand. "He's working on samples for me now."

"It's your money," Adrienne says, with qualified grace.

"It's not the money I care about," Coco muses, "it's the
independence."

Misia says, "That's something you realize after husband number three!"

Resignation thickens Adrienne's voice. "I suppose."

"Here's to us all, then," Coco offers.

"Your perfume."

"Your money."

"And all our independence," finishes Coco. The three of them raise their glasses to the light and clink hard.

CHAPTER TEN

The day after her return from the shop, Coco invites Igor for a walk in the surrounding woods. Above, the sky is vast and blue. Beyond stretch cornfields blotched with poppies. Visible in the distance is the spire of a church.

They stop to sit on the grass, and lean their backs against a cedar tree. To Coco, the tree smells of freshly sharpened pencils. All around them, crickets seethe.

She complains, "I wish *I* could play an instrument."

Igor says, "But you can sing."

"Like a crow!"

"That's not true."

He starts telling her of a soprano who gave up singing because the sound of her own voice made her cry.

She says, "That's ridiculous!"

"Why?"

"It's so precious."

"I thought it was romantic."

"Sentimental. There's a difference."

"I thought it would appeal to you."

Straightforwardly: "You were wrong."

She has this ability to belittle him in a way that no one

else can. Perhaps, he has time to consider, it's because he cares what she thinks.

Coco prefers to talk about more down-to-earth matters: the amount of tax she has to pay, the interest the banks charge, the ever-increasing wages bill. In Igor's loathing of the Bolsheviks, she finds an echo of her own impatience with workers' rights. Having pulled herself up out of the mire, she has no wish now to give others a helping hand. They'll rise, she thinks, if they're talented enough.

Something reckless enters her head. She stands up and strikes out in the direction of an orchard. Moments later, she's back, her eyes bright with mischief. In her hands she holds two small apples. "Here." She offers the more healthily distressed of the apples to Igor and burnishes her own against her chest. She twists off the stalk and takes a large bite.

Leaning back against the tree, Igor closes his eyes. With the sun on his face, he feels buoyed up. The world is good, he thinks. Suddenly the insect hum, the sunlight, and the crunch of the apple inside his head synthesize into a single chord. "Good," he says aloud.

He looks at Coco. He's fascinated by this woman who always seems so much in control. Not only does she cope with everyday problems, she seems able to shape her destiny in a larger sense as well. In short, she's good at life. She has vivacity and strength. He likes that. So different from Catherine, he can't help but observe. And she's shrewd and beautiful, too. He's stirred by her, no question, and feels a strong animal attraction enter his bones. He realizes he hasn't made love now for weeks; months even. A sweet heaviness begins to thicken in his groin.

He has always resisted other women in the past. Here in the present, however, he finds himself tempted beyond measure. He turns his head toward her and sees her lit by the sun. Suddenly he wants to put out his hand and touch her. To prove to her his feelings, to match her audacity. He's so close at this moment he can see the pores on her nose. He feels the veils of flirtation dissolve before a raw urge, a blind will. His fingers stretch tensely. Seconds bend into a new space. His body involves itself in a tropism toward her.

Afraid, though, that some deceitful twist of perspective makes her seem nearer than she really is, he tilts forward to follow the instinct only to lean back, deterred. The moment is lost. She hovers out of reach.

Something of the northern puritan in him has drawn him back; all that formal restraint, that coolness. He hates that in himself. He's afraid to say or do anything irrevocable. Here he is living in Coco's home and, thanks to her patronage, enjoying a fine lifestyle. If he were to make advances, he's not sure what she'd do. She might react badly and tell Catherine. Perhaps her invitation to Bel Respiro was wholly altruistic, after all.

Sweating, he rubs at the reddened dents where the pads of his glasses have chafed in the heat. He thinks of all the love in the world, and none of it for him. He'll never make love to anyone again in his life except Catherine. He sees the possibility, the probability, stretch in front of him, extending to a vanishing point which, he guesses, is his death.

Then sternly he reminds himself, he is here to work. This, for him, is paramount. And there's a strong sense of loyalty in him—always has been. He feels he'll never stop loving

Catherine, or the children. They are, and will forever remain, fixtures in his life. There's something charming in flirtation, but something noble in resisting it, he tells himself.
Yet he knows, too, that Coco's proximity within the villa is
killing him.

He watches her throw away the remains of her apple and
follows suit. Then they set off back through the woods. Dog
roses blossom in the hedges. The grass is thick with butterflies
and fungus. Birds call sweetly from the crowns of the trees.

Coco offers her arm and, with exaggerated gallantry, Igor
takes it. There is an intimacy in their just being together, he
thinks; the two of them touched by the same air. He feels her
lean against him. Their embrace tightens, though visibly they
move no closer. For a time, they are conscious through layers
of cloth that their arms touch. Then without warning he
reaches across to kiss her, quickly and deliberately, in a way
that still might be interpreted as merely playful. A noncom-
mittal kiss on the cheek, soft and moist, lasting less than a
second.

She permits it, and smiles without looking at him, but
doesn't encourage him to go on. He senses it as a rejection.
She has drawn her line. Only so far, but no further, he understands.

Walking in silence back to the house, they disengage just
before they enter the garden. For there Catherine sits, reading in the sunshine. And there the children play.

At night, on the balcony, Catherine stands close to her husband. She says, "It's romantic, isn't it?"

Romantic: the smell of jasmine on the air, the moon in three-quarter profile, and the cicadas fiddling like café violinists. He cannot deny it. "Yes," he says, leaning against the rail.

He feels the need to appease her after their fight the other night. They have not spoken openly for several days now. Humiliated still, Igor has been uncommunicative and sullen. He can sustain a sulk for weeks. Usually it falls to Catherine to make up. But on this occasion, it is he who attempts to be conciliatory.

He moves toward her. They hold hands; his eyes grow soft. Taking her in his arms, he kisses her on the forehead chastely. His fingers stroke her cheek. She inclines her neck to accommodate his touch. His lips wander tenderly to her eyelids. But when he tries to kiss her on the lips, she moves her head so that his mouth meets only her hair.

"No," she says, almost inaudibly.

In avoiding his lips like this, in averting her head, he feels she's withdrawing her whole being. She seems, suddenly, a lifeless doll in his arms. The faintest impulse of desire drains from him. He holds her slackly for a moment, feels her head press against his chest. She's sleepy, she says. It's been a long day. The children are already in bed.

Igor can't remember the last time they slept together as man and wife. She's sick, he knows, and that doesn't make it easy. And perhaps it shouldn't matter, but it does. He aches with frustration. The absence of physical love is burning a hole inside him. He feels a tension within him that is desperate to be released.

With a final hug, he releases her from his arms. At that moment a gust of wind buffets her from one side, causing her to stagger. He can't believe she stays upright. She has to steady herself against the railing. He thinks of Coco and the way she'd find the wind invigorating, the way she'd feed off its energy and make it her own. A vision of her comes to him: her dark hair, her inky eyes and ardent mouth, that wide, shapeless smile. In thinking of her, he looks at his wife. In his mind he attempts to superimpose the image of the one upon the other. Try as he might, the image will not fit. They're too different, misaligned. White note and black note. Together they jar.

Catherine retreats inside. Igor remains on the balcony. He looks up at the starlit sky, listens to the hiss of insects, inhales the odor of the night flowers. The word still haunts him: romantic, he thinks.

Sunday. With the Stravinskys at church, Coco noses around Igor's study.

She enters the room with reverence as well as a remote sense of dread. Looking about sharply, she half expects him to storm in and reproach her for violating his space. She leaves the door ajar, wanting if necessary a means of escape. Each step she experiences as a transgression. There is an intimacy in the act. Something worshipful, yet something predatory, too.

She heads straight for Igor's desk, and touches the ink bottles, india rubbers, pens, and rulers—things rendered precious by the fact of their being his. She opens his glasses' case, which snaps shut abruptly, causing her to start. Lifting his magnifying glass over the table, she sees objects oddly warped and swollen under the lens. The knit of things seems for an instant to be revealed—the weave of manuscript paper, a watermark. A tuning fork thickens under its Cyclopean eye.

With a final thrill of trespass, she moves to the piano. She removes the tiny trefoil key from its place within the stool, turning it once in the lock until it clicks. With both hands, she lifts the lid. It is heavier than she thought, as if a resistant force is telling her she shouldn't be doing this.

She pulls the back of one hand softly across the keys. Too soft to make a sound, but hard enough to feel the tiny hairs on her fingers bristle with a delicate rippling pressure. They feel strange to the touch and not what she'd expected. The white keys seem bony and brittle, while the black keys are harder and more compact. Then she allows her index finger independently to press one of the higher notes. The sound makes a star in the surrounding silence.

Her heart jumps as she hears a rustle. Recoiling a little, she turns around to see Vassily padding in. The cat stares at her through the narrow slots of his green eyes. Igor's familiar. Stealthily he lengthens his body. She feels guilty again before rationalizing the moment: Igor won't be back for another couple of hours.

Once more she presses the key, bolder this time. She presses the note again and again until the room rings with its prolonged vibration. Then, touching it more softly, she listens to the dissolving tone. The sensation she gains is not just auditory, it is tactile. In decaying, the echo sends a spasm the whole length of her spine.

She is struck once more by the thought that she misses him. Each day without him now seems a day damned. And anyway, she considers, why should she compromise? What if this is a chance to experience genuine love? Not the wanton romping of her youth, but something more substantial, more profound. Can she really afford to pass up such opportunities in her late thirties? She's free to do as she pleases. She has the money to finance her desires, and the power to enact them. Catherine has had her chance. Why should she feel sorry for her? She's led such a privileged existence until now. It's up to Igor to choose who he wants to be with. He's not interested in being a martyr, she's convinced. She just hopes she hasn't frightened him off.

Looking out of the window, she feels the world around her widen. Leaves, their heart-shaped shadows, flicker flatly against the wall.

She sets down the lid of the piano and locks it. Then, running an eye over the table, she checks that everything is as she found it and that nothing has been disturbed. She leaves as silently as she came. Behind her, the sunlight shoots through half-open shutters, touching all the objects and making them warm.

Upon their return from church, Igor and Catherine relax in the garden in two reclining chairs. The children play football on the lawn. Their shouts carry a long way. At the far end of the garden, thinking they can't be heard, the two boys begin swearing following a hard tackle. Igor shouts for them to watch their tongues.

His chair is turned away slightly from that of his wife.

Since returning from church, they have not exchanged a word. He is busy scribbling some notes.

She says, "You only ever tell them off. You never play with them." The whiteness of her skin looks incongruous next to her husband's swarthier body.

"I don't see you playing with them either," he retorts, after a pause. Although he has the genuine intention of patching things up with his wife, he nevertheless finds himself tetchy in her presence.

"I would if I were feeling better."

"Well, I'm determined not to waste my time." He continues writing, more urgently this time.

"Theo has been miserable recently."

"Really?"

"You don't care."

Slowly and deliberately, with a pencil in his mouth: "Yes. I care."

"I think he might have heard us arguing."

"No. He heard *you* shouting."

She ignores him. "It's hard for them. They've moved a lot."

"It'd be a lot harder back in Russia."

"I'm not so sure."

Derisively: "You don't think?"

"*You're* the only one who seems happy in the villa."

"That's not true. Ludmilla loves it here, and Soulima's having a nice time. In fact, there's no reason for any of them to be unhappy."

"Well, I can think of a few."

Exasperated: "Catherine—can't you see I'm busy?"

It's no good, it isn't working with Catherine, he decides. He wants Coco and feels miserable without her. And yet it is torture living so close the whole time and not being able to touch. It places an intolerable strain of temptation upon him. He must do something. It isn't right. He admits to himself that he's in love with her but doesn't know what to do. He burns with the need for a different life.

Flight.

It's as if Catherine senses this. "Why bother to spend time with us? Why don't you just go to her? That's what you want, isn't it?"

Igor says nothing, just bites his lip and carries on scribbling.

"You never talk to me anymore. Even Joseph pays me more attention than you do."

It is true; at this moment he resents being with her and has nothing to say. He feels ashamed but is unable to deny it. Part of the problem, he realizes, is that he feels powerless, living here on another woman's charity and subject to her whims. He needs to impose control over someone—and who is more convenient than his wife? Of course on one level he knows this is pathetic. Yet, try as he might, he finds he cannot help himself.

The boys hurry back toward them. "Come on, Papa, come on, Mama!"

Having come to an impasse in his composition anyway, and hurt into activity by Catherine's slight, Igor responds immediately. In a vindictive show of energy, he slides his papers into his wallet, lays down his pencil, and sprints after the ball.

Rising from her chair, Catherine feels her lungs labor

with the effort. She senses the air in her chest begin sluggishly to churn. While the fresh air is good for her, she knows
the emotional upset she's experiencing is potentially calami-
tous for her health.

The sermon today, she recalls, was all about tolerance and
forgiveness; how we shouldn't allow our grievances to get in
the way of giving our love. Ordinarily she'd be quick to forgive him. But she feels hurt and angry still. He's made no
effort, really, to reconcile with her, apart from his grand gesture on the balcony last night. It was clear all he wanted was
sex—to force himself upon her—while what she craves with
increasing desperation is tenderness, affection, and, above
all, respect. She's not willing to surrender just like that. That
would be too easy.

She watches him now as he runs around the garden. It is
as if he is possessed, she thinks. Finally he kicks the ball so
hard against the outhouse that all the parrots squawk.

CHAPTER ELEVEN

Coco arranges a game of tennis with the Serts. A club in a neighboring village boasts several well-maintained grass courts. Igor enjoys playing, and Coco is keen to see Misia again. So, in the heat of the afternoon, the two couples—for so they seem—are driven out by Coco's chauffeur.

Coming to a narrow bridge over a stream, the driver brakes sharply. A car has drawn up simultaneously on the other side. As both approach roads are on an incline, neither is aware of the other's presence until both are practically on the bridge itself. The two vehicles come to a stop. The driver of the other car makes it plain he has no intention of reversing; so Coco's chauffeur starts to back up. But she screams at him not to budge. Both cars are thus stuck on the creaking wooden slats of the bridge for about ten minutes. Igor remonstrates, but she refuses to back down. She grows adamant, instructing the driver to switch off the engine and sit back until the other man yields—which, eventually, in high dudgeon, he does. Driving on, Coco offers a magisterial wave to the driver of the other car as they pass. He is red-faced with indignation, she white with self-righteousness.

"Stupid man!" she blurts.

Looking out, Igor sees the telegraph poles stretch into the distance like bars and bars of rest.

"She's a woman who likes to get her own way," José says, as he and Igor emerge from the changing room half an hour later.

Tanned and glowingly healthy, both men look dapper in their whites. Igor bends to measure the height of the net as José practices a few overhead serves. Coco and Misia still linger inside.

"Catherine, of course, is still sick," Coco says. "She's had Marie up and down the stairs all day."

"Oh, dear."

"And the kids just create havoc around the place."

"Does Igor say anything?"

She laughs. "I'm not sure he even notices. He spends all his time at the piano."

"Ah, yes."

"He says he has a new symphony on the go."

"Exciting."

Sincere for the moment: "Yes. It is."

"I liked his *Scherzo Fantastique.*"

"What was that about?"

"Bees, I think," Misia says, tying her laces. Dressed, she picks up her racquet and bangs the strings against the heel of her hand. The air around the racquet rings. Small white squares are printed on her palm. "If I remember the scenario correctly, the queen kills off the male once he's outlived his sexual usefulness."

Coco laughs. "If only . . ." She copies the gesture of rapping the racquet smartly against her hand.

Outdoors, Igor, a little skinny next to the plumper José, swings his arms gawkily in preparation for the game. Mixed doubles. He is to partner with Misia, while José is paired with Coco across the net.

The women come out wearing white cotton dresses and broad cream hats. They both look swanky in contrast to the men.

After knocking up for a couple of minutes, the match begins in earnest. José is sluggish around the court and rarely comes to the net. But when he connects, his shots are strong. He has an impressive forehand, which fizzes if he hits it right. Igor is quicker and nimbler around the court; his anticipation is good, and while he may lack José's power, he enjoys a surer touch.

Coco, he notices, holds the racquet oddly, and sometimes it is all she can do to volley his serves back over the net. Yet she manages a few deft dabs and perky volleys, and her timing is generally sweet. He's more lenient in his returns to her than he is with José. And twice when, with fat backhands, she hits the ball long, he knowingly calls them in. Seeing this, Misia—to his consternation—winks at him. He pretends not to notice. But she's wrong if she thinks him a pushover. Ever competitive, he's out to win. And as the match proceeds, he scampers after every point until something swells within him and seems ready to burst. He begins to hit the ball harder and harder as if he wants to punish it.

The weather is hot and he sweats profusely. The handle on his racquet grows humid. His grip begins to slip. Released into a life of higher energy, he chases everything, exerting himself beyond measure. The others seem ponderous by contrast. As the match goes on, he ruthlessly exploits José's slowness. A series of exquisite dink shots played into space are perfectly calculated to leave him for dead.

"What's the matter with him?" asks José. "Does he always play like this?"

Then with the score at one set all, and in the middle of a tense final set, he reaches for one of José's whippy, unanswerable, chalk-flirting serves. The ball hits Igor's racquet with a melancholy twang. In the following overheated exchange of shots, Igor feels the "give" of the racquet along with its tautness soften. His shots lose their crispness. The song goes out of them. An inspection of the racquet head reveals a broken string, which crimps miserably as he pulls it out. He raises the frame to show his opponents.

The match is abandoned and declared a draw.

"Well, what do you think?" Coco asks. Exhausted, she slumps down in the changing room next to Misia.

Misia idly straightens the strings on her racquet. "He makes a good tennis partner, that's for sure."

"Come on," Coco urges.

"He certainly puts his all into it."

"He never gives up on a point, does he?"

"He likes to chase the things he wants."

Coco looks across at her. "And what's that supposed to mean?"

Misia's waist may have thickened over the years but she still possesses the aura and frank energy of the sexually voracious. "Nothing," she responds in a singsong voice. "But none of us is getting any younger, dear. You've got to chase what you want, too."

"That's part of the problem." Coco looks despondent. "I don't know what I want." She's finding it hard to resist the instinct that keeps telling her there is something about him that is right. He is talented and sophisticated. He has intellectual weight and the kind of profoundly artistic sympathy that appeals to her. Rather than infatuation, a deep sense of affinity draws her toward him. And the call is becoming stronger with each passing day. "I keep changing my mind. I need to be sure."

"About him, or you?"

"What I don't understand is . . ." She hesitates.

"Go on."

"How can he be so musical, yet so lacking in emotion?"

"He wants people to love him, don't you see?"

"I'm sure he'd prefer them to love his work. Everything else is secondary. He says so."

"He's just shy."

"You think?"

"Maybe he just needs someone to bring him out a bit."

"Perhaps you're right." Then less cheerfully: "But I want someone who's mad about me, who can't live without me."

Misia looks at her. "You think I don't?"

Coco clamps her racquet back in its press.

"Here." Misia tosses two tennis balls to her in quick succession. Coco catches them, opening her hands and closing them over like a mouth.

Misia burlesques the flight of a bee, flapping her arms about rapidly. "Zzzz."

"Oh, stop it!" Coco says. Then, fitting the balls into the bottom of her bag, she pulls the buckles tight.

CHAPTER TWELVE

It is the lifeless middle of the afternoon. Houses across the region are sealed against the heat.

The shutters in Igor's study are half closed. Light filters through them, fashioning shadows against the walls. He is running through a melody by Pergolesi. He neither hears nor sees Coco enter the room.

Stirred by the faint strains of the piano, she has been drawn like a somnambulist toward their source. She stands in a corner of the room, watching him. A white linen suit sets off her deep bronze tan. The skirt is cinched by a dark belt. Light from the shutters stripes one side of her face. Her bare feet feel the coolness of the floor.

Seeing Igor's hands ripple across the piano, she experiences a slow inflammation of her senses. Her mind made up, she shuffles silently out of her skirt, which falls in a wrinkly heap at her feet.

Igor becomes abruptly aware of her presence, sensing her nearness like an animal. He stops playing, but does not turn around, remaining frozen in midgesture, his fingers tense and arrested above the keys. Coco moves like heat behind him. Two deft hands steal over his eyes.

She whispers thrillingly in his ear.

He does not answer, but with supreme self-control he closes the lid of the piano. He turns slowly as she backs off. A line of sweat appears on his forehead. His throat is parched, and his tongue feels like a bone. The sound of a bird outside scrapes across the floor of his mind. He sits facing her, astonished, his hands placed chastely on his knees. They look at one another trustingly for some moments. Then jubilantly she pulls off her top. The fabric snags on the cloud of her hair. Static adheres to a few stray wisps so that they stick out witchily. She lets the top drop with startling casualness the short distance from her hand to the floor. Then, without visible hurry, she peels off her underclothes. The sight of her naked stuns him.

Straightening her hair, she turns around. She knows she's taking a risk, but it's what she wants. She's thought about it, and the only way to succeed, she decides, is to be as open and honest as possible. Despite her frankness, she feels vulnerable and fights a natural shyness.

She lies upon her stomach across the chaise longue, her legs bent at an angle to her body. Slats of light from the shutters extend in bars across her body, improvising a keyboard the length of her naked back. Her face tilts up toward him, her chin cupped in her hand. "Well?" she says. There's a sense of challenge in her voice. She sounds almost cross.

A faint hum hangs in the air, sustained from the ghostly notes of the piano. Igor hesitates, half puzzled, half afraid.

He feels all at sea and moves heavily as through water toward her. He halts for a moment, his shadow occluding the stripes across her back. His glasses sit with a desperate attempt at equilibrium on his nose. A fly fizzes and crackles in a corner of the room.

His fingers tingle as though recovering from numbness. His limbs are no longer solid. Something catches in his throat. It's insane, he thinks. But his chest seems suddenly full with blood. Then, like a piece of elastic that has stretched and stretched and finally snapped back, frenziedly he undresses, abandoning his garments like bad debts. She watches him struggle with the buckle of his trousers, smiles to see him rip off his shoes. His eyes reveal a raw need, a desperate longing.

Desire undoes him. He kisses her hungrily on the stomach. A delicious salinity films her skin. He absorbs the scent of her hair and inhales the odor of her breasts like damp roses, feeling their smearing pressure against his chest. He feels her tongue flutter in his mouth. Quick, oysterish kisses.

"Hey, slow down a little!" she says, sensing his impatience.

He looks up, stunned to hear her voice. Now that it is happening, it seems unreal. He loses any sensation of weight in his body. Appalled at himself, yet unrepentant, he is overwhelmed by the sheer carnality of the act.

Coco smiles at him. "Slowly," she urges. He smiles back, disarmed.

It's as though his life thus far has been a sham. A door within him is flung open. He feels something monstrous in his performance, something utterly reckless released. At this moment, music seems a remote groping, a mealymouthed endeavor, an obscure project that can at best approximate the passion he feels. The compositions into which he has thrown himself seem as coldly abstract as mathematical proofs. The physicality of his love for Coco is what makes life urgent now.

He is permeated by the scent her flesh gives off. His lips cling to her skin and release themselves only to find new undiscovered points of her body. His fingers find with fierce ardor the flute stops of her vertebrae. Fumbling along the warm and tawny insides of her thighs, his hands are cold there and she shivers.

Minutes before it had seemed wholly improper to sleep with her. Now it seems the most natural thing in the world. He remembers the first time Catherine and he made love—a messy, painful defloration. He experiences nothing of that with Coco. It's what he has been waiting for secretly all his life. He feels their limbs mingle as if they were made to.

Slowly Coco feels herself the center of a set of concentric circles, around which everything seems to ripple and blur. A glow spreads itself like an odor across her chest. The low flame on her cheeks spreads to a fire engulfing her whole body. She feels something well within her, quicken, achieve a brief vertiginous rhythm, and then explode. Her insides feel as if they're falling. For a moment, her eyes have a stupid look, then her head snaps sideways violently.

A prolonged shudder runs through her. Her limbs stiffen, and pink spots appear where her fingers press into Igor's arms.

They both rest on the floor. Gently she runs her fingers through his hair and traces the ripened line of his jaw. She strokes the muscles of his stomach and caresses the insides of his arms. He seems immobilized for a moment. But she relaxes him, kissing his head, eyelids, neck, and chest, before coaxing him into her with an ardor he finds almost immodest.

Astonishing how slim she is, he thinks, the hungry young look of her hips pulling him in. He eases deeper until he's swallowed by her heat. A hot slippery softness that makes him think of licorice. With thrilling delicacy, her hands trail over his body, enjoying a series of wondrous contacts. Blindly she sucks his fingers. Lithely she arches her back. He realizes, a little awed, that he is being instructed. Slowly he senses a realignment taking place. He feels his whole life being re-defined, his entire existence reshaped.

Drunkenly he loses himself inside her. Her breath is warm and fluttery against his chest. As his movements quicken, be-coming more urgent, he feels their warm charged bodies move in synchrony like two melodic lines. His face becomes radiant, his lips stretched wide with desire. Then he trembles with fierce pleasure. A single hot charge stings his flesh. The delir-ium suffuses itself long-sufferingly through his body.

Motionless, they lie together for a few moments in a state of mutual dissolution. She rests her body against his. He sets his hand, limp as a leaf curl, on her stomach. Her fingertips pamper the hairs at the back of his neck. Eventually they both rise from the floor. Standing apart, she folds her arms in suddenly discovered modesty.

"Forgive me," he whispers.

"For what?"

"I couldn't help myself."

She asks, "Did I shock you?"

As she turns to retrieve her top, he sees her shoulder blades flex symmetrically like a winged creature at rest.

He finds himself thinking bizarrely of Beethoven's final string quartet. In that piece, the composer asks the violinist to play two notes together without separating them—only directing that the second should be played "with emotion," with a kind of audible sob. All his life, Igor has wondered what that meant. Now, marvelously, he knows. He has felt that sob inside himself, in the movements their two bodies enjoyed in making love.

"You're beautiful," he says, stroking one of her eyelids with his thumb.

"No."

"Very beautiful."

"Stop."

"I mean it."

After a pause, she asks, "Have you ever slept with anyone except Catherine?" She sees him smile. "I mean apart from me."

"It didn't occur to me until I met you." This is not quite true. It has occurred to him with increasing frequency of late. But he's always feared the flat retributive hand of God smiting him in the act. He still does. "I've wanted it to happen ever since."

"Me, too," she says. This is also a lie. It is only in the last week or two that her admiration for him has developed into a powerful sexual attraction. What would have surprised her a week ago, however, seems inevitable and necessary now.

"Are you sure I'm rich enough for you?"

Enigmatically. "I'm used to having a good time."

She sees he is about to say something else and puts a finger to his lips, hushing him. Down the corridor, they can hear the children finishing their lessons for the afternoon. "I must go," she whispers and dresses quickly. She stops to blow him a kiss before slipping in silence out the door.

Afterward, Igor wipes a thin film of dust from the top of the piano. He opens the lid the way a horse might lift its gums to reveal a set of healthy teeth. Bending his head close to the keys, he guddles for a moment in the lower registers.

Music spills from the study for the remainder of the afternoon.

Exhausted, Igor lies in the dark, lengthways, next to his sleeping wife.

Normally he sleeps on his stomach, but tonight he lies on his back. He's afraid he will smother facedown. The moon is full, giving the room an incubatory glow. His eyes stare at the ceiling. His toes point upward. His hands, slightly curled, rest inertly at his sides. He finds it oppressively hot. Stifling. Heat presses in at the window, and a pain presses behind his eye. He experiences an inner tightening.

He feels terrible. Sternly raised by his parents, he finds faithfulness a hard standard to break. Loyalty has always had for him the force of an implacable law. Marrying, he'd taken a sacred vow. And in breaking it he feels guilt like a liquid thicken his blood. Yet when he asks himself if he wants to spend the rest of his life with Catherine, he suffers the realization that the answer is no. Doesn't he deserve to be happy, too?

A wild hope takes over that perhaps Catherine need never know. Better still, she might grow to accept it. But Coco might not want that. Then it crosses his mind: what exactly does she want? A fling? A long-lasting relationship? Marriage?

If a mere fling, he'd hate it. He's too infatuated to want just that. But marriage: that would require a complete and potentially messy renegotiation of the terms of his life. The possibilities branch and fork before him until his future seems suddenly out of control.

Next to him, his wife's head is exposed above the sheet. Her breathing is uneven, her hair fanned out like a shadow behind her head. He reaches across to touch her forehead. It is hot. Her cheeks are hectic with fever. Her body has always generated more heat than his own. She has always enjoyed this caloric superiority over him. He closes his eyes. All he can see is Coco. All he can think of is Coco. She's the first thing he thinks of in the morning and the last thing he contemplates late at night. She has become his whole world. It's as if nothing came before. Everything else is canceled out. He wants his life to start over again, he decides: here and now, with her.

In thinking this, he becomes vaguely conscious of a shape surrounding him. Something dense and vengeful spreads in the dark above his bed. He feels a weight oppress his chest. His scalp freezes. Terrified, he pulls the covers up to his neck. Try as he might, he cannot sleep. And this after having attempted to deaden his senses with vodka until quite late.

He lies on his wrong side as the small hours slide by. And he's bitten alive. It seems the mosquitoes have registered the rise in his blood. All night, they fizz above him like watches being wound. Worse, cats scream like babies outside his window. The sound—its high-pitched whining, its intimations of bristling fur—rips with its claws into his appalled consciousness.

Abruptly, he awakes. A twinge of pain starts from deep within him. Dyspepsia. Little acid secretions set off a burning sensation in his chest.

It is very early in the morning. He feels dizzy with the twin burdens of guilt and fatigue. Sitting up, he senses the room's angles tilt. An unstable sense of gravity seems to have entered the fabric of things. Objects upon their surfaces appear uncertainly sustained, held down by a pressure unseen. As he rises from the bed, Igor is frightened that the floor might fall away beneath him to reveal the abyss beneath. Tentatively his feet reach for the ground. Only miraculous forces conspire, it seems, to keep him upright.

In truth he is preoccupied: blissfully, hopelessly preoccupied, and subject to ungovernable urges. He cannot help himself now. Everywhere he is reminded of her. Her smell crowds his nostrils, her image clings to the mirrors. The gravity of her warm mass drags him toward her. He is in torment. The heat is driving him to despair.

And he is afraid there will be a price to pay. What if Catherine finds out? She would be destroyed. She's already very weak. This might push her over the edge.

He looks across at her. She no longer seems like someone he knows. A distance has opened up between them that calls into question everything they've ever shared. He tries to remember a time when they were happy. A collection of moments is summoned, but they seem in his mind to be stiff as pictures, remote and even vaguely unreal. A seashell on her bedside table gleams creamily with its inner light.

He walks toward the window and peeps through the curtains. The sky is dark still. The usual stars swarm into his vision. Oddly, the universe seems unaltered.

He thinks of the invisible sinews of connection, the unseen webs of contingency that have delivered him here, with Coco in this villa, at this irreducible point in time. He wonders what benign or malevolent effort of destiny has so tugged him toward her.

He's never been one to give up on things, to quit. He likes to stick at a task until it's done. But where is his responsibility now? His sense of endurance, his ability to see things through? And what is it all for, anyway? A glimpse of freedom, wholly unreal? A taste of desire, ruinous?

His face is filmed with perspiration. His pajama top adheres tackily to his back. A white heat ripples across his skin. Fear touches him. He resists an impulse to kneel and pray more fervently than he has ever done before. For what, after all, could he say? What has happened, he wanted to happen. He had willed it, even, and yielded with shameless speed.

He moves into the bathroom and confronts his image in the mirror. A gray, taut face is thrown back at him. He sees his thinning hair, his rotting teeth. The network of fine lines on his palms seems deepened into trenches. Another two years and he will be forty. What is he doing at his age, falling in love? It is absurd. A feeling of utter bliss at his experience vies with a feeling of terror at the possibility of its loss. He wants more of her, needs more of her. Nothing in his life has prepared him for this.

He removes his glasses and turns on the tap, scooping handfuls of cold water onto his face. He winces at the shock.

Then, with the air of a man who has just discovered appetites that scream out to be appeased, he fills a bath and pours jugful after jugful of water over his head. The water cascades over his torso, flattening the dark hairs on his chest and back. He shivers with exhilaration.

Dressed, he makes his way downstairs. Entering his study, he prepares to take on the world through his work. It is still too early for breakfast, still too early to wake anyone by playing the piano. In any case, it is out of tune. It has warped in the heat—or the humidity, which is also very high. At least it is cool right now. Outdoors, the morning light is shadowless. The apple trees are glazed with dew.

He glances at the photographs of his family on the desk. They seem alien to him now, as if overnight someone has changed the frames. He feels guilt perch like a squat bird on his shoulder, its talons sinking deep into his skin.

Seeking respite in his music, he takes out a clean sheet of paper. He picks up a sharpened pencil and shoves his glasses up on his head. Then, taking great pains not to extend his strokes a millimeter above or below the staves, he marks off the bars in regular lines.

CHAPTER THIRTEEN

On subsequent days, always at the same time in the middle of the afternoon, the piano stops playing.

A tense silence establishes itself within the house. Catherine's head stiffens on her pillow, braced for sounds that do not come. She listens as the piano's last note withdraws slowly from the air. Like an acid, the silence works its way through her body, leaving a feeling of afterburn in her guts.

Each day, as the piano comes to an abrupt stop, the cat bristles and arches its back; the birds in their cages tilt their heads; the dogs' ears assume a worried angle. The children freeze for a moment and exchange curious glances, surprised by the lengthening silence that reigns in the middle of each afternoon.

Joseph and Marie shoot one another a knowing look. Both raise their eyes to heaven.

Marie whispers, "It's started!"

"This is all we need," Joseph says.

Each afternoon for the next few weeks the same routine repeats itself. The piano breaks off in the middle of a phrase, only to pick up a little more jauntily about half an hour later. The silence creates a hollow into which everything is drawn.

As the days pass, the hollow deepens into an emptiness

within Catherine, an emptiness she fills with anguish and fear. Part of her wants to investigate this bizarre hiatus, but another part dreads what she might find. She prefers ignorance to the possibility of horror. She is too weak at present to deal with the consequences. The silence widens within her like a wound.

Igor, meanwhile, is bewitched. Coco offers him an unapologetically sensual love, the quality of which he has never experienced before with Catherine. Hers is a passion uninhibited by any residual bourgeois scruple, a passion approaching vulgarity in its frankness. He is astonished by Coco's sexual confidence and her willingness to experiment. He wonders if she finds him sexually naïve.

Catherine in lovemaking has always tended toward passivity. Unresponsive at the best of times, her illness now makes sex a difficult and clumsy business. If her body participates at all, he considers, it is only through a reflex that answers him out of habit. The truth is, she hates the physical demands he makes upon her.

Where Catherine endures making love as a wifely duty, a procreative act that has all too quickly yielded four children, with Coco, Igor experiences it for the first time as a mutually jubilant and rawly pleasurable bliss. It is like the sudden and liberating discovery of jazz. There's something joyous about it, glorious even. It's as if, released from timidity, he feels free to improvise. There are no rules. Emboldened to follow his impulse, it's different every time. There's a gleeful abandon in their lovemaking. An unquenchable momentum establishes itself in their relationship. The bird of guilt is blown from his shoulder. He cannot stop himself now.

The affair makes him see everything in a vivid light. It's as if he's been given new eyeglasses that allow him to see colors more brilliantly than ever before, and, having glimpsed the high tones and contrasts, the vibrancy of life around him, he's reluctant to give them up.

They take to exchanging love notes. Igor writes a note and sets it in the piano stool. Then, in the afternoon, Coco collects it and leaves one of her own in her familiar, sprawling, slightly childish hand. They are simple and effusive and full of endearments, and secret, which makes them more thrilling. Igor writes more than Coco usually. But she has all the emotional delicacy and uncanny eloquence, he thinks, so that just a few short sentences from her can be more moving and tender and true than any well-turned phrases he might conjure up.

In the mornings they both work. Then in the afternoons they make love. At other times of the day, when they meet at dinner for instance, they attempt an outward show of aloofness in each other's company. It's as though there are two distinct and separate levels upon which they can operate. One does not seem to interfere with the other so the two do not, for the moment at least, need to be reconciled. They are like two clarinets playing simultaneously in harshly conflicting keys. The only reconciliation necessary is an acceptance of their duality.

They coexist in a kind of super-key.

Eager to escape the hazardous privacy of his study, Igor and Coco take a walk in the woods.

Coming across a remote clearing, they abandon their usual care. The illicit nature of their relationship generates a sudden heat. A sympathetic seethe of insects surrounds them. Their needs converge in an instant and focus on a scorched patch of ground. They undress rapidly and form a rocking knot that has them both grunting furiously with all the relief of a passion no longer strangled but given voice at last. The whole wood seems to catch the vibration. Birds answer from the topmost branches. A distant dog barks. The minutes of the day for both of them warp and broaden into a delicious and unanticipated second life.

Afterward, as they retrieve their garments, Coco says, "I think they know."

"Who?"

"Joseph and Marie."

"How?"

"They run the house. They know everything."

Fear pulses through him. "My God, what are we going to do?" He stumbles pulling his trousers on.

"Calm down. They're loyal to me. I employ them, re-member."

There's a silence.

She secures the last button on her chemise. "But doesn't Catherine suspect already?"

He looks at her. "I live in fear of her finding out."

"Do you want to stop it now?"

"I can't." He's never felt so alive. It's like when you have your first child, he reflects. You love it utterly and think you could never love another so much. And then the second child comes along, and you *do* love it as much if not more. He feels the same about marriage. He never thought he'd meet anyone he'd love as much as Catherine. And here he is now with Coco, and his world is turned upside down.

She, too, explores the revelation that she is in love. It hits her as something essential; something as necessary as the walls of the house, as the sunstruck windows or the warm tiled roof above her head. There is nothing fussily luxuriant or emptily decorative about the sensation. It has about it the pure clean lines of a given fact. There's no mistaking it. Like a scent, it is simply there.

She says, "I won't smother you, I promise."

"Maybe I *want* to be smothered." Dressed, he embraces her again.

"Let me be your mistress."

"I'd like that."

"You'll be my lover."

They touch foreheads for a moment before he shakes his head in disbelief. "It's crazy, but for the first time in years, I'm really happy." He means it. A feeling of well-being overtakes him.

"I'm glad," she says.

As she looks up at him in the sunlight, everything around her suddenly whites out.

Obsessed with cleanliness at the best of times, Igor is careful always to scrub himself of Coco's scent. He is careful, too, to ensure the children are preoccupied either with their lessons or playing out of earshot in the afternoons. If the affair is reck-less in itself, then his pursuit of it—save for the impetuous episode in the woods—is rigorous in the extreme.

Yet something impish within Coco wishes to buck the regulated nature that their assignations quickly assume. Every so often, she deliberately fails to appear on time. On such occasions, Igor feels an icy void dilate inside his body. Reli-gious about keeping appointments and fanatically punctual himself, he begins pacing around inside his study if she is even a minute late. He grows increasingly frustrated if that one minute then stretches to five or ten. Eventually, of course, she does arrive, and his longings are soon healed. But she takes a sly pleasure in registering his dismay.

With inevitable quickness, Catherine becomes suspi-cious. She watches closely, scrutinizing their behavior for any telltale signs. She knows Igor has been attracted to other women in the past, but this time it's different. There's a grav-ity about his relationship with Coco that none of his previous friendships with women ever possessed. What worries Cath-erine now is that Igor is no longer a young man. This can't be ascribed to some passing infatuation. He's thirty-eight, for God's sake. A mature, grown-up man. This is serious.

For all the lip service Coco and Igor pay to discretion, it is at mealtimes that Catherine realizes, with a crushing sense of helplessness, that something is indeed going on. She sees that, as they speak, there flashes a spark between them. For the first time, their relationship is on display. And Igor, at least, seems unaware of the embarrassing transparency with which he behaves when the two of them are together.

They betray themselves involuntarily. Their closeness

broadcasts itself despite their best efforts. Their voices grow softer in one another's company, braiding into one. A kind of languor steals over them. They eat little. She shoots him dewy glances across the table. He responds with involved stares. Her knee rests heedlessly against his.

Sickened, Catherine is scarcely able to touch her food. She has no friends close by to consult or share concerns with. Lonely, she exists in a kind of bubble. When she's with them, she feels herself go completely numb—the way a body in shock closes down all but its essential functions. The only time she escapes is when she goes to church each Sunday.

With little independent means, she is totally reliant for the moment upon Coco for financial support. And here is Coco with her shops, her Rolls-Royce, her villa, and her servants. Catherine feels trapped, isolated, violated, and betrayed. The servants tiptoe around her as though around an unexploded bomb. The children sense instinctively that she's upset, that something is wrong, and yet she finds herself in the ludicrous position of having to reassure them that everything is fine.

Igor is slow to recognize the children's misgivings about their being there, even though Theodore in particular has been sulky of late. And as regards Catherine, he so convinces himself of his discretion that he feels she must be unaware. It's as if, blinded by desire, he really doesn't feel he's doing anything wrong. So that when she does confront him with her doubts, he laughs it off as her paranoia, telling her she's being silly and demanding that she stop being so possessive. Of course she *wants* to believe in his innocence. And so each time, despite her better judgment, she allows herself to be duped. But she never quite manages to banish her fears.

Questioned further, Igor becomes sullen and grudging of the time he spends with his wife. And Coco, though she remains civil, increasingly keeps her distance. Catherine is in agony. How can she accuse the woman, whose benevolence is seeing them live rent-free, of conducting an adulterous affair with her husband? Where would that leave her? What if, after all, it wasn't true? What if Igor was right: that in her feverish state, she was erecting an elaborate apparatus of deceit that in reality didn't exist?

Still, a kind of poison of suspicion insinuates its way around her veins. Watching the two of them enact their secret pantomime at dinner is an almost unendurable torture. Under the table she pinches the skin of her arms hard. The pain distracts her and in her mind assumes the glamorous shape of martyrdom.

Over the next few days, as the piano stops playing and silence swells around the house, Joseph gets on with his duties, Marie continues cleaning the house, and the children carry on with their games. The dogs, the cat, and the birds cease tilting their heads beyond the merest fraction.

For the rest of the household, the blank space becomes part of the fabric of the afternoon. But for Catherine, alone in her room, wrapped tightly inside the sheet of her bed, the silence burns into her consciousness. Listening tensely, she draws her knees up to her wheezing chest.

CHAPTER FOURTEEN

The medicine prescribed by the doctor sedates Catherine effectively. But it also induces in someone who rarely remembers her dreams a series of vivid and disturbing nightmares, of which this is the first.

She imagines Coco's apartment, which she has visited once, above the shop in the rue Cambon. In the dream, Coco sits at a table surrounded by the day's takings in cash that have just been carried up. There are heavy sackfuls of coins and broad wads of notes. It is dark outside. The shop is quiet and Coco is alone. She begins counting the money, stacking all the coins and pressing the notes into neat piles.

Unannounced, Igor walks up the stairs. It is unquestionably him, Catherine sees. Coco ceases counting. They both undress. Then Coco gathers up the bank notes. Together with Igor, she throws them jubilantly into the air, allowing them to fall and form a dense weave like autumn leaves. The apartment is soon carpeted with crisp bits of cash. Throughout, the dream is silent, but from the motion of their mouths, the two of them seem to be laughing.

After that, she pictures them lying naked and making love. They roll on the notes. The money sticks to their royally sweating bodies, flaking off like bits of grass. Their lovemaking continues until the print rubs off on the couple, until their glistening skins are stained with the color of Coco's money.

Catherine wakes up feeling dirty. She feels a deep need to wash herself clean of her dreams. As she rolls up her sleeves and scrubs her hands, the mingling of her fingers under the water seems to her, for an instant, obscene.

She and Igor have made love only once since arriving at Bel Respiro. And that was in the first couple of weeks of their stay. She didn't enjoy it. In fact, he hurt her. And now she feels grubby. Polluted.

Catherine can't fathom why he'd be interested in Coco. Yes, she's attractive. But she's also coarse, opinionated, and ill-bred. An upstart. An arriviste. She understands nothing of his music, and music is his life. Can he really be in love with her? Is it just lust? Or are his feelings woven of a need for patronage? No doubt, she considers, Coco sees him as a kind of trophy. She collects things. Perhaps he's just a symptom for her of a larger acquisitiveness. He's an object, something she must have. She'll soon grow bored of him in that case. He's this season's fashion. And hopefully he'll soon begin to see through her. But what if the relationship develops? Where will this leave Catherine? And the children, what about them? The questions generate sparks of anxiety in her mind.

She longs to return to Russia, to enjoy the simple dignity of being a wife in her own home. And associated with that distant country is her health, which, too, seems banished. The life she leads now seems utterly unreal. Her existence here, surely, is not a permanent condition? She has faith to sustain her. She prays. Everything will be all right. Normality will be restored. She will once more enjoy a firm grip on her life. Like a smashed glass leaping up from the floor, its fragments miraculously reassembled, the world will be made whole again. Things will knit together. They will heal. They must.

The doctor shakes down a glass thermometer and places it at an angle under Catherine's tongue. Her breathing has worsened recently.

Catherine complains that the medicine he prescribed has left her feeling very tired.

"That's deliberate. It's supposed to make you rest," the doctor responds. The corners of his mouth curl up into a smile. Though meant to be ironic, his grin invites Catherine to laugh at herself.

"It's just that I feel so listless," Catherine breaks out, slapping her hands on the covers in pathetic emphasis.

"But you need to slow your body down if you want to recover fully. You have to rest. It's the only way." He writes out a new prescription and hands it to her.

"What's this?" she asks, trying to decipher the writing. Her voice has thickened with the thermometer under her tongue.

"It should improve your breathing . . ." He's uncertain whether or not to go on. ". . . though the drug does have a sedative effect."

Exasperatedly. "You mean I'll feel even *more* drowsy?"

"I'm afraid that's true. Yes."

Catherine is shocked into silence. The doctor consults his watch and removes the thermometer. Holding it up to the light, he looks intently through his pince-nez. The light makes his lenses opaque.

Igor asks, "Has she a temperature?"

"What do you care?" Catherine snaps. A wedge of bitterness informs her voice. Her lips seem suddenly bloodless.

Warily the doctor looks across at one and then the other. He consults the thermometer once more before lowering his arm. He wavers between talking to Catherine and talking to Igor about her. By way of a compromise, he addresses his remarks to the absent air between.

"Not dangerously high. But I'd still recommend bed rest."

"*More* bed rest!" she hisses dismissively.

The doctor feels piqued by this exposure of his impotence. "It is Nature's way, and it is the best cure." As he chides her, she looks down, smoothing a wrinkle from the coverlet. He goes on, "Of course, I could prescribe you more modern medicines." And then, with odd emphasis: "Expensive medicines. But they'd achieve little more than the bed rest. Not to mention the side effects . . ."

"The expense would not bother my husband. Mademoiselle Chanel sees to the bills."

"Catherine!" scolds Igor. His arms stiffen on the arms of his chair. He colors with indignation.

"Well, doesn't she?" She enjoys this rare moment of superiority. It is not often she sees her husband embarrassed. She's thrilled to discover she still has the power to wound him in this way.

"I'm sorry," Igor offers the doctor. He is angry with Catherine and annoyed with himself for becoming so flustered.

The doctor is discomfited by this reference to his fees. Seeing this, Catherine feels a recklessness enter her temper. She becomes passionate in her anger. "Is she *paying* you to sedate me and keep me quiet? Is *that* what's happening?"

"You're becoming hysterical," Igor says.

"I knew it. You're all in it together!" In her mind, the conspiracy widens frighteningly to include not only Coco and the doctor but also the servants—even the walls of this godless house.

"The doctor doesn't have to stand here and listen to your crazy accusations . . ."

"It's no use denying it. Something's going on. I'm not being told, but I can sense it. I'm not stupid, you know. Just because I'm sick, it doesn't mean I'm totally oblivious of everything that happens around here . . ."

Igor is shocked into utterance. "Catherine!"

"Don't shout at me!" They begin squabbling in Russian.

It is the doctor who tries to calm things down. "It's all right. All right." He rests both hands on the handle of his bag. Then, looking straight at Catherine, he says, "The fact is, you're consumptive. And I'm doing my best to give you good advice—which I hope you'll take." Relaxing slightly: "There's no reason on earth why you shouldn't recover in time. But it's a slow process. These things can't be hurried."

She feels depleted. "All I lack at the moment is a reason to recover." Contained within her voice is a secret appeal. She throws her husband a steely look.

"Now, then . . ." The doctor pauses. A look of benignity

spreads across his features. Lifting his case, he smiles at Catherine. He's trying to convince her that he's on her side.

Igor steers him out, impressed by his calmness and his tact. He apologizes noiselessly and attempts to share the exasperation he feels at his wife's behavior.

The doctor seems unmoved. He halts in the hallway and adopts a solemn tone. "Mental health can be crucial in determining how soon a patient recovers in such cases." He moves toward the stairs. "It's important she gets some attention, that she's pampered, made a fuss of. You understand?"

Igor regards him blankly. What does he know? Has there been talk? Have the servants been gossiping? It is his turn to entertain thoughts of a conspiracy. The branches of possible betrayal ramify in his imagination like the side streets in a town.

"I think you have to be extra patient and generous at this time. Show her you care, and I'm sure her condition will improve."

"Yes." The utterance sounds so equivocal and squeezed out, even to his own ears, that he feels compelled to repeat the word. "Yes. Yes. You're right," he says.

Joseph, who must have heard all this, is waiting at the foot of the stairs. He returns the doctor's hat and opens the door.

Igor winces inwardly. He can hardly meet his eye.

Coco is in the garden, pruning shears in hand. She has cut two white carnations and advances toward them, awarding one each. "A man should have a buttonhole on such a beautiful day," she says.

The doctor looks uncertain.

She removes her fawn gloves and pins the flowers on the lapels of both men.

The doctor adjusts his buttonhole minutely. "You're very kind, Mademoiselle."

"There's no reason why men shouldn't smell sweetly, too." She picks up a long-nosed watering can.

The doctor makes as if to leave. Then, affecting to remember something, he asks, "Would you prefer to settle now, Mademoiselle?"

Coco does not make it easy for him. Her manner is patronizing. After an awkward silence, she says with sudden overweening concern, "Ah, yes! Of course. And how *is* poor Catherine?"

Igor feels a sudden pang of loyalty to his wife. It's not her fault she's sick. She wasn't always like this, he wants to explain. He sees the doctor looking quizzically at Coco, attempting to read the evident complexity of the relationships going on inside the house. Igor watches as the man's eyes sharpen, his intelligence at work, weighing, calculating, inferring. He's terrified that the circle of knowledge and gossip will widen. The situation must be contained.

The doctor replies levelly, "With rest, she should be fine."

Coco's breezy manner gives nothing away. "Good, good. Let's settle, then."

Brisk to the point of impatience, she leads the doctor back inside the house. Joseph stands impassive. Seeing him still there, Igor lurks purposelessly by the door. He represses an instinct to explain, to say something. But what? For a second he remains there feeling intensely foolish. Then he slopes off down the corridor to the refuge of his study.

A clock ticks audibly on the kitchen wall. Marie is washing up, and Joseph is drying the dishes with a coarse white cloth. The windows are open and the piano sounds distinctly from Igor's study. Voices drift in from the garden. A new swing has been installed in a corner of the lawn. It sways metronomically as the children take their turn.

"I don't know what to make of these goings-on," Joseph says, wiping a steaming plate with an overlapping motion of the cloth.

"You don't?" Marie asks, sardonically. She plunges her hands into the soapy water and pulls out another dripping dinner plate. A white cup and saucer follow.

Joseph stacks them on the table. "Has she said anything to you?"

Faintly outraged at the suggestion, Marie frowns. "Of course not."

"Do you think Madame Stravinsky knows?"

"She has eyes and ears like the rest of us. Unless, of course, she's deceiving herself." Marie sees her fingers have wrinkled finely in the water.

Outdoors the boys are messing around with a hosepipe, spraying each other. Suzanne is pushing Milène vigorously on the swing.

Marie carries on, "Even your own daughter's old enough to understand what's happening."

"Don't be ridiculous. She's only fourteen."

"She's not as naïve as you think, Joseph."

A wineglass gulps as she puts it in the water. The dregs in the bottom make a sharp red stain.

"All right. I suppose she must have an idea. But the worst thing would be for it all to blow up."

"God! Men are such cowards," Marie says. And then, with a force that almost pulls her forward: "I've half a mind to tell her myself."

"Remember, darling, where our loyalties lie."

"I *would* tell her if she weren't so haughty."

Joseph wipes away a thumbprint from the side of a glass and puts a stack of plates into the cupboard. Clearing things away, returning each bright pot to its allotted place, is his way of coping with the turmoil that has disturbed the calm of the house. "Like it or not, Mademoiselle Chanel is our employer. Her best interests reflect our own."

"I think it's perfectly disgraceful the way she carries on."

"It's not for us to judge, Marie."

"Somebody has to."

Through the window, Joseph sees Milène on the swing twisting the ropes around tighter until they begin to kink.

"Well, it's not our place. Remember what happened last time."

"I don't need reminding."

"I think you do. Each change of lover brings with it a fresh change of domestics. You know the rule."

As Milène releases her feet from the ground the ropes of the swing unravel, sending her spinning around and around.

Relenting. "All right, I know."

"We can't afford that to happen again."

Marie pulls the plug from the sink. Ringingly she wraps the chain around the tap. She adds, "I don't know what she sees in him anyway."

"Mm."

"It's pretty obvious what *he*'s after, though."

"Oh, stop it!"

Just then, the Stravinskys' cat trots into the kitchen and stalks around.

"Nothing left here, I'm afraid, Vassily."

"Scram!" blurts Marie, less charitably.

The water drains from the basin with a long-drawn gurgle, then a vortical roar. Marie runs cold water around the congealed scum at the bottom of the sink. She swills away the little scraps of food. A few remaining suds crackle softly in the light.

Catherine endures a succession of identical bedridden days.

She awakes each morning feeling the weight of boredom press upon her. She finds it hard to concentrate. Scared of venturing downstairs where she doesn't feel welcome, she's afraid, moreover, of what she might find. Increasingly she feels imprisoned. The bedroom's single window is too high to see anything but birds trace indolent circles. Her horizons have narrowed to this one blank space. And the room is so underfurnished, it still seems to her austere. Hour after hour she lies there motionless, watching the sunlight generate its patterns upon the wall.

She reads a good deal. The poems of Akhmatova, stories by Dostoyevsky and Chekhov. The Bible—Paul's epistles, especially, and the Acts of the Apostles. But not the stories of Colette lent to her by Coco. She reads until her eyes give out. Then in the afternoon she dozes, yielding to the waves of tiredness that lap at her from some far shore.

And when Milène comes to her, pulling at the covers, it all proves just too much. "Get off!" she shouts, pushing her away. Milène, though, continues to hang around the bed, thinking it all part of some game. Again the girl begins tugging at the covers and scratching at her mother's arms. She doesn't realize she is being too rough.

"Get away from me!" Catherine cries, so fiercely that her younger daughter freezes. Poor Milène bursts into tears. She can't understand why her mother, once so affectionate and playful, now appears so wretched and pathetic. Of course Catherine instantly regrets it. But the incident cruelly illuminates her decline. She knows it is wrong, but she can't help herself. She feels too anguished, too harried, too desperate for space and calm. In addition to the physical ailments, she seems to suffer an emotional collapse. Her sobs well in the darkness. Her eyes fill with a liquid thicker than tears. She pushes the children away to keep them at a manageable distance. It is all she can do to survive.

Her nerves are shot to pieces. The dry sound of a petal falling on the sill is enough to startle her. In the room, a faint smell of decay reaches her nostrils, a remote odor of putrefaction. At first she thinks it is the flowers. But the smell is more like meat that has gone off. Then it occurs to her that it must be her insides. It is herself she can smell, her own inner corruption. She feels dead already. Her hair is falling out in handfuls, and now she's beginning to rot. The sensation scares her. She needs to fight to stay alive.

Before Igor retires to their bedroom each night, flush with adultery, Catherine measures out drops of her medicine onto a spoon. The red glob clings to the metal with a tremulous effort of surface tension. Slowly, with the same effort of trembling, she maneuvers the spoon into the dark cave of her mouth.

CHAPTER FIFTEEN

At last, in mid-August, Coco hears from Ernest Beaux. The perfume samples are ready for inspection. Exchanging childishly solemn promises with Igor, she takes off almost immediately, traveling first class by train down to the south.

There are scores of perfumers in the town of Grasse. The whole region reeks with sweetness, flavoring the landscape for miles around. Just as it attracts many people out of curiosity, though, so many blameless residents have also left the town. Not everyone enjoys the olfactory onslaught that assails the houses night and day. A cloud of cloying odors hangs in a permanent pall over the streets, stretching in an invisible film over the roofscapes. There is little wind to relieve the region. And when a freshening breeze blows in from the coast, it is only so that a new wave of fragrances can waft across the town again.

Coco detects this compound of aromas as she alights from the train. She feels excited that, from this mixture of odors, there might be isolated and distilled a single ribbon of scent that will be bottled and bear her name. She's always dreamed of having her own fragrance, of sending her signature into the world in this way.

But steady. She's getting ahead of herself. There's a lot of hard work ahead of her first.

The next morning, she stands outside Beaux's perfumery with its square window and unfussy façade. Nervously she consults a piece of paper, making sure the address written there corresponds with that of the shop in front of her. It does. The shop bell clangs loudly. The reverberation continues long after its last note leaves the air.

A man emerges from the back and stands behind the counter. "Madame?"

"I'm looking for Monsieur Ernest Beaux."

"How can I help you?"

"My name is Gabrielle Chanel."

The man's demeanor changes from that of an obliging shopkeeper to that of a humble subject about to meet his queen. Lifting the hinge of the counter, Beaux walks through to greet her. They shake hands with equal strength and for slightly longer than is necessary.

Like Igor, Beaux is a Russian émigré from St. Petersburg and, Coco notices, he speaks French with the same clipped accent.

"This way, if you please."

He ushers her behind the counter and steers her into the laboratory at the rear of the shop. He is grayer in appearance than Coco had expected. She'd naïvely imagined her perfumer to be a brilliant young man. A paterfamilias beard luxuriates around his broad jaw. His eyes are bloodshot with overwork. But she notes with pleasure his clean hands. A wedding ring glistens on one of his spatulate fingers.

Beaux notes, conversely, that Coco is younger than he

had thought, and much prettier, too. He is struck by her professional air and determined manner, her understated good looks.

Coco is dazzled by the whiteness of the lab. For a moment, she's almost snow-blind. But the sensation does not dominate for long. Immediately she's overcome by the perfumes as they rush at her from all corners. A fabulous amalgam of scents. She feels queasy, experiencing these interwoven aromas for the first time.

She sits down and looks about her. A continuous wooden surface runs seamlessly around the room. On one side lies a set of burners, flasks, and agitating devices. Here, two white-coated assistants bend low over their retorts and swill liquids in glass beakers. On another, measuring glasses rest next to funnels; pestles and mortars share a space with spoons and rods. Coco approves of this careful taxonomy. She likes the fact that he's systematic. She's reassured, too, by the white, germless surfaces.

Opposite, a broad shelf is laden with glass jars. Coco takes a mental inventory. Each container is labeled in black ink: alcohol, volatile oils, and fats in different combinations, plus a liquefied series of natural and artificial odors. A complete lexicon of differentiated scents: ambergris, camphor, frangipani, jasmine, musk, neroli, sandalwood, and violet—scents distilled from southern Europe and the Middle East. The collected sweat of the gods.

Coco asks, "Do you extract the essences yourself?"

"We don't have space. It's an industrial process now. We buy them in already refined. Besides, the way you extract the scents is not so important." Beaux's voice lowers, hinting at the possession of diabolical knowledge. "It's how you *combine* them that counts."

He moves around the laboratory like a celebrated chef in his kitchen, assembling all the flacons he has prepared for Chanel. She recognizes his ability to pick out discrete scents, to isolate a happy or recalcitrant strand, either to distill it down or siphon it off. It is, she thinks, the facility Igor has: to pounce on the single instrument in the orchestra that is slightly out of tune.

It is all going bewilderingly quickly. The brightness, the scents, and the movement of white-coated chemists mingle and make Coco dizzy. Then, after a few minutes, the men cease moving and stand ready behind her chair. Beaux squeezes a dribble from a pipette into a petri dish. She thinks of the hundreds of crushed blossoms that have gone into this thin distillate, this elixir, to create a single liquid drop.

He repeats the operation several times. Then he lays out the samples and beckons her to test them. The odors resolve in a precise spot a few inches below her nose. She's conscious of a vaporous welling. Their blended notes rise up.

Now that everything is still, she hears a sound. An insistent hum. The chirr of ceiling fans, she thinks. She looks up, but the fans make too rhythmical and insistent a noise. There is a more frantic and high-pitched buzzing mixed in, coming from somewhere near the window. She looks across. The window is open because of the heat. But behind the frame is a gauze mesh. And beyond the mesh stirs a thick cloud of flies. Fruit flies maddened by the sweetness of the scents. Frantically they dance against the netting, crazed with frustration.

Beaux sees her register their presence. Rubbing his hands together, he says, "That's how people will react to your scent, Mademoiselle."

Coco manages a sardonic glance that, through an alteration of her features, becomes a shy smile. "I hope!"

In front of her Beaux sets six dishes inundated with perfumes. They are the color of translucent honey, amber, or weak tea. He dips a smelling strip into the first dish, then wafts it below her nose.

As she inhales, each perfume in turn unfurls like a mysterious blossom.

She quickly discounts two of the samples as overripe. Another is a little bitter. This leaves a further three. The smelling sticks swish like wands below her nostrils. She dismisses another one as merely enchanting, which leaves just two more—numbers two and five—still in the running.

After trying another couple of times to discriminate, she says, "I like them both."

Beaux urges her to try again. She must choose one. She inhales generously above each sample. Each is exquisite, redolent, and evocative in slightly different ways.

"I can smell jasmine."

"Yes."

"And tuberose?"

"Yes."

"And there's an animal note in there, somewhere, too."

"I'm impressed."

She sniffs, compares, and reflects once more. And there it is. Slowly it comes to her: subtle but glorious, splendid, and, in its mix of distillates, almost divine. She's never smelled anything like it. A feeling of sickness mixes with desire. And then a strange thing happens. In this state of near reverie, her mind flashes back to the floor of the convent and orphanage in Aubazine where she went to school. Her memory lingers for an instant upon the mosaic tiles in the corridor with their repetition of the Roman numeral V.

She points at her chosen dish.

"Number five."

Beaux looks pleased. His two assistants straighten. They remove the dishes from in front of her.

Like an aura that hovers and vibrates, the scent envelops her still. She takes a few moments to recover.

"One thing puzzles me, though," she says.

"Oh?"

"I can't actually detect any single defining extract."

"There isn't any one thing. There are over eighty ingredients mixed in together."

"Doesn't that make it less natural?"

"You want your fragrance to last for hours, no?"

"I do."

"Well, the problem with most perfumes is that they fade very quickly. You have to reek at the beginning of the evening if you want the scent to last all night. This, on the other hand," he says, brandishing one of the flacons, "doesn't degrade or decay. And you won't have to saturate yourself with it either, I promise. It's much more stable. Just a dab will do."

She looks doubtful.

"Trust me," he says.

She agrees to experiment with it on her friends and so

conduct a kind of trial. Meanwhile, Beaux is to manufacture a small amount to distribute as gifts. The idea is to infiltrate the perfume into her clients' lives. Write off the first batch as goodwill. Then go for the kill! She has already made up a provisional list of about a hundred people. They'll be the first to receive the scent. Beaux is to send the samples, and she'll have them gift-wrapped, enclosing a little note offering her compliments.

"But before that, I want you to tell me everything. If I'm going to invest in this, I need to learn about the process from first to last."

"Of course."

Coco leaves late that afternoon following a detailed tour and commentary and several celebratory glasses of champagne: Krug, her favorite.

She feels a little heady. The pavement beneath her feet appears distant and unreal. The echo of her footsteps seems out of sync with the rhythm of her feet. She clutches a black valise containing two dozen flacons of her perfume. The vials fit snugly into the red velvet casing like the articulated bits of a musical instrument.

She feels the bubbles of champagne continue to rise within and make her giddy. She resists the temptation to telephone Igor. She's too excited to talk properly. She'd only gush, and he'd think her silly. She misses him, though. In fact, she has made up her mind to donate three hundred thousand francs to Diaghilev for a revival of *The Rite*. She'll donate the money anonymously, so that no one will feel obliged by the gift. With the perfume starting up and the salon doing so well, she can afford it. Probably.

Leaving Beaux's shop, she notices something odd. A squadron of flies settles in a dense vapor about her case. Many of them peel off as she steps into a taxi. A few more flake away when she enters the train. Others fall, exhausted with thwarted longing, as she alights from her carriage. Some are still with her, fiercely tenacious as she returns to Bel Respiro almost twelve hours later. One even clings intoxicated as it is placed inside the safe.

The plucky little insect suffocates in the airless vault. But it dies a sublime death—achingly drunk and happy. Stiffening, its brittle body quickly corrupts, its atoms mingling with the perfume, becoming one with the powdery air.

CHAPTER SIXTEEN

Following a set of vigorous exercises, Igor springs up from the floor. His movements are light, almost rubbery. And if his limbs are thin, then his muscles are nevertheless well-defined. With a sweet strain of extension, he stands in his underpants before the bedroom mirror, rotating his head, then tilting it from side to side.

Catherine watches him, repelled. His health and vigor mock her in their ostentation. "Is Coco back today?"

"Tomorrow, I think."

"I thought you were looking happy."

"I'm happy because it's a nice day, and I'm alive. Is that so bad?"

"It's not bad for you, no."

"Why do you have to be so sour?"

"Why do you have to be so cruel?"

"Cruel? You're well looked after. You receive excellent medical attention . . ."

"Ha!"

". . . the children have a private governess . . ."

"And who have I to thank for all this? Little Miss Nouveau Riche?"

"Well, I think you should be a little more grateful, that's all."

"Grateful? Fine."

Catherine twists away from him on the bed. Igor makes as if to say something, then, shrugging, moves to the bathroom. He fills the basin with hot water and hums in a low voice as he shaves. He pretends to be indifferent, but he isn't. His heart is thumping, and it's not from the exercise. He can't stand arguments. He hates being made to feel ashamed. But, at present, their every conversation ends in acrimony. He can't say anything right.

"I'm going to get on with some work now."

"Go!" She waves him away. She wishes he'd vanish. His presence is a living rebuke to her. She feels like a prisoner. Even staying in the most cramped apartment, she never felt as trapped as she does now.

Leaving the bedroom, Igor feels as though he is quitting one country and entering another, where the climate is healthier and there exist different rules. It's as if in crossing the threshold he enjoys new constitutional rights: rights to freedom and happiness; even silence, if he so wishes.

Downstairs he drinks his coffee. The noise of the children playing drifts in from the garden. Combined with the sunlight and the taste of his coffee, the sound seems especially sweet. Coffee he loves more than anything in the morning. He relishes its fierce aroma, its astringency. Sipping it quickly, he peruses the newspaper for the results of the Olympic sports. Though in exile, he still finds his sympathies tend most strongly toward the Russian athletes. He feels a secret satisfaction when they do well.

He works without stopping until lunch. He revises cease-lessly, with his glasses pushed up onto his forehead and a magnifying glass hovering like a monocle over the score. Themes are restated, motifs reconfigured. He explores com-binations of chords that converge at different centers, varying the intervals between the notes. Testing various phrases on the piano, he achieves fortuitous collisions on the keys. He experiments with major and minor chords together, relishing the complexity of their moods. He is learning to follow the emotional lead of the music, allowing it to take him into areas previously closed, territories he's never explored before. There's a new flexibility and freedom in his composition, a willingness to try things out, a new openness to accident and chance. Maybe it's better, he thinks, not to be always so in control.

He makes good progress. Always at his best in the morn-ing, he works hard so that in the afternoon he can relax.

Some new books have been delivered: the works of Sopho-cles, plus new Russian-French and Russian-English diction-aries. Cutting the leaves of the Sophocles volumes, he enjoys the slow tearing sound of the watermarked paper and the leather smell of the spines.

He looks up "coco" in his dictionary. He discovers it is argot for snow, cocaine, and coconut milk and means "eggy" in babyspeak—definitions which cluster associatively around the color white. It also means licorice powder: black. He likes the monochrome simplicity of the word. White, the spin of all colors, and the no-color of black, with a whole spectrum of feelings implied in between.

Toward late afternoon, Soulima knocks at the door to his

study. The boy knows that if he sees the door closed, he is not to interrupt. This is a long-established prohibition. But, with his mother ill in bed, Coco in Grasse, the servants busy preparing dinner, and his siblings too torpid from the heat to want to play, he feels drawn toward the forbidden door. His knock provokes a low grunt. Sheepishly he enters the room.

"Soulima? What's the matter?" Seeing the boy's blue eyes gaze timidly up, affection wells inside Igor's chest.

"I'm bored."

"Why's that?"

"Because I am."

Igor laughs at his unanswerable logic. "What do you want to do, then?"

Seeing that his father is in a good mood, the boy says, smiling, "Can we have some dancing again tonight, please, Papa?"

"Come here," Igor says, setting aside his books. He beckons his son over, inviting the ten-year-old to sit on his knee. "Now, you know your mother doesn't like dancing . . ."

"Why not?" Soulima says.

"Because it makes her dizzy."

"But she doesn't have to dance."

To the children, Igor knows, Catherine's ailment remains vague. "Yes, but when she watches, it makes her head spin."

"Then she shouldn't watch."

"I'm afraid she's made her mind up. No more dancing."

"But *why*, though?"

"Anyway, it's too hot."

"Not at night, it isn't."

"Well, it upsets her all the same."

"It's not fair!"

"Oh, come on now."

"But it isn't."

"You know your mother isn't well, and we have to be considerate."

Sulking. "I suppose."

"That's a good boy. We love Mother, don't we?"

Speculatively. "*I* do."

Startled: "What's that supposed to mean?"

"Nothing."

Soulima looks solemn. Igor scrutinizes him. Has he guessed? Does he have any inkling of what is going on? Has somebody spoken to him? But he looks so sweet and innocent and shy. It's just a mood he's in, Igor decides, nothing more. Still, it's a reminder of how careful he must be in front of the children. And he realizes at this instant that he absolutely does not want them to know anything about his relationship with Coco. He'd be desperately upset if they were ever to find out.

Momentarily lost for any means of consolation, he offers to show his son some tricks on the piano. He's coming on promisingly and is the most gifted of the children in this respect.

"No," the boy says, stiffening. There is a pause, filled by Igor stroking his son's fair hair. Soulima relaxes. His head falls back against his father's chest. Igor watches him closely. That same frown. It's like seeing a picture of himself as a young boy.

"How about a game of chess, then?"

Soulima looks up without enthusiasm. He smiles weakly, then seems to brighten. It doesn't much matter what he does as long as he can spend some time with his papa.

"All right."

Igor retrieves the board from a high shelf. A faint marbled pattern runs through the squares. He hands an oblong wooden box to Soulima, who slides the lid across and tips out the pieces. The boy readies them for battle. One black pawn is missing. It's nowhere to be found. A small brown button functions as a substitute.

Picking up one black and one white piece, Igor shuffles them behind his back. He presents his son with two clenched fists. Soulima slaps the left one.

"White."

The boy kneels intently over the board, his chin almost touching the pieces. Igor sits back in his chair and lights a cigarette.

Having failed to find Soulima in the rest of the house, his brother and sisters track him down to their father's study. In no time, they are all gathered jealously around the board.

"Can I play?"

"Can *I*?"

Igor blows smoke into the air and groans. "All right, all right! But not in the study. You know you shouldn't be in here. There's not enough room."

He won't tolerate this invasion of his work space. He is afraid, moreover, they might disturb him one day when he is with Coco. The vision of this happening flashes pinkly through his mind, making him wince. He emits a noise that is almost a groan, and the children turn to look at him. He covers it up by clearing his throat. It is his prompt to move them out. They decamp to the living room.

"And after you've played me," Igor insists, "you must also play each other." They agree.

Igor beats Soulima. The lumpen button proves the boy's undoing, wriggling its way to the end of the board. In fact he wins all his games with ease. But the tournament between the children continues until the early evening.

Catherine comes down to join the family group. Still in her dressing gown and looking exhausted, she is nevertheless pleased to see the children so content. At the same time, she rather resents the ease with which Igor has achieved this. It is always on his terms, and at his convenience. There he is, presiding like a deity in his chair.

The children go to bed around nine o'clock, arguing over the significance of their triumphs and defeats. In the quiet that succeeds, Igor and Catherine sit together. Igor tosses off a vodka.

"How are you feeling?"

"Rotten."

Regarding her response as automatic, he chooses to ignore it. "The children had a nice time tonight."

"Did they?"

"Don't you think?"

"I don't know what to think anymore. I feel as if I hardly know you."

"You're in one of those moods, again." He stoops to pick up a chess piece. His fingers toy with it restlessly.

"Don't I have just cause to be?"

"That's not for me to say."

"It never is, is it?"

In the silence, she adjusts her dressing gown around her legs. He notices how thin his wife has become. She has lost so much weight, her wedding ring slips constantly from her finger and needs to be resized.

She makes a direct appeal. "Let's leave here, Igor."

"What?"

"Let's go somewhere and start again."

"Where?"

"I don't know. The coast, maybe."

"I can't." He continues to fiddle with the chess piece, picking the green baize at its base.

"Why not?"

"I'm working well here."

"You've shown me nothing new in weeks."

"I've not finished anything yet. But the ideas are coming like never before."

"I'm not happy here."

"Well, *I* am."

"That's very selfish."

"Then I'm sorry."

"Really?"

The look in his eye is unrepentant. They've had this argument before.

"Your talent doesn't excuse you from acting decently."

"If it wasn't for my talent, as you call it, we'd still be in Russia."

"Would that be so bad?"

"If it's decency you're after, then, yes, it would be. Very bad."

A fold of her dressing gown slips, exposing her knee. The glimpse of leg afforded him is quickly eclipsed as she tightens the gown around her. "At least we'd be with friends."

"We'd be penniless."

"We're penniless now."

"It's a good chance for us to save."

"I'd rather be happy."

"You will be."

Unconvinced: "You can't say I haven't supported you."

"I've never said that."

"Then why can't you support *me* for once?"

"I have supported you. For years. Since you became ill."

"I've got a bad feeling about this place. I want to leave." The weight of her entreaty bends her forward. "Please?"

Sighing: "Look, it makes sense to stay here at least until the new year."

"Sense to you."

"We're on holiday, here."

"We're not on holiday," she corrects him. "We're in exile."

"Catherine, if you're going to snipe at everything I say, why don't you just go back to bed?"

She gives him a hard accusatory stare. "You'd prefer that, wouldn't you?"

After a silence: "Yes."

Catherine bites her lip, twisting her mouth sideways. She feels defeated. Having demeaned herself utterly, she's still failed to move him. In an instant of clarity, she realizes her life here is a sham. "You've changed, Igor. You know that?"

Her lips narrow in mute fury. Her eyes seem to burn a hole into his brow.

He says, "And the problem is, you haven't."

Hurt, she rises and withdraws from the room. She closes the door behind her with a strange quietness. The undramatic nature of her exit startles him. The door's click operates like a spring inside his mind.

Gravely he shakes his head. The evening was going so well. The children had enjoyed themselves. Even Catherine had seemed pleased at first. Yet each time they come near each other, some invisible force contrives to push them apart. It grieves him to know that he's hurt her. He has no wish to. At every turn he finds himself ambushed by guilt. But what can he do? The fact is, he's in love with someone else, and there's only so much love within him he can give.

He looks at the repeated pattern of squares on the chessboard, at the piece still in his fingers, and, via a knight's move of his attention, his gaze switches to the window.

Outside he sees the moon float in and out of sight behind dark trees.

CHAPTER SEVENTEEN

Coco is back. She rattles the vials of perfume inside their little box.

Hearing the muffled clatter, Igor looks up from the piano. He is meant to be impressed. She undoes the latch with a click. Inside, luxurious in red plush, are two dozen flacons of scent. She removes one from the box and unstoppers it.

"Smell!" she says, trailing it beneath his nose.

"Are these the samples from Grasse?" He recoils slightly as the bottle is thrust toward him.

She nods. "What do you think?"

"I'm no judge." He brings his face closer, steadying the flacon with his hand. Inhaling, his nose is spiced with the beginnings of a sneeze. He pinches his nostrils to forestall the explosion.

"Careful," she says.

Unstoppering another, as if teasing him, she draws it under his nose. But he breathes in too deeply. His eyes water and he starts to gag.

"Well, come on. Tell me what you think!"

He hides his admiration. He's never thought of perfume being created before, of having a specific human source. For him, it has always just been there, always existed like the sun. He says, "It's better than the stench of resin from the orchestra pit."

"I'll take that as a compliment."

"If *I* had to create a perfume, it would be something like the smell of coffee when it first comes out of the tin."

"Ugh!"

"I told you. I've got a hopeless sense of smell."

"Like most men."

She replaces the bottles and sets the box down on the floor. He looks at her and realizes again how beautiful she is. Her face has taken on a deep honey color he didn't think achievable in human skin. As she straightens, he embraces her. They kiss, and he feels again that trembling warmth he experiences whenever she is near him. Hung loosely at their sides, their hands intertwine.

After a few moments, Igor says solemnly, "Catherine wants to leave."

Alarmed, Coco's face tilts upward. "She does?"

"Yes."

"She said so?"

"Yes."

"When?"

"Yesterday."

"Why?"

"Why do you think? Because she's unhappy."

"What else did she say?"

"Nothing." He sees himself toying with the chess piece, with the moon floating outside.

"Did she say anything about me?"

"Not directly."

"Does she know?"

"Not for sure, I don't think."

After a pause. "So, what are you going to do?"

"I'm not leaving, if that's what you mean."

"Are you sure?"

He wasn't, but he is now. "I couldn't." He realizes his life with her has a fullness, a repleteness he has not known before.

"Good." A look of trust and vulnerability deepens in her eyes.

"Good," he echoes, smiling. He finds the notion of adultery alien, still. It's too hard and unforgiving a noun for the contagion of love he feels. Adultery is what other people do. "I'm not going anywhere," he says. His expression grows tender. "I need you." Then, after a pause: "That's if you still want me?"

"I do, very much." Her eyes in emphasizing the point squeeze tight.

In the silence that follows, Coco moves close to him once more. She can smell the perfume where it has leaked onto his skin. He feels it burn and experiences its sweetness. She whispers his name. And in hearing it issue from between her lips, he feels he possesses her completely. They kiss again. Both succumb slowly to an inordinate longing.

Later, music swells epically from the study, occupying the rooms of the house. Harmonies advance in a cloud across the garden. Driven like a theme, the music enjoys a buoyancy, the soft summer breeze sustaining its miracle of self-belief.

———

Alone in her study, Coco sketches a cube. She adds with abrupt strokes a short neck and oblong stopper. At the base swells a dimple—the one curve amid all the lines in the design. Then, in large black capitals against a white background, she frames the letters of her name. Angling her head to one side, she sucks at the faceted head of her pencil. She wants something simple. Nothing fancy. A plain square bottle, unfussy and clear.

She can't stand those exotic titles such as "Dans la Nuit," "Coeur en Folie," or "La Fille du Roi de Chine." They're just pretentious and silly, she thinks. She wants something more cryptic, something simple but mysterious. Something strong. A number, maybe. Her favorite: five.

It will be the first time, she recognizes, that a couturiere has put her name on the bottle. And why not? She's designed it, after all. Why shouldn't people know who's responsible? That's not arrogance; it's just natural pride.

The first reports from clients seem very promising. Beaux was right: they like it. It's discreet, and it endures a whole evening. And, what's just as important, their husbands and lovers seem to like it, too. If men like inhaling it while making love, she considers, then its success is virtually guaranteed.

Down the hall, Igor slides a record from its sleeve. On the turntable it appears slightly warped. Light curves on its uneven surface. He winds the gramophone up and lifts the lever into position. A staticky *scrik* leaps from the bell as he sets the needle down. He watches the furrows run into a thin continuous line of music. The divine Franz Schubert. Beethoven's

Hammerklavier. A harpsichord concerto by Bach. As Igor puts on disc after disc, he feels his insides slip.

Upstairs, Marie takes Catherine a glass of water. Catherine sits up with a grateful smile.

"I hope the music isn't keeping you awake, ma'am."

"I've had enough sleep, Marie, to last me a lifetime."

"And I hope you're feeling better."

"A little, thank you, yes."

"Can I get you anything else?"

Catherine sits up. "No, but tell me"—she sips at the water—"how long have you worked for Mademoiselle Chanel?"

"Nearly three years now, ma'am." Marie knits her hands together primly in front of her stomach.

Fishing: "And you find her a good employer?"

"How do you mean, ma'am?"

"Well, is she honest and straightforward?" Catherine senses Marie hesitate. She laughs, hoping to disarm her. "Don't worry, I'm not one of her spies."

"She's been good to us, yes." On more solid ground: "And Suzanne likes her a lot."

"She can be very generous, I know."

"Yes."

"It's a shame she doesn't have children of her own, though, isn't it?"

"Yes. It is."

"She's a modern woman."

Becoming wary: "Modern, yes."

"I mean, you know, independent."

"Very."

Catherine senses herself getting nowhere. She feels as if

she's picking at a splinter beneath the skin. She decides to be more direct. "Sometimes I wonder, though . . ." She nerves herself to complete the sentence. "Sometimes I wonder how moral she is." There, she's said it. The thought is out.

It burns like a hot brick in Marie's hands. "Excuse me, ma'am?" She sees where the conversation is going and doesn't like it.

Awkward: "Well, is she? Moral, I mean."

Marie feels an abyss open beneath her, creatures catching at her heels. "Well, ma'am, that all depends." Her words are carefully spaced.

"Depends on what?"

"People's ideas have changed since the war . . ."

"Have they?"

Marie begins wringing her fingers. She doesn't want to get into trouble. She feels a weight upon her chest. "I don't quite know what you want me to say, ma'am." She decides to play for time.

Catherine's eyes plead fiercely. "I want you to tell me the truth." Abruptly any social distance between the two evaporates. She makes a direct appeal to Marie as another woman.

Marie wants to blurt out what she knows. The impulse to confess is strong. It pulls at her jaw like an unseen string. But the tact that is an habitual part of her employment eclipses any sisterly instinct. The answer that comes—almost ghosted from her mouth—is practiced, diplomatic, cruelly neutered. The effect is like a racing car dragged off the track.

"Mademoiselle Chanel has endured her fair share of tragedy, ma'am . . ."

To Catherine, her answer is maddeningly oblique. "And her fair share of good fortune, too."

Marie remains wary. "Indeed."

"She's very rich."

"I believe she is."

"And powerful."

"Yes."

"Unlike me?"

Marie squirms under the continued pressure of questioning. The creatures from the abyss are now pulling at her legs. One of her knees feels as if it's about to buckle. She bites her lip, surrenders. "Ma'am, I'm just the maid. I'm not qualified to answer such questions."

Dissatisfied with the evasiveness of Marie's responses, and keen to reestablish the gap between them, Catherine adopts a tone now close to condescension. "No, of course you're not. I'm sorry."

After a pause: "Will there be anything else, ma'am?"

Absently: "What? No. You may go."

Marie withdraws and breathes easier once she has gone beyond the door. Her hands are shaking. Her back is damp with sweat. Yet, relieved as she is that the ordeal is over, she also feels distressed. She has become a coconspirator, one more opaque part of the betrayal. Given the opportunity, she did not reveal what she knew to be the truth. She feels profoundly that she has let herself and Catherine down.

Catherine meanwhile feels ashamed. Closing her eyes, she can't believe she risked humiliating herself like that. What did she expect? Of course Marie was loyal: she'd never say anything against her employer. Her silence has been bought. It was unfair and stupid of her to ask. Yet she feels so desperate. As much of her fist as will go, Catherine now shoves into her mouth.

Back downstairs, Coco hears the music float from Igor's study. She sees the square shape of the bottle on the pad in front of her. Then she thinks of the circle of the disc delivering its notes from down the hall. And an odd thing occurs. In her mind the two shapes begin to interpenetrate, the square and the circle; and just for an instant they even seem to fit.

Her lips pucker tautly around the pencil's stem. She begins to sketch, more tentatively this time. On the paper, a kind of black seal appears: an overlapping back-to-back double C. She has in mind the initials of the Cour des Comptes on the rue Cambon close to her shop. A kind of heraldic device, a signature. Like an attenuated version of the Olympic rings, a buckle of some sort. Or two profiles locked together in intimate silhouette.

CHAPTER EIGHTEEN

Joseph hands Stravinsky the telephone.

It's Diaghilev. He informs him that they've just received a donation of three hundred thousand francs to finance a revival of *The Rite of Spring*.

Igor's hand darts to his brow. "Who?"

"I don't know. Anonymous, it seems."

"I can't believe it!"

"I thought you'd be pleased."

Apprehensive suddenly: "I want it performed properly this time, Serge."

"Of course."

On an impulse. "And I'll conduct it."

"Let's not jump ahead of ourselves."

"I want it to be good."

A rider pulling on the reins. "Don't worry. Things will be different."

"What makes you so sure?"

"Those people were brought up on Swan Lake and Sleeping Beauty. They weren't prepared for what they heard."

"You think they've changed?"

"They wanted a fête. You gave them a female orgasm. Not even Dr. Freud was ready for that."

Igor laughs. "And now?"

"After a war and a revolution, they should be ready for anything."

Igor continues, breathless with excitement, and with a confiding if not quite confessional air, "I'm working well, Serge."

"You've been busy?"

Igor tells him about the five-finger exercises, the concertino and symphony, how he's experimenting with different tempi, different instruments operating in different time signatures, how he's working on it in blocks, but that he wants to get on with *The Rite* now, and is desperate to revise the string parts, and has already amended the second horn group in his head.

A silence follows.

"How's Catherine?"

Shrinking visibly: "Not too well still, I'm afraid."

"I'm sorry to hear that." After a pause, his voice deepening: "Have you been behaving yourself, Igor?"

He doesn't answer.

"I've heard a couple of whispers, I must say."

"Who from?"

"Never you mind."

"It's Misia, isn't it?"

"It might be . . ."

"She's a real snake-in-the-grass, that one!"

"She's a generous patron."

"She's not to be trusted."

"Never mind her. You just make the most of your time there, old boy."

"You think it was Coco who donated the money?"

"I doubt it. She has other ways of supporting you."

"Not you, too!"

"You should be happy. We've just received a huge donation."

"I am happy."

"Good."

After setting the phone back on its cradle, Igor curses, "Misia. That bitch!"

Friday, Coco and Igor go to the races. Saturday, they can be seen together at Le Boeuf sur le Toit—a small bar in Montparnasse where a black band plays Mozart and jazz and the regulars dance on the tables. Monday, they rendezvous along with the Serts at the cinema in the center of Paris. They both enjoy watching films. They've already seen *The Cabinet of Dr. Caligari*. And tonight they have tickets for *The Mark of Zorro*.

Inside the cinema it is warm. The chairs are square and uncomfortable. Coco's legs move away from some ache and come to rest against Igor's. In the dark they feel an intimacy, a restfulness that contents them both. It's good to get away from the house in the evenings, and away from their work, too. Here, together, they feel heedless and free.

The movie is exciting with plenty of action. Seeing Douglas Fairbanks perform his acrobatics makes Igor itch to rehearse his own exercises. His legs flex involuntarily with each new stunt.

He is struck, too, by the accompanist. A young man in his early twenties, he sits openmouthed in the pit, staring up at the screen in front of him. He accents the motion he sees, adding chromaticism to the black-and-white images as they drizzle across his face.

There is no question of any connecting music or bridging passages. The jumps are too abrupt. He needs to respond instantly to the visual effects. Igor nods with approval at the young man's ingenuity, his precise sense of timing, his sensitivity to mood. But he winces at the flatness of the piano, especially in the higher registers. It seems almost to slow the action down. He wonders if the pianist has managed to rehearse, and has seen the film before, or whether the performance is genuinely spontaneous.

At the same time he's galvanized by a moment on the screen: Zorro roughly embraces his woman, pulling her toward him with an encircling arm. The woman—blowsy, dark-haired, gypsyish—arches submissively as he bends low to deliver a kiss. Witnessing this, Igor feels a sweet ache, a remote throb of semiengorgement tighten inside his pants. He shifts awkwardly in his seat, surprised that the film has stirred him in this way. Coco guesses correctly the source of his unease. And with a note of throat clearing to cover his dismayed excitement, he allows her fingers for a few frank seconds to steal across his thigh.

Seeing this in the corner of her vision, Misia raises an

eyebrow. A little later, she whispers to Coco, "I see things are going well."

"Satisfactorily, thank you." Coco nods, smiling.

Emerging from the cinema some time later, they are surprised to find it dark outside. The two couples head for a nearby bar. Seated at a table near the window, José and Igor discuss the film. José thinks Zorro improbably athletic. He argues that he couldn't possibly throw himself about like that and survive. It is all camera trickery, he maintains. But Igor is convinced that the action is authentic. He has read somewhere that Fairbanks is a gymnast and that he performs all of his own stunts. They make a small wager.

Across from them, Coco tells Misia about her jaunt to Grasse to see Ernest Beaux and how she's been busy this last week dispatching samples to clients. Then in whispering tones she updates her on the latest from Bel Respiro. Igor tries hard to listen. He resents Coco confiding in her and wishes she wouldn't do this. He is more than a little concerned about the looseness of Misia's tongue. She's an incorrigible gossip. He hates the way she twists and distorts things. And if she has blabbed to Diaghilev, then who else has she told? He can't stand the woman; her flame red hair and her oriental fans. It is all he can do to be civil to her.

They leave the bar around midnight and relish the cool night air. The sky is thick with stars. The couples kiss and part, and the Serts hail a cab.

Coco says to Igor, "We could stay the night above the shop."

"Shouldn't we get back to Garches?" He is thinking of Catherine and what she will say, but he is also mindful of his work. If they were to spend the night in Paris then by the time Coco was up and ready, and by the time they returned to Garches, a whole morning would have been lost. And he has so much to be getting on with.

She draws a cardigan jacket around her shoulders. "It's late. The apartment's only minutes away."

"I know, but . . ." Igor shrugs apologetically. ". . . It would only mean trouble."

"All right, all right." She's disappointed. She's worked hard today. Tired, after a few glasses of wine she is also vaguely amorous. "I just thought you might like to spend the night with me, that's all."

"I do . . . It's just that—"

Frustrated, suddenly: "Save your excuses. I don't want to hear them."

But something has been niggling him, too. After a silence, he asks, "What were you saying to Misia?"

"Is that why you won't come back, because you don't like me talking to her?"

"Of course not. I'm curious, that's all."

"Mm."

Insistent: "So? What *did* you say to her?"

"Nothing."

"You were talking for a long time."

"We talked business."

"You weren't gossiping about us."

"And what if I were?"

"Is that wise?"

"If you must know, I think she's jealous."

"Jealous? Why?"

"Of my helping you out."

"Oh?"

"She's rather seen herself as your patron, and I'm not sure she's keen on me butting in like this."

"She doesn't own me."

"She's a jealous woman."

"She's a gossip."

With a new firmness in her voice: "She's a friend."

"Well, I'm sick of her interfering."

"Interfering?"

"Yes."

"You should have said. I thought you liked it when people gave you money."

Cowed: "You know what I mean."

"And I'm sure you know what I mean, too."

"Well, I'm not sure I like her knowing too much . . ."

"No?"

"In fact, I don't like her knowing anything about us." His features stiffen; he knows she's watching him.

"Are you ashamed of people finding out?"

He finds her intensity disconcerting. "Ashamed? No."

"What, then?"

"You're being ridiculous."

"What other reason can you have for not wanting people to know?"

Painted into a corner: "Be reasonable, Coco. I have a family. A wife, children."

"Well, I *don't*." The gap between her eyes narrows into a

frown. "And if I want to confide in my friends, that's my business, not yours." Were there a door between them, he knows that it would slam.

They reach the car. The presence of Coco's chauffeur puts an end to any further discussion. It is their first real fight, and both of them feel agitated and upset. Each feels the other has been unreasonable and stubborn. Driven home, they both surrender to a juvenile impulse to sit apart and say nothing. Their grievances harden in the silence.

Igor can't understand why Coco entertains a hanger-on like Misia. It's true, he has accepted her money in the past. But the alternative for him was destitution, poverty. Ordinarily she'd never be a friend of his. And as for staying the night in Paris, perhaps he should have seemed more eager. But can't she see that it would be terribly insensitive given his position, and that anyway he has work to do in the morning? As it is, the two of them enjoy a nice routine in Bel Respiro. Why spoil it? There's no need.

At the same time, Coco can't fathom his unwillingness to spend the night together for once. It seems so little to ask, and this after she has given him so much already. She can't believe that he's so selfish. She finds their life back in Bel Respiro sordid, suddenly, mean and cheapening. She's furious at what she sees as his rejection. For a minute, her mouth is lipless, grim. In the darkness next to him, her profile is a stone.

Staring out, Coco sees the moon appear, now to the left, now to the right of the car. Leaves in the hedges glimmer vividly. Headlights pick up the flicker of insects an instant before they smash against the glass. For a split second she glimpses a fox. Then there's a sound, a muffled thud. She thinks they hit it. Her fists clench instinctively and she winces, sure of it now. No one says anything, not even the chauffeur, who must sense the tension behind him. A horrible taste enters her mouth.

As they round finally into the drive, the house seems drowned in shadows. A single light burns in Catherine's room. The car slides to a halt. For a moment Igor thinks he sees a patch of shadow amid the general glow, before—and this time he is certain—he sees the curtains twitch and close.

CHAPTER NINETEEN

Click. Catherine stands pale and emaciated, her chest pressed flat against the X-ray machine. Her condition has worsened over the last few weeks. The doctor has advised she visit a hospital in Paris for a scan of her lungs. Stone-faced, she braces herself as though expecting a blow.

The radiologist calls her into his office later to confront her with the spectacle of her own insides. "The good news is, it's not galloping," he says.

He slides the X-rays one by one against a luminous screen. She regards the images, this glimpse of the invisible, with an eerie calm. There is her body exposed in all its materiality. Revealed is a secret scaffold of white bones. Blackness fills the vacuum between the ribs, except for these transparent sacs that look like jellyfish, and which she guesses are her heart and lungs. She's disturbed, though, by the dark, vacant spaces that seem devoid of any soul.

"As you can see, however, the tuberculosis has taken a slow hold."

The doctor points out the white swirls that cloud her lungs. Numbed, she hardly manages to take in anything he says. Horror mixes uneasily with an impression of magic at what she sees. A chill runs through her, making her shiver.

Moving closer to inspect, she cannot resist touching the X-rays on the screen. What fascinates and shocks her most, though, are not the white shadows on her lungs. Seeing her own slow dissolution frozen in an image is too disembodied a notion really to spook her. No, what strikes her most keenly is the appearance of her left hand, which has also crept into one of the exposures. She places her hand tentatively against its skinless image, finger to sinister finger. And around the thin third digit she registers her wedding ring floating in tender negative—like a halo around the white bone.

The ring hovers, ghostly. It is as if she has penetrated layers of mystery suddenly to discover a truth. But if this is a revelation, then it is without grace. There is no accompanying lift of the spirit, no attendant radiance or bliss. Quite the opposite, she feels tugged down. She becomes conscious of her own mortality as never before. And it fills her with dread.

She tries to think of God inhabiting the calcium of those bones. But the two things—the X-ray in front of her and the existence of God above—seem at this moment wholly incompatible. Instead of God, all that comes into her head is a huge nothing, an appalling sense of cancellation, a final blank that wants to swallow her up.

She has always clung to the belief that there is something out there—something powerful and stubbornly opaque, yet something splendid and ultimately good. It is a crumb to hold on to, a comfort, a reassurance, like the small studded crucifix that hangs around her neck. Until now it has given her hope that the sorry forlorn deplorable business of this life is not all there is. But what, after all, if it is? Thinking about this frightens her. The prospect of oblivion she finds horrific. She feels again the weight of her gold ring like a zero into which everything is pulled.

Even though Igor accompanies her, she has never felt so alone.

"Thank you," he says, shaking hands with the radiologist.

Fine, she thinks, he doesn't want to panic her, but must he thank the man quite so heartily? He has just been informed that his wife has consumption. Doesn't he realize that she has just received her death warrant? Doesn't he grasp that she might die? Her own handshake, when she offers it, is more grudging, guarded.

Afterward Igor says all the right things, and reassures her in appropriate ways, but as with the X-ray there seems to her to be something missing. She finds it hard to say what it is: a deeper sense of conviction behind the words, perhaps, or a greater sense of consolation in his tone. All she knows is, there's a gap, a barrier between them, some kind of wall. Maybe, she considers, it's that he is alive and well and that she is sick. Can it be that simple?

Next morning she wakes up, terrified and sweating, with a feeling of depletion, of lives sloughed off. Turning to see the empty pillow beside her, she experiences a vivid sense of diminishment.

Igor is already at work downstairs, hammering away at the piano. She hears, too, the voices of her children rise from a remote corner of the house. And, leaking also into her consciousness like a detectable stain, she hears distinctly the voice of Coco. She is singing to them.

CHAPTER TWENTY

Igor finishes a morning's work at the piano with a flourish. The keyboard ripples under the backs of his hands like strips of film being fed into a projector. Leaving his room, he walks along the corridor until he arrives at Coco's study. She has avoided him these past two days since their argument in Paris.

As he enters, she's sitting at her desk, working; endlessly pinning and cutting. She has assembled material for a white tunic and sable hat. Watching the film the other night, she had been struck by the contrast of white shirt and dark mask; the chiaroscuro of white horse and black cape. The experience reinforces for her again how black tends to dominate other colors under the lights. She recalls her own years at convent school, forced to wear a black and white uniform like the nuns.

His face cuts into the side of her vision. Seeing him, she leans back into her chair.

He says, "Don't you ever stop?" He's not used to seeing women work; not society women, anyway. Like his wife, he's always thought it somehow improper.

She picks it up, his resistance to her working. Yet, she reflects, it's what fires her, what has always pushed her on: a determination to prove herself, to reconcile a new sense of feminine elegance with the everyday needs of her sex. "I never finish." She wants him to know she's still cross with him.

Igor hesitates in the doorway. She nods for him to come in. Then she leans across the desk to grab a length of wool. Her hands are quick in manipulating it.

"Here," she says, improvising an intricate cat's cradle. Expertly she transfers it onto his fingers. An olive branch. "Go on, then."

In Igor's hands, the threads soon tangle and the structure falls apart.

"You're hopeless," she says, teasing him. "Watch me again." Coco again contrives the cradle about his hands. "There. Have another go."

Once more he tries, and once more the whole thing yields feebly in his fingers.

"All right," Coco says, with mock exasperation. "Let's try something different."

"Something easier," he protests.

She strings the wool out like a necklace in front of his eyes. "Now, the trick is to pull one of the threads so that it untangles. Watch!" She tugs gently at one of the threads, and the whole net undoes simply. "See?"

Quickly Coco reworks the wool into its web. Then she holds it up for Igor. His tongue touches the top of his lip in concentration. After wavering a moment, his hand suspended in the air, he pulls at one of the depending threads. The wool clots hopelessly.

"It's no use," he says. Setting it aside, he reaches toward

her. His fingers brush her lips, then trail backward across her cheek. "I'm sorry about the other night."

"That's all right," she says, looking away.

"I was tired."

Unwilling to forgive him yet, she wants more. "So was I."

"I wasn't thinking straight."

"Clearly."

"You know Catherine's not well."

At this new mention of his wife's name, Coco lowers his hand from her face. She finds his apology gauche. "I don't want to talk about that at the moment, thank you."

"But you're the one I want to be with," he pleads.

Turning on him: "Then do something about it!"

"What do you suggest?"

Exasperated: "You don't make things easy for me, Igor."

"Easy things are not worth having."

"And difficult things aren't always worth pursuing."

"But sometimes they are," he insists. Reaching toward her this time, he's more resolute. "And I *am!*"

He recognizes the need for a gesture, something brave but self-abasing. Abruptly he gets down on the floor and lies flat on his back. He lifts up his shirt to his chest. Then, tensing his muscles, he invites her to stand on his stomach. "Come on."

"Don't be silly."

"It's not silly. Come on."

It's his way of making up, she recognizes, his way of regaining her trust. But in seeming to belittle himself, she sees, he is actually showing off.

"All right," she says, making it clear she's humoring him.

Slipping off her shoes, she plants her stockinged feet squarely on his midriff, wobbling for a moment. He supports her weight for several seconds without flinching. His face goes taut with concentration. She can't resist a smile. She steps off; but before he has a chance to roll down his shirt, she reaches for a knitting needle lanced in a ball of wool. He looks up, alarmed.

"You don't get off that lightly," she says.

"What are you going to do?"

"Give you the mark of Coco!"

In imitation of Douglas Fairbanks, she grazes his stomach below his shirt, incising nimbly a monogram of her initials: two big interlinking letter Cs.

"You're mine," she says, dragging the knitting needle upward and following the seam of his shirt until the point is at his throat. "Do you understand? All mine!" she continues in a singsong tone, but with a serious undercurrent to her words. "And I don't want to share you with a-ny-bo-dy else." Suddenly pulling the needle down, she ends with a remonstrative jab in Igor's groin.

"Understood?"

He's conscious that he's under her control and feels a kind of panic at the fact. Yet it's a panic that possesses a sweetness, too. In yielding to the regime she imposes, he feels the challenge of a slave to please a master; the thrill of willing submission; the humility of having to lick a woman's shoes only to discover suddenly that they are smothered in honey.

"Understood." He gulps.

The next few days, he accompanies Coco into Paris in the afternoons. While she goes to the shop, he walks around the capital. He enjoys the city's trembling energy, its radial symmetries, its broad avenues, and its bridges spanning the river like the frets on a melting guitar. He loves the birch trees that are everywhere, with their blistered trunks and their leaves that catch the sunlight spottily. There's a grandeur to the parks, too, that he likes, and a shameless love of spectacle. France may be a republic in name, he thinks, but everything about the capital seems to scream out royalty: its arches and spires, its monuments and tombs, its gardens and palaces. It reminds him of St. Petersburg.

Regularly he visits the Pleyel office, where he submits his transcriptions for mechanical piano and picks up orders for further work. It's lucrative, he finds. And while not particularly stimulating, it's easy enough to do. More importantly, it gives him an excuse to be there, in Paris with Coco, and for this he is grateful.

While she finishes work, he strolls in the Tuileries and takes coffee in one of the nearby cafés. Afterward he invariably retires to Coco's apartment above the shop, where they make love.

One afternoon she surprises him with a present.

"Well—what do you think?" Igor allows the children into his study to show them his new toy.

"What is it?" Milène asks. Tilting her head, her ponytails dangle sideways, unevenly exposing two pink bows.

Soulima answers, "A pianola."

"Watch!" Igor says. His eyes flash like a conjurer's with the promise of spiriting music from the air. He winds the instrument up. Then as he releases the handle, the music starts. A little flat, perhaps, and the rhythm seems to drag at the end of one revolution then quicken at the beginning of another, but jaunty nonetheless. He recalls Coco's remark that it sounds like something you might find in a brothel.

The pressure of invisible fingers depresses the keys. A perforated scroll revolves on a cylinder in the central panel of the piano. The children are thrilled. As if witnessing a miracle, they move closer, openmouthed.

"Careful — don't touch!"

"How does it work?" Theodore asks, stirred out of his moroseness by the apparent magic of the machine.

"You see the scroll?" The children watch the perforated paper turn thickly at the front. "Well, the little holes give information to the keys about what notes need to be played. It's clever stuff."

Igor is delighted to see his children interested. He's been stung by Catherine's criticism that he doesn't spend enough time with them. She says that Theodore isn't sleeping, and this upsets him, and she tells him that the others are feeling insecure. He realizes he's become distant recently, as a consequence probably of his wish to protect them from his secret life. This afternoon is an attempt to reestablish good relations, to reinforce the fact that he cares.

"So what do you think?" he repeats.

"I like it!" Milène says.

Ludmilla complains, "But there are too many keys going down at once."

"That's the beauty of it."

He explains that you can code the pianola so it has the equivalent of four hands, eight, or even more.

"Four hands and no feelings," Soulima mutters, less impressed than the rest of them. In recent weeks, a saddle of freckles has developed across his nose and cheeks. They seem in their sudden eruption to underscore his disapproval.

"It's true you can't vary the tempo or volume as much as you could if you were playing it yourself. But it's very useful for working things out without having to rehearse lots of instruments. And it saves having to pay the musicians as well."

Milène says, "Well, I think it's great!"

"I do, too," Igor says.

"Is it expensive?" Theodore is becoming more practical by the day. Physically he has grown fast, too, Igor notices. Though still in shorts and with the thin limbs of an adolescent, he is only an inch or so shorter than his father now. His lankiness serves to exaggerate his height.

"Yes."

Theodore persists. "How can we afford it?"

"We have Coco to thank for that," Igor says. The slight delay in his response reveals his discomfort. There is something forced about his smile.

Of the children, only Theodore seems troubled by this. Perhaps sensing something hostile in his mother's attitude toward her, he has always been wary of Coco. Being the eldest, he is the most sensitive to the family's dependency on their host. Instinctively he resents it. He finds it demeaning and undignified, an affront to his imminent manhood. His thick, almost Mongolian features grow tense. His mouth narrows a little. For a moment, the air between father and son seems a fabric that might tear.

"Did she get the gramophone records, too?" Ludmilla asks innocently.

Igor's heart goes hollow. "Yes, she did."

"Can we hear them again?"

"Later, later . . ."

Igor is determined that the unveiling of the pianola should remain a triumph. He won't allow Theodore's bad mood to spoil it. To amuse the children, he presses the palm of his right hand under his left armpit and squeezes in time to the rhythm. The rapid movement of his arm up and down makes a farting sound. They all laugh, except Theodore.

Igor stops. In an effort to appease his son, soon to be fourteen, he puts an arm around him. He notices for the first time the fuzz on his upper lip. "Just looking at you now, son, you know what I think?"

Theodore has retreated into his habitual surliness. "What?"

Igor smiles broadly. He has an idea. "I think it's time you and I had our first beer together. What do you say?"

Theodore brightens. Soulima looks on in silent awe. The two girls beam at their big brother, who cannot resist a bashful smile.

"Come on, let's share a drink. And for the rest of you, there's a jug of lemonade."

"Hooray!" cries Milène.

With the pianola still instructing itself blindly in his study, Igor leads his children to the kitchen to enact this new rite.

CHAPTER TWENTY-ONE

Coco and Igor sit late on the balcony. Now early September, the weather still holds. An outside light illuminates the two of them as they talk and smoke in the evening air. Mosquitoes swarm in a halo of fluorescence, maddened by the dazzle of the lamp.

"Damn things!" Igor says, swatting them away.

Coco pulls a black angora sweater close around her shoulders. Fingering the string of pearls around her neck, she says, "Look at the stars! They're all shaking." She plays the pearls to her lips, nibbling them.

It is true. The more they look, the more the stars seem to jiggle minutely in a kind of dance, like animalcules in a pond. Solemnly the constellations present themselves. Igor watches for several seconds, trying to locate the unseen threads that connect them. He listens to their music: a celestial insect hum.

"If you look down at the city, you get the same effect."

In the distance they see the amber glow of the capital thrown up into the sky. To Igor's left, Coco's face makes a heart-shaped shadow.

"The stars above us and the city below. What more could you want?"

"I used to dream about coming to Paris when I was a boy." The city hovers at the edge of his attention like a tint or perfume flavoring the night sky.

Coco draws on her cigarette. "And now, given the chance, would you return to Russia?"

Nursing a wineglass in his hand, he says, "There are things I miss."

"Such as?"

"My mother. Friends. My piano. My house. And spring when the ice melts and the earth seems suddenly to crack and creak into being. You feel as if you're coming alive."

A gust of wind blows, rattling the door. The light flickers momentarily. Leaves make a gentle chafing sound. Reaching down, he picks up a half-empty bottle of red wine. He gestures to Coco. She traps her hand over the top of her glass. He shrugs and pours himself another. The wine looks black in the moonlight.

"You know, you've never told me how you met her."

Until now they have avoided speaking of his wife. He has made it clear previously that it is not a subject open for discussion. And Coco has indulged him. Indeed, the physical fact of her existence in a bedroom upstairs has been quite enough for her to contend with. It has taken a huge unspoken effort of will on Coco's part to diminish her presence within the house. Yet it is beginning to seem ridiculous not to acknowledge her. Catherine has become a hole in their talk. An unhealed gap. Now the wine has fortified Coco

enough to quiz him. And it is evidence of their growing intimacy that he feels relaxed enough to answer.

"I was practically brought up with her." Released from the
tension of silence, his words seem weightless.

"Childhood sweethearts, how romantic."

Ignoring her: "But the first time I can remember being
drawn to her in any way was when we were about fourteen.
We were in a cathedral."

"Don't tell me. She was in the nativity scene, playing the
Madonna."

"Not quite. She was in the choir."

As a formal prelude to his tale, Igor again offers her more
wine. She relents this time, permitting him to pour a further
inch into her glass, accepting it as a ticket of admission to this
episode from his life.

"It was a crisp spring day. Inside the cathedral, though, it
was cold. The choir was singing some hymn, and light streamed
in through the stained-glass windows and hit a point near the
altar where they stood. The smell of incense was overwhelming, I remember, and the music rose high to the cathedral
ceiling. You know what the acoustics of churches are like?"

"Yes, yes, get on with it."

"Anyway, just as the priest intoned, 'Thou shalt be admitted into the garden of eternal delight,' it happened. I saw
Catherine standing at the end of one row, and . . ."

"What?"

"She was wearing a thin white shirt and, with the light
hitting her sideways from the window, it became completely
transparent."

"She must have been wearing something underneath."

"I'm sure she was. But in silhouette the effect was devastating to a young boy. She was all . . ."

"Standing to attention?"

"That's right."

"It was probably the cold inside the church."

"Churches are very erotic places."

"What?"

"If you think of the architecture of the cathedral, it's totally erotic. The spire, the cupola, and the arches with their ribbed insides just waiting to swell and contract . . ."

"Tender Mary."

And then rapidly, burlesquing the catechism: "Exalted Sister of Peace."

"Grace of the Redemptrix."

"Celestial Queen of Heaven."

"Holy Mother of God."

They both laugh. Coco's eyes shine glassily. Filaments of her hair shake loose, catching a glisten of light from the lamp.

"What happened next?"

"Well, neither of us had had much contact with the opposite sex. We just became used to each other's company. And soon we were great friends."

Her mouth twists sideways. "Friends."

Igor's tone grows serious. "Yes, actually, friends."

"Brother and sister?"

He shrugs.

"You didn't have to marry her, though!"

"I know all you see is this bedridden invalid, but she's an intelligent woman. She's well-read. She has taste and refinement . . ."

"It seems to me she's in danger of refining herself out of existence." Coco finds it hard to disguise her contempt for Catherine. She didn't even try to come down once today. Yet she still wants Marie to minister to her all morning and afternoon. Coco can't stand that kind of weakness in people. There's no fight in her, she decides.

Picturing his wife listening to this, Igor winces. He doesn't like her being so summarily dismissed. He wants her accorded more respect. Their bodies mock her enough as it is. "She's not well," he says.

"I know. I'm sorry."

"Well, that's that." It is obvious he does not wish to go on.

Sensing that the conversation needs to change key, she asks brightly, "So what did you think of me when we first met?"

Igor lifts the wineglass from his knee. He turns the stem slowly, watching the wine lap darkly against the sides.

"What did I think when I first met you?" He repeats the question aloud to himself and ruminates for a moment. Involuntarily he squeezes one eye shut to look at the glass as he raises it. The surface of the wine seems to form a disc that retains its shape however he tilts it.

"Come on, tell me the truth."

He says, "I thought you were quite aggressive."

"Aggressive?"

"Verbally, I mean."

"And what else?" Coco lights a cigarette and blows the smoke out quickly.

"I thought you were clever and generous . . ."

"Is that all?"

"Well, I obviously found you attractive if that's what you mean. Shapely and slim . . ." Igor continues ritually to twist his glass on the point of his knee. "Must I go on?"

Coco stares out at the garden and the needlepoint of stars. "No. That's fine."

"And *me*? What did you think when you first met me?"

Decisively: "You seemed a bit remote and cold."

"I'm sorry."

"But vulnerable underneath it all. And passionate."

"Passionate?"

"I saw that the first night of *The Rite*." Her voice lifts. "And I made it my duty to bring it out in you."

"Have you succeeded?" He inspects a leaf made glossy by the outside light.

"I've done a pretty good job, I think. Under the circumstances." She looks at him and they share a smile.

He touches the back of his hair. "I've grown grayer as a result."

"But you look"—she hesitates—"more distinguished."

Why is it, he thinks, that women find gray hair attractive? Perhaps it reminds them of death, and they find that exciting. Maybe they find it appealing to consider the perishability of their men.

"I'm starting to dress better, that's for sure." He hears a buzzing about his skull.

"That's not hard."

He falls abruptly to scratching his arms. "I'm being eaten alive out here!"

"So am I."

"It's your perfume. It's driving them crazy."

Lifting his glass with one hand and grabbing the bottle with the other, Igor is quick to lead the way inside.

CHAPTER TWENTY-TWO

Catherine is sitting up when Igor enters the room. It has become his custom, after working for a couple of hours in the morning, to pay a dutiful visit to his wife. He always comes at the same time. It's part of the rhythm of his day.

Catherine has readied herself. Since experiencing the terrifying sight of her own insides, she has become more aware of her appearance, too. In an attempt to spruce herself up and look more attractive, she has combed out her hair and rouged her cheeks. She has even put some lipstick on. She greets Igor smilingly as he walks in the door, continuing to comb her hair.

His heart sinks. He can see what she's doing. He responds with a forced smile. "You look very nice," he says, complimenting her. But she wants more than compliments. He knows that. She needs attention and tenderness. She wants his love. And this he is unable, or at least unwilling, to give. There is a reined-in element to his voice that communicates the glum unenthusiastic truth.

He finds he needs to remind himself that she is a good person. He loved her once, with youthful ardor and with a passion that seemed reckless. They had braved their parents' opposition to marry, and risked alienating their good name; such was the strength of their innocent love. He remembers his family's disapproving glances at the wedding, the sparsely attended ceremony, the shamefaced priest. He can still smell the musk of incense prickling his nostrils, still see the gold ring, and her face trembling beneath a veil as she recited her vows.

But that seems like a lifetime ago, now: before the war, before the Revolution, before *The Rite*. Since then their lives have changed beyond measure. Looking at Catherine, he no longer recognizes her as his bride. His love for her, like her health, has slowly eroded so that only a sense of filial attachment, like a last tenaciously clinging bit of ligament, remains to connect them together.

"Very nice," he reiterates. He hopes somehow the repetition might invest the phrase with the weight of truth.

He cannot, though, bring himself to say anything more. He does feel bad at the way he has treated her. But he is also repelled by her sickness. Atom by atom, she seems to be decaying, whereas with Coco there is always some kind of shimmer or sparkle that affirms her own existence and his. It is as much as he can do to regard his wife blankly, in the hope that she might understand.

Catherine's eyes fill with sadness. Her scalp stretches tight with the pressure of her thoughts. She continues brushing her hair in short, robust strokes. But there is something automatic about the gesture, which is no longer necessary. "Why do you hate me?" she says, throwing the brush onto the bed. She wants the action to produce a noise, but the brush hits the covers with a muffled thump.

"I don't hate you."

"What have I done wrong?" So much heat is contained within the question that her tongue seems almost to burn.

"You've done nothing wrong."

"I don't *want* to be ill, you know."

"I know."

Guilt sweeps through him. The air around him seems to turn thin. Relenting, he extends a hand to her cheek and makes pathetically to stroke it.

In that vulnerable face of hers he has a glimpse suddenly of Catherine as a young girl—her lips set prim and her blue eyes sparkling. But her lips have become blurry, he sees, and her eyes seem squeezed of brightness.

In a voice gone calm again, she asks, "Do you still feel anything for me?"

"Of course."

"Is she so different?"

He looks inside himself and tries to be honest. "No."

"She understands nothing of your music. She collects people. Can't you see?"

"That's a little harsh."

After a pause: "You know, you're not yourself when you're with her."

"Oh?"

"You become someone else."

"You've never seen us alone together."

There is, implicit in his too-quick answer, a confession. Her look sharpens. He makes to elaborate, to diffuse the element of revelation involved in his unthinking response.

She seizes the moment. "Are you in love with her, Igor?"

His lips seek to frame a statement. In vain, his mouth tries to conjure the right words. Outdone, he refuses to meet her gaze. Repelled, she pushes him off.

The look of pleading in her eyes is replaced with an expression of rancor and hurt. All the tiny antagonisms of her life are magnified and focused into this one moment. Each small torture she has endured at mealtimes, each brief meeting of Coco and Igor's knees, the anguish of every complicitous grin distills itself vividly into the mixture of pain and humiliation now visible on her face.

"You disgust me!"

"I'm sorry," he responds inadequately.

The energy she has generated in an effort to be conciliatory discovers now a fresh outlet in bitterness. "Why do you pretend? And who do you think you're fooling treating me like this, as if I'm an idiot?"

Igor thinks this time before answering, "It's not because I don't love you."

"Don't try to justify your actions, Igor, please."

"You're still my wife."

"How privileged that makes me feel!"

"Catherine . . . try to understand . . ."

"I understand all too well."

"I've tried not to hurt you."

"Am I supposed to be grateful?"

"What can I say?"

"You can say you're sorry!"

"Sorry," he says. But he's not; not really.

"You wouldn't behave like this if your mother were here,"

she flings at him. "It's very convenient for you, isn't it, that she's still stuck in Russia?"

Igor remains upright and unmoving on the bed, saying nothing, stung by the remark about his mother. It is true, of course. Adultery and exile, like everything else that holds him up, are interconnecting simplicities. Banished along with him have been the usual prohibitions governing his behavior. Deracination grants certain permissions, licenses certain acts. A stern moral ombudsman, his mother has always operated as a kind of conscience for him. While he wouldn't wish her ill, he has felt obscurely liberated since they were forced apart.

Catherine is right, he recognizes. He is a coward. Though isn't this scene somehow inevitable—as unpleasant as it is necessary? Things can't go on as they are. He has an urge to confess as well as to conceal. He wants to tell the truth. Yet how do you tell your wife you don't love her? His mouth is crammed with the unsayable. It would be wrong to stay with her merely out of pity. There lingers still an impulse to reach out, to hold and reassure, even though ultimately this might prove more cruel.

"I take it you've slept with her."

He can't bring himself to lie any longer. He looks away. His silence is the affirmation she requires.

"How often?"

"Does that matter?" The impulse to reach out is beaten back.

"I'd like to know."

Wearily. "Catherine, I don't keep count."

She is wild-eyed, not so much with rage as with disbelief at finding herself trapped like this. The room around her seems to change shape.

For Igor, the weight of his past life with Catherine slides against the now of his existence with Coco. He feels the friction, jarring his insides. He loathes himself at this moment. In bristling self-defense, he senses something ruthless, even brutal, enter his head. "I thought you'd be glad," he hurls at her.

"What? Are you insane?"

"Well, you hate making love."

Catherine shakes her head slowly, then more fiercely. "I do not!"

"How can you say otherwise? You're revolted by it."

"That's not true!"

"That's not the impression I get."

"You're saying that Coco's doing me a favor? Is that it?"

"I have needs, Catherine."

"And I have needs, too. Enormous needs."

"Well, perhaps the fact is, we can't fulfill each other . . ." He hates what he's saying, but it is how he feels. Cornered, he knows no other way out.

"I can't believe you can be so heartless. I find this so hurtful, I can't even explain." Her neck swells. The vertical cords at her throat grow taut, and her chest begins to heave. She wills herself, with an urgency that might move objects, not to cry. Her whole being strains to contain the misery that sweeps through her. "I've supported you, endured your moods, borne your children . . ." She turns away from him. Pulling the covers up to her face, she chokes off the sobs that rise inside her.

She has been content until now with his long hours at the

piano, his frequent absences due to recitals and tours. She has tolerated his anger and his pride, his arrogance. But she has never before had to reckon with his adultery. She feels obliterated. A crushing sense of redundancy descends upon her. "I'm suffocating here," she gasps.

The shadows of leaves agitate darkly against the wall. Objects in the room seem conspiratorial suddenly. The lilies are vicious tongues. A shell becomes a secret ear. The curtains exist to conceal things from her. Her fists tighten in the covers. Something in her wants to explode. A surge of violence rises within and makes her face stretch wide.

"You bastard!" she hisses. Her voice is choked. "And with that whore!"

The primitive in her takes over. She feels like slapping him across the face, grabbing his hair and yanking it, kicking out at him. But the impulse only lasts a split second. Violence is not her style. There's nothing savage in her. She's too decorous and restrained. The layers of politeness are too thick within her, and she curses herself for it. For just a moment back then, she might have brought her fists down upon him. She might have felt better for it. He may, she has time to reflect, even have respected her more. But such brute instincts soon drain from her, along with any remaining energy.

His voice is level in correcting her. "She's not a whore, Catherine."

Sensing a rawness enter her throat, she says, "I feel sick."

Continuing to sit there, they avoid touching. He looks at her, conscious of the cruelty of his words. He can't believe he's uttered them. He's propelled by a momentum that cannot be stayed. He had to tell her. It was spilling from him. He regrets not doing it more gently, but he feels now strangely unburdened, relieved.

In seeking a gesture of consolation, he offers, "We still have four beautiful children." Saying this, something clenches in his chest.

It is not clear that Catherine hears it. The effort of constraint has become too much. Her whole frame shakes. "Why don't you love me?" Her voice in its attempt at a scream sounds hoarse and broken. Silently she yields to tears. Crumpling darkly, her face is transfigured. Her jaw shudders with a grief remarkable both for its intensity and her attempt to suppress it. She manages, "I'm scared, Igor."

"Don't be."

"I'm afraid."

"Why?"

"I'm really sick. I feel like something is pulling at me, dragging out my insides." The air around her seems unbreathable. A sense of terror crams her chest.

"But the doctor says the prognosis is good."

"I know, but I saw it with my own eyes. I saw my death."

"What you saw was just an X-ray."

Her voice lowers suddenly. "Can I ask you something?"

"Of course."

"There isn't anything else, is there?"

"What do you mean?"

Her eyes shine, hopelessly benign. "I mean this is it, isn't it? There isn't anything beyond."

"No, I can't accept that."

"But take away the fact of our bodies, our physical existence—strip that away and what's left?"

Igor hesitates, puzzled for a moment, his face radiantly attentive to everything around him. His eyes pass over the icons around her bed, the curtains stirring at the window. He hears the birdsong outside. Then the answer comes, as though it were so blindingly simple a child might supply it. A world held together by chance rhythms, invisible strings. A sublime incarnation of His voice, hovering solitary, suspended above the void. "Why, music, of course."

She stares at him in a state of deep incomprehension. Baffled and saddened, she shakes her head.

His response is instinctive but, he is aware, profoundly unsatisfactory. He opens his mouth in an effort to say more, but the words won't come. After a long pause, which deepens the gulf between them, Igor rises solemnly, touching his fingers to his throat. He makes to kiss her but she draws away. He stands there motionless for a few moments. Then he leaves the room without a further word or look and returns to work in his study.

Catherine weeps stonily. Her face is contorted, her eyes bloodshot and scoured. Her sorrow seems bottomless.

Downstairs, the piano's tone of self-congratulation mocks her. For some minutes afterward, her chest rises and falls with the effort of deep unmusical sobs.

———

10 September 1920

Dearest Mother,

I hope all is well. I need hardly tell you we all miss you here. Catherine and the children send their love and kisses.

I have written again to the embassy, requesting they grant you a visa. The ambassador is a reasonable man. He foresees no real difficulty. But there is a backlog of such cases, he says, piled up at the ministry, and they are taking their time in processing each one. Be patient, and we continue to pray that you will join us very soon.

The children are all well. Theo is growing into a fine boy. He enjoys his drawing more and more. He completed an excellent sketch of the house yesterday, which I enclose so you'll have an idea of where we live. Soulima is coming along nicely on the piano. He has the self-discipline, I think, to become very good indeed. His fingers are supple and he has a quick mind, too. Ludmilla is growing taller all the time. She has shot up over the last few months. She needs larger sizes already in all her clothes. And Milène is adorable. She has taken to one of the puppies in the house and wants to keep it, I think.

Catherine is still unwell, however. Recently she underwent tests, and I'm afraid she's been stricken again with a mild form of consumption. She remains positive, though, and the air and warmth here are all to her advantage. In addition, the doctor who tends her is splendid—full of encouragement and good sense.

I'm working regularly and well. With Diaghilev I am to revive The Rite *again next year. A copy of the score has been sent from Berlin. I'm revising and developing it assiduously. It's good just to be able to work. And it's a blessed relief not to have to think about rent and bills. My patron is generous and hospitable, and I'm sure you'd like her very much.*

*Anyway, keep well. We all give you hugs and blow you
tender kisses. We miss you.*

Your loving son,
Igor

Late that afternoon, Igor feeds his parrots. All the birds are
kept in an outhouse along with the garden tools and furniture, spades and forks, and bits of netting. A pair of shears
hangs on a hook, its blades splayed so wide it seems almost
improper. A musty smell rises from the timber of the shed.
Inside, the humidity is tropical. Outdoors, for a change, it is
quiet. Thanks to Coco, the children have been enrolled in a
local school.

Ritually Igor fills the birds' bowls with water. He pours mil-
let and seed into the food troughs and removes the odd torn
feather and droppings from the bottom of each cage. Placing
his head next to the wire, he scrutinizes their quick, spasmodic
movements. The space in the shed is echoey. Collectively
they generate quite a din.

Behind him, he hears the door click open. It's Coco.

"They're beautiful, aren't they?"

"They are," she concedes. She looks at the parrots and
lovebirds with renewed attention as they move on their
perches like tightly wound toys.

"Look at the engineering that's gone into those wings. There
must be a God to have managed that, don't you think?"

"Oh, come on, some birds are just one step up from ver-
min. They're pests, most of them."

"Not to me."

He tickles one bird's underside. With a crooked forefinger he strokes the feathers on its head.

"Watch this," he says.

He extends his tongue with a few bread crumbs on it through the bars of the cage. The bird looks at him. Its narrow skull twitches in response. Then its beak pecks unerringly at the crumbs on his tongue.

"Ugh!" Coco exclaims. "Don't they nip you?"

Igor sniggers. "No. They're very precise, and their eyes are much sharper than ours. Than mine, anyhow." Igor caresses the beak of the bird, which purrs in appreciation.

"They must have tiny brains."

"That doesn't stop them singing."

"I know. I hear them."

Igor whistles. He tuts and clicks with his tongue behind his teeth, angling his neck with comical stiffness. The birds shift their feet and tut back, their heads twitching absently. He opens the cage and encourages one of the parrots to perch on his finger.

"Do you want to hold it?"

"Are you sure?"

"Go ahead."

Cradling it, she feels the bird's heart beat rapidly against her palm.

"They love it here," he says. "The climate is just right for them."

"Unlike you?" Coco suggests. She continues to pet it.

"I do find it hot, still."

He thinks of his argument with Catherine this morning.

It depresses him to consider what might happen next. At the moment, he and Coco just steal what time they can alone. They have their afternoons in Paris. But it would be better to spend the nights together, to get used to the sound of one another's breathing, and for each to feel the skin of the other close and touching all night long. At the same time, Igor is determined to keep the relationship discreet. He has no wish to humiliate Catherine or to hurt the children. And since the dreadful scene this morning, the truth is he's not sure what he feels. Numbness, chiefly. And sadness. Looking after the birds, he finds, grants him a kind of monastic calm.

"Well, it's soon going to get much cooler, if that's any consolation. Maybe the birds will have to fly south."

"The need to migrate can drive some birds mad. They've been known to dash their heads against the bars."

She hands the parrot back to him. Gently he replaces it inside the cage. Slipping his finger between the wires, he allows another to peck playfully at his nail.

"I hope you don't feel the same way."

Being with Coco, he reflects, is like being drunk all the time. It's marvelous, but he wonders how long he can sustain it. The sensation is intoxicating. He has never felt so light-headed. It's extraordinary, like the giddy sensation you get with a first cigarette. He finds it impossible to concentrate. Sometimes, he longs just to come up for air. And physically she drains him. A fellatricious little minx, like a snake she seems capable of swallowing someone twice her size.

"Well, do you?"

"What?"

"Feel the same way?"

Turning from the cage to face her, he says, "You know what I miss?"

"Tell me."

"Snow," he says. It matches the present blankness of his mind.

"Snow?"

"Yes. Real snow. Not the powdery stuff you get here, but huge piles of it billowing all over the place and falling for days."

Coco touches Igor's hands and beckons him closer. "Come on."

"What?"

"It's the heat. It affects me, too, you know."

"Now?"

"Yes. I want you in my room."

"But . . ." He remembers the children are at school now. The decision is made for him. He submits. The stronger woman wins, again.

Slinking out of the outhouse, they slip quietly upstairs, Coco leading him insistently by a single finger for the first time to her bed.

An hour later, sitting at her window, she sees Igor in the garden below. On an impulse, she grabs a pillow and begins ripping out feathers by the handful from inside. She walks back to the window and undoes the hasp.

Hearing the window open above him, Igor looks up. He needs to raise a hand to shield his eyes against the sun. Coco smiles broadly, leaning out. He gives her a quizzical look. Her lips lift into the tension of a smile.

Abruptly, "Here's your snow!"

And she lets fall a blizzard of feathers that land in a white cloud on his head and on his jacket. Several more fistfuls are released in a soft white storm, each feather shilly-shallying airily to and fro. They almost blind him as they catch and scatter the sunlight in their spinning, almost dazzle him with their promise of a brightness beyond.

CHAPTER TWENTY-THREE

Igor paces the floor of his study in time to the music in his mind. His head is bowed and he hums to himself in a low, barely audible tone. His steps register the rise and fall of a rhythm that haunts his skull. Then he sits down to transcribe this inner music, to seize and hold it fast.

Setting himself limits, restrictions, constraints, he finds, is the best way of achieving imaginative solutions. Total freedom, the absolute permission granted by the blank page, most often proves a freedom merely to jump in the ocean. He needs something to jib against, the equivalent of a net in tennis: something to hit the ball over. With the *Symphonies of Wind Instruments* he has set himself this obstacle of writing simultaneously in different time signatures, of juggling synchronous yet dissonant rhythms. He tries, in writing it, not to control the direction of the piece too much, but rather to pursue lines that suggest themselves and see how they turn out.

He has become interested lately in the tension between chancy, pell-mell elements and more conventionally orchestrated compositions. There seems to him a kind of accidental beauty in the simultaneous sounding of adjacent chords that he wants to explore further. He sees in the pattern of black and white keys potential chords, melodies unplayed, previously unreachable harmonies suddenly heaving into view. He tries to capture and transpose them, trusting his impulse to follow them through.

He likes to start with the bass and build upward. He plays phrases at different speeds regulated by the metronome. He superimposes arpeggios in C major and F sharp. White and black notes. Tonic and dominant chords. Major and minor both in the same register. A hum is set up in his head. A polytonal sympathy. It resonates like a vivid patch of paint upon a wall. He can almost see the shape of it, vibrating like a stain on the retina once his eyes are closed. He strives to align the noise inside his mind with the sounds available on the keyboard. Determined to make it fit, he scribbles notes on the stave. For a few minutes, there seems an absolute correspondence between these inner and outer sounds.

Then a strange thing happens. He feels his existence beginning to take shape according to an unseen pattern of keys. He remembers the celestial insect hum he heard in the garden, and he stops to ponder to what extent his life here is given and preordained—like the scrolls of music for mechanical piano. Abruptly he feels weightless, as if manipulated by the tricky fingering of something outside himself.

He writes furiously. He can't fill in the bars fast enough. The act of composition takes him over. For a man so used to controlling every detail of his life, this is a strange sensation. The impulse overwhelms him, and a buoyancy enters his body at the unstoppable flow of notes. He feels his head grow hot. The thin skin of his ears burns.

Finished, he sits back with exhaustion. But he wants to look over what he has done. Examining it, he's excited. Is he deceived? Is this not brilliant? His instinct is to sound out Catherine. She's usually the first to see his work. She's his best and fiercest critic, his finest copyist. He can always rely on her for an honest opinion. He itches to know what she might think. Would she like it? Would she approve? But he realizes he can't ask her. It would be an insult to give her something so clearly illustrative of his vigor. To offer this up now as an example of how he's thriving would serve only to sharpen her suffering. It would be like presenting the nude portrait of another woman and asking, What do you think?

Igor rolls a cigarette, registering the taste of tobacco on his tongue. Lighting it, his eyes are blinky for an instant from the smoke. He glances at the portraits of his children on the desk and at an oval frame containing an early picture of Catherine. The photographs and their fervid details seem remote studies in happiness, images from a previous life.

Since the revelation of his infidelity, she seems to have withdrawn almost completely into herself. She no longer comes down to lunch or dinner. If she takes turns about the garden, she does so alone. Ceasing to heap insults upon him, she now suffers noiselessly, choosing to turn away when he enters the room. She has stopped crying, too, he has noticed. Emotionally bankrupt, she no longer has the resources even to make a scene. A new mute hardness has entered her features. A look of numbness beyond sorrow. For the moment she has become a ghost.

Down the corridor, the clattering preparations for lunch

are under way. It's odd not hearing the children, he thinks, now they are at school. The house is so quiet without them.

Igor thinks back to his own childhood. He recalls long walks in the woods outside St. Petersburg with his brother, the clinging haze of summer mornings, the clouds of midges by the river. Though similarly dimmed, his recollections prompt within him a moment of deep melancholy, a recognition of profound loss. Like a wrong color, there is something about his memories that chafes with the tone of his present locale. The tension generates a noise within his head. And there it is—that burning sensation again. Recognizing the moment, he grabs a pen and begins to scribble, launching himself into a last half hour of work before lunch. His hand can't keep up with his head, and he feels a welt develop on his finger from gripping the pen so tight.

In the afternoon, Coco strolls with Igor about the garden. The children won't return for another couple of hours.

She says, "Doesn't it bother you that we don't hold hands?"

"What makes you ask that?"

"It just occurred to me—we never do."

"Does it bother *you*?"

"I don't know. I've only just realized." A scent of cut grass lingers in the air, a polleny burden that scrapes against her sinuses and almost makes her sneeze. "It might."

He says, "I'm not sure I'd like it much if we did."

"Why not?"

"We're beyond that stage, now."

"No one should be beyond that stage."

"No, I mean, ours isn't a boy-girl kind of love. It's mature. We have an affinity deeper than man and wife. I feel it."

"Deeper than cousins?"

They come to a curve in the lawn. "All right," he says.

"I suppose it would be unseemly for your wife to see us holding hands . . ."

"That has nothing to do with it."

"Really?"

"Don't be absurd."

"Why is it absurd? Aren't you worried she'll find out?"

"Find out? What if I tell you she already knows?"

Coco halts. Stunned, she turns to face him. "She knows? How? Did you tell her?"

He does not meet her eye. "In a roundabout way, yes."

"Why?"

He feels her looking at him. "Why not?"

"I can't believe you told her."

"Who else would I tell?"

"Well, you didn't tell *me* you'd told her."

"You didn't consult me before you told Misia."

"It's not a game, Igor."

Realizing he has some ground to recover, he blurts, "Look, how can you question the fact that I love you?"

They begin walking again. "I just wish you were more honest with me, that's all."

"I adore you," he says. "You know that."

"Mm."

As though to prove his point, Igor, in the open, kisses the nape of Coco's neck. Her perfume rises into his nose. He feels the heady familiar ache of longing that has haunted his body all summer.

He has been more attentive of late, she concedes. He's taught her a few things on the piano, written her ardent notes, and given her drawings of the two of them together. But she knows it is also his way of trying to take control. And she must guard against that. She wants to keep the upper hand.

"Anyway," she says, "there's something I need to tell *you*."

"What?"

"Something that concerns us both."

"Well?"

"My period is a week late."

His heart freezes. "Are you sure?"

"Of course I'm sure."

"Is that unusual?"

"I'm regular as clockwork."

His next step seems not to land, but to go on falling. His color drains through a hole in the center of himself.

"Does it alarm you?"

"Should it?"

"I don't know."

He offers, "Catherine is often late."

A note of protest rises in her throat. "Well, I'm *not*, as a rule."

"Do you feel any different?" He stays her with his hand. "Catherine always said she felt strange. Something chemical. Her breasts used to be tender and sore. She felt tired. That's how she knew."

"I don't feel that way." Come to think of it, though, maybe she does.

"What are we going to do?"

"There's nothing *to* do. Yet."

A fear is touched off in him. "Have you tried taking hot baths?"

"I always do."

"I mean scalding."

"And what if I *want* a baby? Have you considered that?" She thinks of the times she spent trying with Boy, all to no avail. She hasn't so far contemplated it with Igor. Now that it might happen, though, and she hears herself discussing it, she quite likes the idea. She feels a sense of pride in her possible fertility. Her view of the garden, giving on to the plum and cherry trees, seems projected from within. She says, "You're not happy about this, are you?"

The sunlight dyes the insides of his eyelids red—a willed counterpoint to her refusal to bleed.

"Are *you*?"

She withdraws sharply at his question. She's not sure what she thinks. And what's that burny feeling in her abdomen, or is she just imagining it? "No," she offers solemnly. "But I'd like to be there when you tell Catherine about *this*!"

He can't find the breath to answer. In front of him on the lawn, he sees a green ball covered in dog's slobber and a shuttlecock stripped of all but one feather. The unsayable fills the next few seconds. There's a cacophony from the parrots in the outhouse. Blameless clouds float high above his head.

Walking back into the house, a coolness washes over them. The heat leaks from their skin and clothes.

CHAPTER TWENTY-FOUR

Of Igor's four children, Coco's favorite is Ludmilla. The twelve-year-old doggedly follows her about the house. She listens to her on the telephone, runs after her into the garden, even pursues her into the bedroom to see her change clothes. And, just when Coco's patience is stretched to breaking point by her clinging attentions, Ludmilla, sensing it somehow, will summon a winning, irresistible smile.

Keenly aware that she has made a favorite, Coco doesn't care. She has no problem showing her affection openly. She's not the girl's mother, after all, she reflects.

Catherine quickly comes to resent the rapport her eldest daughter establishes with her host. She can't help but notice that Ludmilla is more often downstairs playing with Coco than she is upstairs ministering to her. A kind of unannounced competition for the girl's affection begins within the house.

This sense of challenge merely quickens within Coco an already instinctive liking for the girl. The two of them enjoy a developing warmth. She allows Ludmilla to play with her jewelry and encourages her to try on some of her clothes. The girl is excited by the different fabrics. She's intrigued, too, by the way materials can be transformed from their raw state into a skirt or jacket. The whole process fascinates her, and she's keen to know more. So one day Coco takes Ludmilla to the shop. The girl comes back dazzled and impatient to tell her mother about the fabulous things she has seen. She also wants to show off Coco's present of a dress.

"Isn't it marvelous?" Ludmilla gushes to her mother, showing off the mantle of black Chantilly lace. Catherine manages a tight smile. The dress whispers sinisterly to her. In twirling around, the girl displays an instinctive flirtatiousness, a native sexuality that makes her mother look at her in a different light. She's horrified at the thought that Coco is educating her in the ways of the world. That bitch. Her baby. She feels a hard knot inside herself: something twisted, kinked.

She complains to Igor. She feels Coco is stealing Ludmilla away from her, buying her affection with expensive gifts. It is enough to lose a husband, but a daughter as well! That is too much to endure.

Igor, of course, does nothing. Anyway, what can he say? He can't very well scold Coco for befriending his daughter, for generously spending some time with her. She'd laugh at him. Besides, he wonders how much of this new closeness to Ludmilla is due to her own possibly pregnant state. Each day he waits to hear that it is all a false alarm and that there is nothing to be worried about. But nothing has happened yet, and he's growing ever more anxious and preoccupied. Then, when Catherine complains that if anything the situation has become worse, and that Coco and Ludmilla are spending more time together than ever, he snaps, "I don't see what the problem is. There's no harm in it. It's perfectly natural. And," he adds with impatience, "it's just as well at her age that the girl gets some attention."

Catherine feels the jibe keenly. She doesn't deserve this. Energized by fury, she retorts, "Even when I'm sick, I still do more for the children than you."

It is a sore point all around. Coco is careful not to involve herself in this new row. Ludmilla meanwhile remains oblivious of the crosscurrents of affection that eddy around her. And while her mother and father continue to argue over whom she spends more time with, she grows, to Catherine's chagrin, ever closer to Coco.

One day, the girl remains in her room, crying. She's inconsolable. She fails to respond when Catherine asks her what the matter is. She refuses to speak to her father, too, and seems oddly ashamed. Her sobbing continues all morning. Only to Coco does she reveal, toward lunchtime, the broad red stain, clammy and stickily intimate, that weeps from her knickers, ruining her new dress.

Coco doesn't need to be told. As she walks into the room she can smell it.

It is her first period, and Ludmilla feels afraid and upset. Coco's mouth frames a smile. The ghost of a maternal impulse burrows at her chest. She congratulates the girl at twelve and a half upon her graduation into womanhood, giving her a sisterly squeeze of the hand. Immediately, she sees, Ludmilla feels better about herself.

Coco's period arrived this morning, too. The two of them are in sync. It used to happen when she lived with Adrienne. A blood sisterhood. She feels silly for having said anything to

Igor, for frightening him like that. She never *felt* pregnant, though perhaps she imagined a few telltale signs. She told him partly to shock him out of what she saw as his complacency. And partly because by articulating her fears, in a superstitious way, she thought she might even help bring the period on. Besides, apart from Igor, who else could she confide in? If she mentioned it to anybody else, Misia in particular, he'd kill her.

She feels relieved, she thinks, that the scare is over. The fact is she's not pregnant. It was what she wanted. But at the same time her relief is complicated by a remote sense of disappointment. She'd begun, she realizes, to carry herself differently: more stately, more serene. She recognizes now from the responses of her body that she enjoys a secret urge to have a child. And if not now, then when? She knows that time is running out.

Ludmilla has brightened. Flattening a tear at the side of the girl's nose, Coco advises her to tell her mother. "She'll be proud of you."

Ludmilla twists her lower lip sideways with worry. "She'll think I'm dirty."

"No."

"She will."

"She won't, I promise. She'll think you're growing up."

"Can't *you* tell her?"

Smiling: "I don't think that would be right."

"Why not?"

"Why don't you talk to Suzanne about it? She'll explain everything."

"Really?"

"Yes."

The thought provides a ledge to which the girl clings. It seems to reassure her. She looks up. "All right."

Ludmilla fingers the dark stain on her dress. She laughs nervously. "I feel strange."

"You *will* to begin with. Everyone does."

"Does it mean I can have babies?"

"That's right."

"Are *you* going to have a baby ever?"

"I don't know. Someday, perhaps." The words scald her throat. Looking at the toilet paper in her hand this morning, darkened with her unpunctual blood, she had felt cheated. In its stain, she had seen the evidence of her failure: the one thing, she recognizes, she cannot do. She thinks now of the two abortions from her early lovers. Cavalrymen, both. What had those operations done to her insides? Reduced her to this empty spot of red; this nameless blank, this absence.

"Mama likes babies."

"Does she want any more, do you think?" Resentment shades her voice. She wonders how Catherine can be so effortlessly fecund, and she not. Four children. It just doesn't seem right or fair.

"Not since she got sick with Milène."

Coco says nothing.

After a silence: "So you don't think I'm dirty?"

"It's perfectly natural."

Then, shyly: "You think I ought to tell Mama?"

Coco smiles. "I think that's right."

Ludmilla is not quite sure how to hold herself or her dress. She shrugs. Her body seems to have grown heavy. It's as if something inside her drags.

Coco leans toward her, and awkwardly they embrace. She pats her back, then holds her by the shoulders. Ludmilla's eyes grow moist again. Placing both hands on the girl's cheeks, Coco wipes away the tears with a deft, symmetrical motion of her thumbs. "You're a good girl," Coco says. "And don't worry about the dress. We can soon get you another one of those."

Yellow-brown leaves fall plenteously. A cold October wind crimps the grass.

A Sunday, Catherine makes an effort to rise early and go to church. She takes the children with her, holding Ludmilla by the hand. Along, too, go Joseph and Marie with Suzanne. Igor has too much work to do, he says. Coco is still in bed.

A little later, Igor dresses for the second time that morning. He's in Coco's bedroom. They have tried and failed to make love. It's the first time since her late period. Igor burns with shame. "I'm sorry. I'm preoccupied at the moment."

"That's all right."

Irked by the tolerance in her tone, he protests, "I can't perform to order, you know."

"I said it's all right. It doesn't matter." But the warmth in her voice sounds ambiguous.

When she told him she wasn't pregnant, she was shocked to discover how exhilarated he was. He must think he leads a charmed life, she reflects. He'd seemed pleased with himself and said he'd prayed for it to happen. He'd even attended church. She felt annoyed at this. "It doesn't matter," she repeats.

"You always make me feel as if I have to compete."

"Compete? With whom?"

"With you." He can't finish dressing quickly enough and fumbles clumsily with the belt on his trousers.

"With me?" She starts up from her languor. "I see." For a moment an odd silence organizes itself around the bed. Then she asks, "Are you afraid of me, Igor?"

"Of course not."

"Well, I don't understand what you mean."

"Don't insult me."

"I didn't mean to." She lies back again.

Igor struggles with one of his socks. "You always want to be the one in control."

"I just try to be happy, that's all."

"And I do my best to *make* you happy."

Not wholly convinced: "I know you do." She sits up in an attempt to appear sincere. He has spoken recently of dedicating his next symphony to her. When it comes to it, though, she doubts he will. It's too reckless a gesture for him, she thinks.

He tightens his laces with a tug. "I'd better go. They'll be back any minute."

"Yes."

Fear of discovery has been overtaken by a new fear: that he doesn't measure up to Coco's other lovers. She makes him feel inadequate at times, inexpert, inept. And he still can't shake the feeling that what he's doing is wrong.

His heart lurches between the two women of his life like

a pendulum in an unvarying arc. Catherine his wife, and Coco his mistress. Two interlinking letter Cs. Blindly he hopes that through some miracle of merging the two women might become one: with Catherine's delicacy and Coco's ardor, with Catherine's gentle intelligence and Coco's native charm, with Catherine's sensitivity and Coco's taste. Alas, the gap between them seems to widen with each passing hour. And his heart, like an atom trapped, smashes against the cage of his ribs, leaving a burning sensation in the center of his chest.

He starts to leave, then turns to kiss her. A formality. She permits the gesture. But his face lingers next to hers. The moment becomes tender.

She whispers, "Why can't you just relax?"

Breathing in deeply, he smells the musk of her body. For an instant her vulnerability and his lust are renewed.

"I'm sorry," he repeats. "I find it difficult with everyone in the same house."

"They're not here now." She's getting tired of his rushing.

"I know, but they will be soon." He fastens up the button he missed earlier on his shirt.

Puzzled: "I thought you said she knows."

"Yes, but still, I don't want to rub her face in it."

"All right." She sighs, turning away from him on the bed. It's as if, she feels sometimes, she's not real to him the way Catherine is.

"We'll speak later," he says and steps toward the door. They share a half smile before he leaves the room.

He returns to his study, flinging the window open for fear

of her perfume lingering. But he finds little sense of respite here either, for immediately he's confronted by another problem: his work. He is trying to complete his symphony, while at the same time revising *The Rite*, while at the same time ranscribing scores for mechanical piano. He feels overwhelmed and admits to himself that he's not sure he can cope.

Plagued by indigestion, he sits up straight, squeezing a fist against his chest. He punches himself, urging a stubborn bit of food down to his stomach. Cleaning his teeth this morning, he noticed the water he spat out was pink. Somewhere his gums must be bleeding. He shakes his head. He remembers what Catherine told him. He's convinced that he, too, is decaying from within, slowly falling apart. The knot in his chest, and now this bleeding. The evidence is mounting up.

He surveys his sketchbooks for a minute. The ills of his personal and professional life seem kindred. What seemed brilliant on paper the other day, on reflection seems less good.

He's distressed by the lack of order his compositions enjoy. Pasting together ideas over the last few days, inserting fragments into what were fragments already, he's not convinced that any of it hangs together. He feels blocked and quite at a loss as to how to go on. The turbulence and messy ongoingness of his life here have muddied the clarity of his thinking. The complexities of his existence in Bel Respiro seem to be spilling over into his music, making his work unusually fussy and inert.

He notices the silence that surrounds him, like a vacuum

that sucks everything up. And suddenly it strikes him that the insect hum has ceased. It is as though someone has lifted a foot from the sustaining pedal of summer. The knowledge shocks him. How did he miss it? When did it stop? And why?

Again he looks at his sketchbooks. He has twenty-four wind instruments to score simultaneously: layers of sound intricately worked. But he can't yet hear them distinctly enough or see how they might converge. When he tries to imagine each in relation to the whole, they either blur into a generalized sound or seem so independent as not to synthesize at all.

"It's no good," he utters.

He keeps hoping that all the unrelated scraps will suddenly fit, like the bits in a kaleidoscope, into some meaningful whole. But so far, despite his best efforts, the pattern has eluded him.

He feels the need to strip away the blurriness of his music. He wants to win through to something pure and distilled, something clean: the thing itself. The only way to achieve real tautness, he thinks, is through the discipline of conflicting rhythms and by generating tensions from opposing melodic lines.

He looks again at *The Rite*. Sitting there, he is revisited by an intuition. Rhythm. That's it!

It hits him again with the strength of a revelation. Rhythm rather than harmony is the organizing principle. Rhythm is what connects everything together.

We all walk to a melody we hear inside our heads, he

thinks. But that rhythm beats differently for each of us. Perhaps love, then, he considers, is where an absolute synchrony establishes itself between two people.

This revelation leaves him feeling liberated but also obscurely afraid. For it makes him confront his own existence in time, makes him aware of the changes in tempo his own life has undergone. With an urgency that seems connected to his pulse, he begins testing the spacing of notes against the settings of the metronome. There exist nuances, he knows, delicate variations of measure that can't be captured exactly by notation. The fractions afforded by quavers and semiquavers are not absolute. There are spaces, margins of freedom in between that cannot be registered or set down. And it is in these spaces, he feels, that the key to something new and undiscovered lies. If only he could focus in close enough to explore these secret interstices, these in-between bits of time.

Just then, he hears the front door open. The children pour in with a sudden rush of sound. He sees Catherine through the window. She walks slowly but unaided. An aura of sanctity surrounds her as she returns from church. It always does. Piety suits her. It lends her a kind of glow.

He goes to greet his children as they enter the house. Flattening himself against the door, he allows Catherine to pass. She ignores him, placing her folded parasol between them like a shield. Palely she floats past him, like a ghost.

It's as though the two of them move in different worlds, to different clocks. They're misaligned, out of sync. Two melodic lines going off in different directions with no hint of a resolution. It's as if they don't exist for each other anymore.

Back in his study, he adjusts the speed of the metronome. On his way to lunch, its rhythm, slower than his heartbeat, ticks with a hallucinatory minuteness inside his head.

The sun is low. The trees are almost leafless. Overhead, a V of geese honks.

Joseph helps Marie hang out washing on the line. The bed linen is cumbersome and difficult to maneuver. Unfurling a sheet, a cloud of dampness is released like an odor from the folds. Joseph holds one end and Marie the other. Together they snap out the creases. They approach one another, touching corners, as if enacting a formal dance.

Joseph asks, "Has she mentioned holidays to you yet?"

With two wooden pegs in her mouth, Marie mumbles, "No. She hasn't." Positioned at evenly spaced intervals, the pegs make dents of shadow on the sheets.

"We're due a few days before the end of the year."

"You should speak to her."

"Me?"

Holding the laundry basket clumsily under one arm, she turns to her husband. "Yes. You."

"But you're the one who spends time with her. You *are* her maid . . ."

"You're better at these things." The sheets flicker whitely off to one side.

"The situation is just so damn tense. I feel I should be going around on tiptoe."

Suzanne and the other children step into the garden. This

being a Sunday, they are not at school. They form a straggly group. Theodore is bouncing a football. As they move, there is an impression of bony arms and luminous shins; a lolloping uncoordinated march, heedless of the events around them.

Walking back toward the house, Joseph says, "It's the children I feel sorry for."

"You know what Milène said the other day?"

"What?"

Marie glances around to make sure no one can hear her. "She said, 'Is Coco going to be our new mama?'"

"What did you say?"

"No, of course! And then she asked if her mama was ever going to get well."

"Oh, dear!"

"She's very sensitive. She cries all the time. You can tell that something's worrying her."

"It's very sad."

"I don't think he has any idea."

As if in answer, from Igor's study come the first promptings of the piano. Notes float across the lawn like scraps of fallen laundry. The rhythms are awkward and syncopated, with a fury fed from within.

Back inside, behind the kitchen door, Joseph says, "His music isn't exactly comforting, is it?"

"I'm sure his playing scares them."

The cry of geese above the house strikes a sharp angle with the sound of the piano.

"I'm not surprised," he says. "It scares me sometimes, too."

———

Catherine sits in the garden, a plaid blanket folded across her lap. A book rests, closed, upon her knee. She is examining a bottle of perfume given to her as a present by Mademoiselle Chanel. The children play in front of her on the lawn.

"Thank you," Catherine says, raising the bottle as she sees Coco emerging from the front of the house.

Coco approaches, taken slightly by surprise, but smiling. "I hope you like it."

"I'm sure it's enchanting."

"It's the least I can do."

"Yes." Catherine looks away at some far point beyond Coco's shoulder.

There's a silence between them filled with the noise of the children playing. Catherine sets the perfume down on her lap next to her book.

Coco shifts her weight from one leg to the other. "What are you reading?" Coco says.

"It's all right. You can stop pretending."

"Excuse me?"

She still won't look at her. "You needn't worry. I won't start a row."

Coco says nothing.

Catherine brightens like a light switched on. "I'm happy for him. He needs distracting. He gets so caught up in his work."

Milène shouts to Soulima, who is chasing her round the flower beds. "You can't catch me!"

The two women look at the children as they sweep by, and smile.

"I know what you're doing," Coco says, holding her smile.

"Don't think I like myself for it."

"I didn't plan any of this."

"Mind the flowers!" Catherine shouts at her children as they skirt the borders of the lawn.

Coco looks on in silence.

Catherine feels in this instant like the still center of a whirling circle as the children run frantically around the garden. But she experiences with it a sense of calm and even a strange kind of power which she has not felt for a long time. Now she steels herself to look Coco in the eye. "Just don't interfere with his music," she says. "It's everything to him."

A brief silence.

"And to you?"

"He sleeps with the light on. Did you know that?"

Coco says nothing.

"He's afraid of the dark."

"Why are you telling me this?"

She grows solemn. "He can't work when there's chaos."

"Are you afraid of the dark?" Coco says, straightening, still holding that smile. "Or is it the light you can't stand?"

Catherine almost laughs. "You're quite something, aren't you?"

Coco doesn't answer.

"And you know the odd thing in all this?"

"What?"

"I actually like you."

Coco nods gravely, accepting the compliment, but now any trace of a smile has vanished.

On an impulse, Soulima races Milene to get to her mother and, when they reach her, they each dangle their arms affectionately around her neck. Catherine kisses their fingers and beams at both of them. Her children.

Slowly Coco walks away.

CHAPTER TWENTY-FIVE

Ludmilla, shirtless and a little cold, bends low over the basin as Coco washes her hair. Three-quarters warm and one-quarter cold, she feels the mix of temperatures spill in ribbons over her scalp.

Afterward her cheeks shine pinkly and her eyelids glisten as she peeps from beneath a towel. Coco administers one last playful rub of the head before drawing a tortoiseshell comb through her hair. "There," she says. "All done." She passes the girl a bar of chocolate. "Don't tell your mother I gave you this."

"Why?" Ludmilla asks, removing the wrapper from the bar.

"She might think chocolate is bad for you."

"Is it?"

"Only if you eat too much of it."

"Is this too much?"

"No."

Content with this information, Ludmilla takes another bite. She chews strenuously, the whole of her young jaw engaged. Chocolate adheres to the corners of her mouth.

"Be careful to clean your face afterward."

Before Coco can add anything, Ludmilla asks, "Do you like Mama?"

"Of course I do. Though I don't know her very well."

"Why is she always sick?"

"I don't know."

There is a pause while Ludmilla contemplates this. She snaps off another swatch of chocolate. With her mouth still full, she asks, "Do you like Papa?"

"Yes."

"You prefer Papa to Mama?"

The simplicity of Ludmilla's French makes her seem more childish than she really is. Coco detects a canniness beneath the naïve questions, however. Wary of delivering too frank an answer, she says, "I like them both."

"But you spend more time with Papa."

"That's because he's up and about when I am."

"Does Papa prefer you or Mama?"

"He prefers your mama, silly." This is terrible, she thinks.

"And you prefer me to the others?"

"I suppose I do. But it's wrong to have favorites." She holds the girl by the shoulders. "You mustn't tell," she continues in a whisper, fixing her gaze. "It can be our secret."

Ludmilla takes a last bite of chocolate, scrunching the silver paper into a ball. "Finished!"

"Good. Now go and wash your face."

Ludmilla runs from the room. Her straight wet hair accentuates her hipless figure. Coco reaches for a cigarette, her mouth compressing into a circle as she lights it. She feels the tension of the girl's questioning drain away. Her eyes tip into glassiness as she inhales.

Noticing strands of hair clinging to the fabric of her dress, she picks them off and deposits them in an ashtray. Afterward she jabs her cigarette out on them. She watches the hairs flare briefly and blacken to a crisp.

On an impulse, she telephones Adrienne. The shop sounds busy in the background. She realizes she misses that. She hates being away—always has done. Suddenly she yearns to return to rue Cambon, to throw herself back into her work. She doesn't possess Igor's self-discipline. He can work alone and regulate his days. She needs to have people around her. Though she's been going in three times a week and putting in long hours at home, it's not enough, she thinks. She'll be there, she decides. Tomorrow.

Looking in the mirror above the telephone, she sees a pallid spot on her cheek, a blanched oval where the skin has lost its pigmentation. And her fingernails, she notices, are tawny from so many cigarettes. She's been smoking too much here.

It's worry, she concludes. And why? Because she has time to worry: about what she's doing and where she's going and who she wants to be with. For the first time in weeks, she thinks of Boy. How *could* he have wed someone else? He loved *her*. It didn't make sense. It was wrong. What grotesque snobbery was it that had prevented him from marrying her? Just because she'd had other men and wasn't highborn? She feels angry suddenly, as if she wants to spit.

She recalls with pain the days immediately following his death. Allowed to sort through his personal effects to retrieve anything that belonged to her, she came across some letters. Going through them, she registered with dismay one mutual friend's advice: "You don't marry someone like Coco . . ."

She couldn't believe anyone would have written that. She couldn't believe, moreover, that Boy would have taken it to heart. Yet in some deep recess of her mind, some obscure corner of her being, she knew this to be exactly what he had thought. She lacked the necessary pedigree. People of good breeding knew better than to marry beneath them. "You don't marry someone like Coco . . ." The phrase stamped a white-hot iron into her soul.

Abruptly, from down the hall, she hears the piano thunder in Igor's study. It shocks her into consciousness. The skin on her hands feels tight. The smell of burned hair touches her nostrils. She begins shaking her head.

She knows there is little prospect of her relationship with Igor developing much further. He is frantic enough as it is at the prospect of anyone discovering their affair. Is he secretly ashamed of her? Catherine, she knows, regards her with the disdain reserved for the ineligible, for those whose blood has no hint of blue. She can hear the superiority inform each of her remarks. The way she insists on speaking Russian with Igor whenever Coco is around. Perhaps that's why she's able to endure the humiliation of their affair. Maybe she knows, ultimately, that her position as his wife will always be secure. For her then, Coco feels, she poses no enduring threat.

This realization is sharpened by a profound sense of abandonment, the roots of which lie, she recognizes, in her mother's early death, her father's absence from the family home, and her subsequent removal to an orphanage. She has a deep need of love and a frank need for physical passion. But these needs, she knows, are shot through with a wish, equally deep, never to get hurt and never again to be dependent upon anyone else for anything. She can cope alone if necessary. Her whole life so far has steeled her to accept loss. She's strong; she knows that. And talented, she reminds herself, even though Igor sometimes tries to put her down.

Entranced by the burning of Ludmilla's hair, she goes on idly to light the loose end of a ball of wool as though it is a fuse. She watches the spark take hold and run smolderingly up the thread. But it fails to travel very far. After frazzling the wool for about a foot, the tiny flame gives up the ghost. Still, something catches inside her. It's as if she internalizes the fire. Taking a pair of scissors, she snips the burned end off.

Coco, her voice thinning with the pressure of utterance, looks at the italicized print on the card. "It seems you're invited, but I am not."

A cigarette rests between Igor's forked fingers. His legs are foppishly crossed. There is to be a party held at the Opéra. Everyone who is anyone in the arts world will be there, including Satie, Ravel, Picasso, and Cocteau.

"I'm sure you wouldn't enjoy it," he allows. "It'll be very tedious. Just a lot of backslapping artists talking shop."

Her voice deepens noticeably. "No, it wouldn't really be my style, would it? A bit too intellectual for me. A bit too sophisticated. I wouldn't want to show you up, now, would I?"

"What are you talking about?"

"They don't invite tradespeople. I know that. You don't have to patronize me."

Bewildered: "What are you saying?"

"I know when I'm being snubbed."

The ferociousness of her tone provokes him. "Don't be absurd. You're imagining a slight where none exists."

"You'd obviously prefer it if I didn't come."

"That's not true."

"You're still not sure about being seen with me, are you?" Framed against the window, the frizzed edge of her hair forms a kind of halo.

"That's preposterous. I'd love you to come. I'll be bored silly without you."

"It's all right for you to fuck me in private, but you don't want to be within ten yards of me outside the house."

Igor is shocked by her language and embarrassed by the loudness of her tone. She doesn't seem to realize that there are servants around and that Catherine is just upstairs. Her features, which he has seen idiotized by desire, close over. Her eyes and mouth seem holes in a flat mask.

"I repeat," he says with emphatic calmness, "I think you'd find it tedious."

She answers, "All right. As it will be so tedious, I don't suppose *you'll* want to go either." Abruptly, to his astonishment, she starts to rip the invitation in half.

"What are you doing?" he asks, startled.

The card makes a thick tearing sound. Her lips purse with the effort. "There! You see?"

"I can't believe you just did that."

"No slight intended, and none received." Her voice rises with the assumption of hauteur. In profile, her chin lifts as if it has been hit.

"It will be extremely rude of me not to attend." The skin tightens across his face. His scalp moves backward visibly.

With severe politeness, Coco says, "Then you'd better telephone and explain. Tell them your wife is ill or something, that you have to look after her. That should do the trick."

She feels a tingling in her hands. Glancing down, she's surprised to find blood on the skin around one of her nails. A paper cut. There's a russet smudge on the torn card, too. The appearance of blood seems to spice her temper even more.

"It's fine to invite me to parties as a patron where there's a good chance of a handout. But it's not all right for me to be with you when you're consorting with friends. That's it, isn't it?"

His expression grows stern. "I do *not* seek handouts."

"Oh, really?"

He warms to a theme. "No. Though, of course, it's not unknown for people to support artists in order to further their own social ambitions."

"You ungrateful bastard!"

She recalls her donation for the revival of *The Rite*. She knows she gave anonymously, but he might have guessed, she thinks. She's certain Diaghilev has told him, yet he hasn't so much as mentioned it to her.

More heated: "In fact, the way people sponsor the arts these days is often quite insincere."

Her words come faster now, with venom in them. "You can never quite get over the fact that I'm a woman, can you? A woman who is intelligent and successful, and an artist in ways that you'll never understand."

Incredulous. "An artist?"

"Yes, an artist, who works every bit as hard, if not harder, than you do."

"If you spent more time making and less time selling, then I might agree with you."

"That's called reality, Igor—something you seem immune to in your own little world."

He discovers a raw burst of energy. "You're not an artist, Coco."

"Oh, no?"

Contemptuously: "You're a shopkeeper!"

"I don't have to put up with this." She moves toward the door. "Remember where you're living, dear," she hurls at him. "One of these days, you'll see." Then, turning smartly on her heels, she leaves the room.

He feels the draft from the door as it slams behind her. With his legs still crossed, though more stiffly posed, Igor's head tips sideways in thought. His heart is galloping. He hates it when they argue. But she shouldn't have torn up the invitation like that. He leans to pick up the fragments from the floor.

She's too easily seduced by surfaces, he thinks. She's too much moved by the glisten of things. He finds it hard to take clothes design seriously. He can't deny that her outfits are ravishing, but it has more to do with vanity, he considers, than any claim to art. There's something too palpable about its manufacture. He can't help taking it for granted somehow. With the perfume, he admits, there's a mystery, an elusiveness, an unseen quality he enjoys. It appeals to the senses in the same way music does; and he's prepared to concede it needs artistry, genius even, to produce it. The trouble is, she's become so obsessed with the business side of it, he's lost interest. She seems to speak of little else.

Looking down, he adjusts the angle of his ankle minutely to align with the shadows in the room. He closes one eye to achieve an exact fit. Then outdoors he hears a scream. He jumps up and looks out the window. Vassily is scrapping with one of the Alsatians. Fierce snarls and barks accompany a series of tussles that seem to take place in a furious blur.

He rushes into the garden and manages to separate them before any real damage is done. But, of course, the cat has come off worse. The poor thing has several deep cuts about the eyes. And where a patch of fur is missing around his neck, there's a raw wound of matted blood.

Igor winces. It had to happen sooner or later, he reflects.

Pathetically the cat dabs at his injuries with his paws. Igor strokes him and inspects the vivid welts already swelling on his skin. Vassily's claws are still extended as Igor picks him up. Cradling him in his arms like a newborn baby, he carries the cat inside.

CHAPTER TWENTY-SIX

Petite but fierce, Coco strides into 31 rue Cambon. Her shop. She's wearing a trim dark jacket, an open-necked white blouse, and a flared, softly pleated beige skirt whose hem stops midcalf. She half acknowledges the greetings from the shopgirls but does not stop to talk. Continuing on through the salon, she mounts the stairs to her suite of private rooms. The carpets are beige, the chandeliers smoked crystal. Carvings of lions rest on the tables. Lilies in vases open like stars.

Adrienne is kneeling over a piece of material with a fat piece of tailor's chalk in her hand. She makes quick unerring lines across the cloth. Hearing footsteps on the stairs, she looks up. "Coco?"

"Adrienne."

Adrienne rises, wiping her hands clean of the chalk. The two embrace. Then, disengaging, Coco rummages in her bag. She takes out a small box with a brushed velvet exterior. She undoes the clasp and lays bare the contents. There is a moment of awed silence as though the relics of a saint are being unveiled.

"The new samples—they've arrived."

"At last!"

"Here. Try some."

Coco removes the stopper from one of the flacons. The glass feels tepid in her hand. Upending the bottle for a second, she allows a quantity to seep through and wet her fingertip. She applies a smidgen to Adrienne's wrist. Lifting it to her nose, Adrienne inhales.

"Well?"

"It's . . . good," she says. Adrienne smells more carefully. There is caution in her voice. "I'm not sure I can place the fragrance, though."

"I'm not surprised. There are over eighty ingredients in that bottle."

Adrienne raises an eyebrow. "It's very delicate," she says.

"But the idea is, it lasts longer."

"And you think it'll sell?"

"I'm convinced it will. The samples that Beaux sent out got a very positive response."

Coco stoppers the flacon. She replaces it in the valise and snaps it shut. "I propose we spray it in the changing rooms. Then, when clients ask what it is and whether they can buy it, we say we've just had a small amount made up as gifts."

"The girls in the shop can wear it, too."

"No. It must remain exclusive."

"But what if the clients *don't* ask?"

"We'll tell the old ladies they need it if they still want to be kissed."

"And the younger ones?"

"I'll tell them it's all they need to wear in bed."

Adrienne laughs.

"We could have bottles displayed across the salon." Coco

leans forward conspiratorially in her seat. Her hands link together around her knees. Her toes just touch the floor. "The point is to flatter them. We say that if, in their opinion, the perfume will sell, then we might consider manufacturing it."

"So you include them in the process."

"We make them think we do."

"You're such a fox, Coco."

"It's a matter of getting people to know and talk about it, and then to buy the damn thing." She readjusts her skirt and sits back.

"So when do we begin?"

"Here I am, and here's the perfume. Why don't we start right away?"

"I could get some of the girls to start spraying now . . ."

Coco looks suddenly tired.

Adrienne notices. "I'm sorry, I haven't asked how everything is."

"Everything's fine," Coco says, too quickly. Yesterday Joseph approached her, asking about the possibility—if it wasn't too inconvenient or impertinent, et cetera—of a holiday. The poor man is afraid of her, she thinks. She does vaguely recall promising them a few days off. It's just so inconvenient, though.

"And how is Igor?"

In response, she seems poised and cool. "Very well, thank you." He has not gone with her to Paris for the last few afternoons.

In a low voice: "Are you in love, Coco?" Adrienne fixes

her with a look that will admit nothing other than a reply of absolute candor.

Coco returns the look. She expects to feel uncomfortable but doesn't, and finds herself saying to her own surprised ears, "My work comes first. Always. Men come second." They regard one another challengingly for a few moments.

"Good," says Adrienne.

"Good," Coco says.

"Shall we spray?"

"Let's spray."

The two of them walk abreast down the stairs with a slightly intimidating rhythm, Coco clutching her bag as though it is a pack of high explosives.

Returning unexpectedly early from the shop next afternoon, Coco rushes to Igor's study. She has to talk to him. She wants to make up. She finds she misses him after all. And it was unforgivable of her to tear up the invitation. She knows that now, and she wants to say sorry. But no sound comes from the piano, and Igor is not there. She moves upstairs and hears low voices coming from the Stravinskys' bedroom. Inching toward the door, which is fractionally ajar, she listens to the conversation going on inside.

There is a tone of intimacy between Catherine and Igor. Coco dares to move closer. Through the thin strip of light between the door and the wall, she glimpses them together. Catherine is in bed. Fully clothed, Igor lies next to her propped upon one elbow. He has pressed her head like a child's to his breast and is lifting her hair in tender caresses. He speaks to her in reassuring tones. Coco strains to hear. She doesn't need to understand Russian to catch the atmosphere that hangs between them.

Catherine's cheeks shine wetly. Her eyeballs seem to tremble beneath closed lids. Her complexion is hectic. Igor kisses her tears.

Coco stands unseen, jaw firmly set, with one hand on the doorjamb and the other sunk into her pocket. She feels the skin on her face stretch tight and experiences a collapsing sensation inside her chest. Flinching, she turns away. Vertigo afflicts her as she stands at the top of the stairs. They seem steeper suddenly by several degrees. She needs to grip the banister hard for support.

She wonders why she bothered hurrying back from the shop at all. Adrienne had wanted her to stay. A wave of blankness breaks inside her, and she realizes she hasn't eaten for hours. All the radiance of expectation drains from her face. She feels utterly betrayed.

Although she has seen nothing revelatory, she senses something tip like a balance inside her head. There are things between Igor and his wife she will never be privileged to know or understand, things that can never be completely canceled out. She realizes that now.

Igor will never leave Catherine. That much is certain. That is an act of riddance to which he will never submit. And yet, Coco thinks, it is craven of him to stay with her. It is becoming too much. For all the loving tenderness he has afforded her over the last few months, the one thing he will absolutely not do is sacrifice his wife. There's a whole history of care and affection from which Coco feels excluded. And this latest glimpse of intimacy serves to estrange her still further. Their marriage will always be there: gnawing, irrevocable; a hard contractual fact.

It all seems so wildly obvious now. And the hurt is worse because she feels she's connived in her own blindness. Was she insane? Did she not see? Could she ever have imagined he would give her up? And is that what she really wanted, anyway? It is the most banal of realizations, yet it does not prevent her experiencing a swelling sense of dread.

Seeing them together, Igor and Catherine, man and wife, has started a pang of jealousy within her. A terrible sense of illegitimacy assails her again. For an instant, she feels physically sick. Back in her study, with one violent movement, Coco sweeps off the table all the fabrics that lie in neat piles. In a fury, she picks up the racquet that Igor used that day in August with the Serts. It has lain there in her study ever since. She pulls at the broken string until its whole length unravels from the head. Scrunching up the catgut, she throws it across the room. Then she bangs the frame so strenuously on the desk that the wood begins to splinter. Hearing it crack, she continues smashing it down until the head snaps off completely.

The truth is tortured into her. He might dally with her, but at the end of the day he will always crawl back to Catherine.

"Bastard!" she curses, sinking into her seat. Impotently she hits the dinted surface of the desk and lays her head down, defeated. She sobs fiercely. A feeling of emptiness possesses her. After a time, she manages to calm down. Supporting her face with both hands, she plants her elbows on the desk. Silence surrounds her, pressing through the darkening afternoon.

Biting her lip, she remembers what she said to Adrienne about her work coming first. Something within her tightens. She begins thinking hard.

CHAPTER TWENTY-SEVEN

Six days after Coco telephoned inviting him to stay, Grand Duke Dmitri arrives with little ceremony but several trunkloads of luggage. He also brings with him his majordomo, Piotr: a hairy, bearlike man, utterly servile and grimly inarticulate.

Coco first met Dmitri in Biarritz last spring, where they established an immediate rapport. Dashing and handsome, with impeccable credentials, he is the grandson of Alexander II, cousin to Czar Nicholas II, and one of the assassins of Rasputin. She passes off his arrival as a gesture toward Igor. He can speak Russian to his countryman and enjoy some male company at last. But Igor senses that Coco has other, more shadowy and as yet undefined motives. And he's a little perplexed as to why Dmitri, and why now.

Immediately he feels jealous and resentful. Swashbuckling, and with a confirmed reputation as a lady's man, Dmitri brings into the house a sense of irrepressible energy and force. This dispirits Igor, and he can barely conceal the fact. He manages to be polite but cannot avoid a certain curtness in addressing him. It is one thing to owe allegiance to a czar whose portrait you fix on the wall. It is another to have some jumped-up courtier come in, look up at the print, and say, "Ah, Cousin Nicholas. A good likeness."

Dmitri radiates an uncommon aristocratic vitality. Tall, he towers comically over Igor. And his acid green eyes seem, with each hurled look, intent on dissolving Igor's features.

Eleven years her junior, at first Coco thinks him immature. But this, she sees, is just in contrast to Igor, who always seems so solemn. She begins to appreciate his bluff good spirits and his pranksterish love of fun. Such a change from Igor's self-regarding earnestness. It's funny seeing them together, she thinks. They stand off like prizefighters. Igor bristles every time he comes near.

She realizes with a thrill that he's becoming possessive. The two men rarely speak, though they greet each other with near military courtesy. When they do converse, it is in rapid bursts of Russian. Usually they end up disagreeing. Privately Igor calls Dmitri a dolt. Dmitri speaks of Igor's social constipation, relishing the potential for mischief in imposing himself upon the house. Coco sits in the middle and watches as each heatedly debates, then shrugs and translates—or willfully mistranslates—what the other has to say.

Unlike Igor, Dmitri was in St. Petersburg when the Revolution broke out. And, acting quickly, he managed to rescue some of his wealth before the Bolsheviks took over. But his finances are not so robust as to allow him to resist the offer of free accommodation. Especially when his hostess is the charming Mademoiselle Chanel. Shrewdly he has come armed with a present: a set of Romanov pearls. There is even talk, to Coco's unashamed delight, of him securing for her a Fabergé egg.

Igor looks on with bitterness. He could never afford to give such gifts. Meanwhile, it occurs to him, he still hasn't finished his symphony.

Increasingly irritated at having to tiptoe around the rooms of her own house, Coco feels the novelty and excitement of her relationship with Igor quickly diminish to indifference on her part. Her frustration modulates to nonchalance in his company.

She resolves to spend more time at the shop. Determined to break free, she stops seeing Igor completely in the afternoons. After a week in which they fail to meet alone even once, Igor seeks an explanation.

It would be inappropriate, Coco says, now that they have a guest, to sneak off together. Besides, it would be that much riskier with Dmitri around. They must take care not to be exposed, especially given their efforts in previous weeks to keep the affair hidden. They don't want people to start gossiping now, do they? Least of all Dmitri, who would quickly spread news of Igor's peccadilloes among his network of expatriate friends. No, a cooling-off period is necessary, she insists.

Igor assents, but smarts unhappily at his displacement from the center of Coco's life. He sees the sense in her argument but is less certain of her sincerity. If she feels strongly enough about him, he thinks, then why is she jeopardizing the success of their relationship by inviting Dmitri in the first place? He tries not to appear too upset by the new arrangements, but he detects a new languor in her behavior. At times her attitude toward him borders on a coolness he finds shocking.

Then one morning, Coco wakes up to find that she no longer loves him. There is no moping, no anguished reappraisal or tortured self-doubt. Enough is enough. She was seduced by Igor's talent and his power. She liked his seriousness. He was interesting to be with. But now when she looks at him as a man, rather than as a musician, she finds she's not attracted to him anymore. She has time to consider that this will delight Catherine. Maybe this is the cure she's been waiting for. She wouldn't be surprised if, anyway, the real ailment lay inside her head.

New routines establish themselves within Bel Respiro. In the mornings, while Igor is at work, Coco and Dmitri go riding together. Igor does not ride and, anyway, to forsake a morning's work would cost him more guilt than it was worth. Dmitri, by contrast, is a keen and accomplished horseman and constitutionally averse to hard work. He rides invigoratingly quickly. Even Coco, a practiced equestrienne herself, has trouble keeping up with him.

Igor sees them each morning in the broad ramp of sunshine outside his window. Piotr brings the horses from a nearby stable. He harnesses the mares while Coco and Dmitri flirt in the garden. Igor watches as, gallantly, Dmitri helps her up onto the saddle. For a moment she lords it over him.

Then they are off at a smart pace. Plumes of dust trail behind them as they disappear down the lane. The clatter of hooves remains in Igor's ears long after they have gone.

Since coming to Garches, Coco has not ridden once. It's absurd, she thinks. And she used to ride so much. The muscles of her horse ripple tensely beneath her. She sees the broad blaze of white that travels the length of the animal's head. Immediately she feels less jaded. Her skin feels taut, as though renewed.

Heedlessly the two of them race through the woods and through the undergrowth that erupted unchecked during the months of the summer. Now a November sun cuts through the leafless trees. The whole wood is visible for the first time since she moved here. And everything in her life seems suddenly transparent, too. There's a new crispness to her vision. A vista within her is opened wide.

Dmitri spurs his horse until it is hurt into a reckless gallop. Coco gives her mare a deft flick and works hard to keep up. Her legs tighten as she leans forward, and the wind quickens against her face. Around her, the smell of wet soil is cut with the pungency of horse. Her face is ruddy, and her breath bursts in long shapeless clouds from her mouth. She feels her back start to trickle with sweat. Her legs tremble with the effort. And after a few minutes of this hard gallop, her lungs begin to burn. When she does finally catch up with him, and she feels her breathing slow, it is as if the world—still galloping around her—continues to pour past.

She feels giddy then as they saunter through the burned-out remains of a bluebell wood. Poplars surround them on all sides. She remembers from the summer its smoky bluish gloom. Within lies a pond. The horses snort. Steam eddies visibly from their skins. All around, and despite the season, there explodes a jubilant riot of chartreuse-green ferns. The light is blue-green and reflective. Dmitri's eyes vibrate with the same color. Everything seems filled with quietness and mystery. Coco feels closed in and secure.

She experiences an inner heat generated by the exertion of the ride. A faint shiver passes through her. And it is here in this secluded spot, as the light ebbs from the woods and the air around them cools, that something happens. She didn't mean it to happen. It takes her by surprise. But with her eyes half closed and her head to one side, she slides her arms around Dmitri's neck and surrenders to his kisses.

Restless, Igor plays solitaire. His fingers are quick with decision. Ripping a waxed card from the top of the deck, he snaps it down. The sound accents the hollowness he feels inside.

Outdoors, shadows drag across the lawn. Thin slices of cloud, like the cards seen edgeways, linger overhead. Coco and Dmitri have not yet returned. Already late in the afternoon, they have been gone for several hours now. Igor's leg shakes in agitation, making the table vibrate.

Eventually he hears the clatter of hooves grow louder as they approach the drive. Quickly he switches off the lights in the room. Wanting the controlling power of observation all to himself, he stands at an angle to the window, ensuring he remains out of sight.

The horses slow and two figures dismount. He sees Coco and Dmitri, their heads bent familiarly in conversation. As Piotr leads the horses off, they walk toward the house.

Igor stiffens. His fear enlarges in the dark. Hearing her thrilling laugh fill the hallway, he recollects himself. He resumes his game of solitaire as though he'd never broken off. Coco calls him from the hallway. He answers as casually as he is able. She follows his voice into the living room.

"Why are you sitting here in the dark?" Her tone is faintly mocking.

Affecting absentmindedness: "I can see."

In mild admonishment, she switches on the lights. He turns to see her silhouette filled. Glowing with vigor from the ride, she looks marvelous in her tight-fitting gear. Her eyes are full of warm tones and her cheeks are touched with color. Still carrying the crop like a baton, she pushes back her hair.

Hurt once more into the knowledge of her loveliness, he asks, "How was your ride?"

"Good, thank you." A small silence follows. "And you? How was your card game?"

"Good," he says, slapping down another card, his attempt at nonchalance strained.

"I'm glad," she says and promptly leaves, closing the door behind her.

Her sudden removal stuns him. He holds the next card frozen between his fingers. Then he flips it nervously around and around. He hears Dmitri say something funny, followed by Coco's whinnying laugh. This acts as a trigger. He smites the cards from the table, scattering them everywhere. Fists clenched, he rises abruptly from his chair. He paces around the room for several seconds, cursing in Russian under his breath. If the cat were there, he'd kick him. But he realizes after all how powerless he is in this situation. He can't very well accuse *her* of being unfaithful. Then, with mad fastidiousness, he gathers up the cards, packing them tightly into their box.

He goes to the outhouse where the birds still chatter away merrily in their cages. An outside light casts a glow around the shed. Entering, he is startled. For there, after weeks of training, he hears one of the larger parrots for the first time speak her name. He's been trying to get them to repeat it for so long, he'd almost given up. And one of them chooses to do it now. There it is again, clear and distinct, strident even. The sound of her name starts to echo, amplifying to a chant inside his head. He can't believe it. It's so awful, he almost laughs. He stares at the bird, which inclines its head and stares back at him self-importantly. The gods are cruel, he concludes.

One by one, he drapes the black cloths that Coco cut for him over the bars like shrouds. There's a sense of finality in the act, a kind of closure. The blackness stretches to cover the evening.

Slowly the birds grow silent in the dark.

The children adore Dmitri. Full of native energy and ideas for new games, he plays with them most afternoons. Theodore and Soulima are bewitched by his stories of bravery and adventure. They are transfixed in particular by his account of killing Rasputin. Rasputin, whom they have heard so much about.

"How did you do it?"

They ask him to tell the tale over and over. He obliges willingly: "And then Yusupov shot him again—pow!—and again—pow!—and still he wouldn't fall!" With each retelling, Rasputin's ability to recover from the bullets becomes more and more miraculous.

The children are dazzled, too, by Dmitri's collection of medals. Ludmilla fingers the low relief of the czar on one side of a beribboned decoration.

"He awarded that to me personally . . ."

"What had you done?" Theo asks, a little awed.

"Oh, nothing really. I led a battalion of men against a German gun battery. We captured the position."

"Were many killed?" Soulima asks.

"Yes, quite a few."

After a pause in which the boys take this in, Dmitri becomes more animated. "Here, let me show you. If this spoon is the gun battery, and these knives represent the advancing battalion . . ."

Igor leaves the room before the rest of the cutlery is engaged. All *he* knows about the war is that the shells whistled over the trenches in E flat.

He is repelled by this ebullient new fellow, who seems to enchant everyone around him with his exaggerated gallantries and military grace. To Igor, he seems an oaf, a blustering buffoon. There were no books in his luggage, Igor noticed. Culturally impoverished, he has little interest in music or the arts. The man is intellectually empty, he decides. Yet something in his manner, he concedes, makes him compelling. At first he can't fathom what it is. Then he realizes. It is a kind of refined cruelty. Like a leopard he might kill you, but he would do it with great style.

Coco seems fatally taken by him. And Igor is shocked by

the coltishness with which she acts in his company. Quickly he realizes he cannot compete with Dmitri's vigor. Rather, he must trust Coco's faithfulness and taste. He hopes nothing is going on between them, but the suspicion gnaws at his heart. Desolate at the thought of losing her, he yet senses her slipping away.

Later, at dinner, Igor feels humiliated. Suddenly vulnerable and insecure, he recognizes the selfsame intimacy—the brimming illicit smile, the hands brushing secretly, legs sliding one against the other under the dinner table—that he enjoyed during the months of the summer. His anguish deepens into despair. He only controls his emotion thanks to an immense effort of will.

Look at her! The way she pushes her hair up showily in front of Dmitri. The way she seeks his eye first for reassurance or to share a joke. That giddy coquettish habit she has of tipping her head to one side when she speaks to him. This is awful, he thinks. And yet there is more. The helplessly tender glances. The melting way she looks at him, chin resting upon her hand. Her equine snort at everything he says. Igor blanches. His heart shrinks. Her love for Dmitri announces itself from every angle. A chill enters his kidneys. It is more than he can bear.

Over the table, Dmitri waves his hands wildly in illustration of another heroic deed. Clumsily he knocks over a wineglass. The wine spills irremovably onto Igor's white trousers, leaving a vivid rubicund stain around the groin.

Igor jumps back as if he has been burned. He dabs haplessly at himself with a napkin. Dmitri apologizes, but something subtly scornful in his manner makes Igor irritated and suspicious.

He looks down at the darkening stain, as at a wound. He feels the dampness against his skin and a growing sensation of cold. And in the wildness of his imaginings he thinks he sees the emblem of his helplessness, the badge of his emasculation, reflected in this shapeless blot.

CHAPTER TWENTY-EIGHT

With Dmitri, Coco can be heedless and tender, demonstrative and bold. Moreover, she does not have to care who sees or hears her.

Catherine, meanwhile, experiences a fresh feeling of disgust for her husband. Igor is fine when Coco is away at the shop. But as soon as she returns he begins slavering like a lapdog. Catherine cannot resist a wry smile at the way things seem to be turning out. A feeling of sweet vengeance seeps deliciously into her veins. She has more color in her cheeks. She feels more self-possessed. A measure of strength returns to her, and she finds she has more time for the children, who respond with overdue embraces. She is even able to undertake a few short walks.

Igor begins to act more warmly toward her. He becomes openly affectionate. But perversely she grows cooler toward him. She can see what he is doing: hedging his bets, looking for succor, for someone to lick his wounds. Well, he can look elsewhere, Catherine thinks. To his annoyance, she makes it plain that she quite likes Dmitri. He's a breath of fresh air around the house. He's courteous and charming, she finds, and she enjoys speaking Russian to him. She discovers in him an unlikely ally. Besides, he's wonderful with the children. And he makes her laugh. The laughter sounds odd in her own ears. It's so long since she's heard it. Perhaps it gives her the confidence for what she wants to do next.

Some days later in a willful act of strength and resolution, Catherine begins packing her things and announces she is leaving Garches. She is going to Biarritz with the children: on the strength, ostensibly, of its climate and superior schools. She calculates she has enough money saved to be able to rent a small place there. She no longer requires the charity of Mademoiselle Chanel. In fact, it has reached the point where she'd live in a hovel if it meant getting away from her.

Igor is outraged. "You can't do this to me!" he shouts, as she folds her clothes into her suitcase.

"I'm not doing it to you. I'm doing it for me and for the children." Her voice, eroded by so much crying, has lowered a semitone, grown a grain or two huskier in recent weeks.

"But I want you to stay."

"You do? Why?"

"Because . . ." He falters. ". . . you belong with me, here. And I need you."

"And I needed you!" The use of the past tense stings him.

His whole frame shakes with fury. But, even in his anger, he is sensitive to the fact that others in the house may hear him. He proceeds in a fierce whisper: "You're my wife!"

Shrill, she doesn't care who hears her: "You should have thought of that before."

A few weeks earlier, she had been desperate for him to come to her. She had begged for his affection, pleaded for his emotional support. He had not responded. He had failed her then. Why should she be loyal to him now?

"The fact is, we're still married. Nothing alters that. That's sacred."

"You haven't acted as though you believe that!"

He fights a rising panic. "But what will you do?"

"I'll cope."

"Are you sure?"

"No. But maybe it's what I need." She flattens a dress into the case.

It's come as a relief almost, knowing she can expect nothing from him. She no longer aches for caresses that will not come. Strange to say, being dead to him has given her a kind of freedom.

"Have you thought it through?"

"Long and hard. I can't stand it any longer."

A repressed hysterical note hovers in his voice. "Stand what?"

"Don't insult me, Igor."

"But it's nearly over with Coco . . ."

"Nearly?" She stops her packing for a moment. "What do you want? Another week, another month, a year?"

"But it is. We're not right for each other." He hears himself talking, but is oddly powerless to stop the words issuing from his mouth. What surprises him most is that he doesn't agree with anything he says.

"And what makes you think we are?"

"Haven't we proved it over the years?"

Resuming her folding: "I think the last few months have proved otherwise."

"Why, though?"

It's as if a mist has risen between them. "Because if it's not Coco, then it will be somebody else." She goes on, "And it just doesn't seem worth it anymore."

"That's unfair."

"Is it?"

"You're acting out of pride."

"And about time, too!"

Igor feels a sudden admiration for his wife, for her resourcefulness and inner strength. From the beginning, he had been attracted by what was placid in her. Now he recognizes this stronger side to her character. It is as if he sees her anew. He makes to hug her. An act of reconciliation. But it's too late. She tolerates the gesture coldly, her face withdrawing from his. She continues pressing clothes into the open suitcase.

"And the children?" he goes on, more quietly this time.

"Yes?"

"Have you considered their welfare in all of this?"

"Absolutely. Why do you think I'm doing it?"

"But they're just getting used to their school. They won't want to start all over again."

"I've thought of that," she responds hotly.

"Don't you think it's worth us staying together for their sakes?"

Catherine ceases packing again and looks him straight in the eye. "You've got a nerve!" With a conviction that almost frightens him, she explodes, "When have you ever given them a thought in the last few months?"

Defiant: "But they're sensitive to such things. This will upset them."

"They'll be even more upset if they stay much longer, given the musical beds that goes on around here. It's precisely for that reason I'm taking them away." Her voice rises like the pitch of indignation in her cheeks. He makes to speak, but she doesn't allow him a chance to answer. "Don't you realize, Igor, they know? They might not say it, but deep inside they know what's been going on. They know that you don't love me. Only you could be so blind."

"But I do love you."

"You'll have to do better than that!"

Catherine has managed to come through her crisis. She has learned to cope in her own way and learned to live without his love. Here he is, coming to her again, and she feels sickened. It is intolerable. His love is cheapened, bankrupt; his affection pathetic. She pushes him away. The simple fact is: she doesn't want him in the same way anymore.

"What about *us*?"

"Who do you mean by *us*?"

The question stuns him.

"Don't worry." She can't resist belittling him. "I won't tell your mother, if that's what you're worried about."

"For God's sake!"

"I'm not changing my mind, Igor. I'm leaving in the morning." She closes the suitcase with a click of the buckles. The act possesses a solemn weight. "If you want to see us, you know where we are."

He stands still, frozen into immobility. For an instant he feels like hurling her suitcase out of the door. He looks around for something to smash. His fists clench in suppressing the instinct.

Catherine moves with renewed purpose, wrapping up the ornaments that have constituted for both of them a family home. The room is quickly stripped of its domesticity. Lastly she packs away the objects from her bedside table: a photograph of her children, an icon, and a seashell with its single nacreous horn.

Igor retreats to the comfort of his study. He is shocked and upset, as well as embarrassed. Yet there is a sense, he knows, in which he's gone through the motions. His initial fury modulates into a conviction that this might not be such a bad thing after all. While it is a blow to his pride, Catherine's removal along with the children might help transform his relationship with Coco. It will leave him free to fight for her. It will give him a respite from the constricting guilt he feels when his wife is there. And then his mood changes again, from hope to fear. Fear that his betrayal of Catherine will be met with another, this time visited upon himself. Fear that nothing will resolve itself. Fear that he will become estranged from both Coco *and* his wife. Fear that the energy and inspiration he reserves for his work will be dissipated in emotional turmoil. Fear, simply, that he will end up with nothing.

In the hours that follow, the sound of the piano wanders across his study like a crack in the ice of a pond.

That night, Igor sits down with Catherine and tells the children they are quitting Bel Respiro. They are to leave for Biarritz with their mother the next morning. Because of the better climate, they are told. And because the schools are more suitable to their needs. And because the villa in Garches is becoming too full, now that Dmitri is here. Their father, it is explained, is staying on to finish his work.

The children are stunned. They greet the news with a morose silence. Only Theodore seems pleased to be leaving. But Igor and Catherine's hand-wringing excuses communicate their nervousness to the children. Oddly none of them asks any questions. Probably because something tells them they do not wish to know the answers. Soulima and Ludmilla both look at the floor, bewildered by the prospect of yet another move.

Later, once they are all in bed, Igor visits his children's rooms. In sleep, their lips are parted, where bubbles seem about to form. The picture of his children asleep is invested with a kind of holiness, always.

Already Theodore has the look of manhood upon him. Milène still wears the frowning expression of an infant in her bed. Soulima is the one he worries about most. Igor sees himself in the boy. The same shaped face, the same eyes and nose. It is himself he is looking at, thirty years younger, the combination jiggled.

Igor had loathed his father, who was cold and unloving toward him as a child. He always promised himself that, as a parent, he would be far more affectionate to any children of his own. But when it comes to it, he discovers his instinct is also to withdraw. He follows the model responses of his own papa in pushing the children off. Emotionally his reflex is to keep them at a distance. While he was proud and delighted at each of their births, he resents the perpetual demands they make upon his time. He finds the domestic music they generate too competitive with his own.

Leaning over them now, though, and regarding their sleep-ing faces, he experiences the sorrow of imminent loss. He puts his fingers to his lips and kisses them in turn. They stir minutely. He mouths the words "good night" just loud enough to make Ludmilla respond blindly in her sleep. The star of her hand tightens, then slowly unfolds again. He notices they all sleep with the light off. As a boy, he remembers he could never sleep in the dark. They're so very brave, he thinks.

The next morning, after much weeping, the children stand prepared to leave with Catherine at the door. Coco is there, too. Dmitri, having bidden his farewells, has gone out hunt-ing in the woods. Coco offers Catherine her hand. Slow to obey the impulse, Catherine's hand moves involuntarily to meet it. For one absurd moment, she even feels privileged, obscurely grateful. Then a surge of anger rises, opening its wings inside her head. As Coco makes to kiss her, she turns, averting her hot cheek.

Soulima asks, "Why is Papa staying?"

"I've explained already," Catherine says.

Ludmilla complains, "But I still don't understand why we're going."

Joseph and Marie exchange a glance.

These late, awkward, tactlessly candid questions act like stabs in Catherine's side. Lost for a response, she picks up the cat. He's been wandering in and out of the space between her feet, gently bumping and nudging her leg, brushing his fur against her exposed ankle.

Little Vassily! Igor experiences a pang of dismay at seeing

the cat. He has failed to register the fact that he, too, will be going along with the children and his wife. This detail, small but overlooked, operates like a lens through which he sees the true extent of his loss. The cat's self-sufficiency away from him is another mocking blow to the notion that he's needed. These few moments, he reflects, are perhaps the worst of his life.

Joseph's announcement that the taxi has arrived breaks the silence and robs the children of their answers.

Gravely Igor shakes his sons' hands and kisses his daughters on both cheeks. He tries to press a lifetime of affection into these gestures. But Theodore sternly refuses to meet his father's eye. Silent and aggrieved, even Soulima remains stone-faced. Igor regards them with admiration. He tries to imagine his own father acting out this scene, allowing his wife and sons to leave him. But he cannot, and his mind fills with shame.

Catherine bids him a stiff good-bye. Then, after a few hurried and guilty hugs of the children from Coco—including a prolonged embrace of Ludmilla—they are gone. The door clicks shut.

It is all so sudden. Igor looks at Coco. He feels weightless. His solemnity wars uneasily with the complex sense of relief he feels. Coco remains tight-lipped. The silence thickens around them.

"I'll let you get on with your work now," she says, turning away from the door.

Igor lingers for a moment before returning to his study. How stupid, he thinks. The one moment that should be touched with triumph, the very instant that should see them leap into each other's arms, is instead clouded by resentment and doubt. A crushing sense of guilt and waste descends upon him. Now that he has all the quiet he requires, he has nothing left to fill it with. Has he abandoned his family for this? He feels the weight return to his body, almost forcing him to the floor. He's always believed his life to be ordered by some pattern, by some obscure allegiance to form. But he can't conceive of the design behind it now. His existence seems purposeless, and for a second he feels utterly desolate. Then with equal quickness he feels buoyed up by a renewed sense of conviction that what he is doing is right. He refuses to give in. To his feeling of dread he attaches a hope that all will be well. Coco *will* come back to him, he vows. She will see through this idiot, Dmitri. She must. Something, he knows, will bring them back together. He feels it in his blood.

Virtually the first thing Catherine sees as she takes a motorized taxi down the high street in Biarritz is Chanel's shop. She pretends not to notice but winces inwardly, as if she can never escape the name. It is the children who eagerly point it out. The impression grows within her that she can never get away. Like the Lord's, her signature is everywhere.

But the new house with its stone façades and timber beams seems a sturdy defense against Coco's presence. They're safe here, Catherine thinks, at least for a while. Not even Mademoiselle Chanel can penetrate these walls.

She sends a telegram to Igor's mother, informing her of their change of address.

———

Two days after Catherine's departure, Coco grants Joseph and Marie a week's holiday. At least with Piotr around, there will be someone left to serve in the villa. And better that there is one person in charge rather than Piotr and Joseph both fighting over who is boss. An unspoken hostility has already established itself between them.

Piotr acts like a bodyguard to Dmitri, steadfastly protecting his master and tending to neglect everyone else. What's more, there is some confusion over household duties. And because Piotr can speak little French, and Joseph knows no Russian, mutually uncomprehending arguments erupt in the kitchen over exactly who is to do what and when.

Joseph and Marie are relieved when the time comes eventually to take their leave of Bel Respiro. Glad to escape for a few days from Garches and its bizarre goings-on, they head for their native village in the north.

So with Coco and Dmitri increasingly away, either horse riding or working in Paris, and everyone else gone, the house is finally silent. And Igor—except for the monosyllabic Piotr—is suddenly alone.

CHAPTER TWENTY-NINE

Igor sits at a table in the living room, his glasses pushed on top of his head. He has just received a telegram from Diaghilev. It reads, "Shopgirls will always prefer grand dukes to geniuses. Ballet off to Madrid. Come with us!" He scrunches it up and hurls it against the wall.

Diaghilev must have heard from Misia. Igor had been right: the woman was poison. His instinct is to telephone Diaghilev and set him straight. Then it occurs to him — set him straight about what? About Catherine leaving? About why he is staying on at Bel Respiro? About Dmitri? His cheeks burn with the humiliation of it all.

Coco, too, has received some news. A letter postmarked Biarritz. She opens it to see blue, thready handwriting open its veins across the page.

6 December 1920

Dear Mademoiselle Chanel,

I am writing to thank you for your generosity over recent months in having us to stay. It has been a difficult time for the family of late. We are still unused to our status as exiles, fattening the ranks of Europe's dispossessed. And you have done much to aid the children through this troublesome period. I appreciate your helping to settle and educate them in this country. It may be their home for several years to come.

I would like to thank you also for your efforts as regards my health. Without your support, I could never have afforded the doctors' fees. And an X-ray would have been out of the question. For this, I am indeed deeply grateful.

The next subject is, however, far more difficult to broach. I have kept it, as I believe is customary in polite society, until the end. It is clear to me that over the past few months you have enjoyed an unnatural closeness to my husband. This fact, as I'm sure you are aware, has caused me a great deal of pain and—I'm bound to say—has been a contributory factor in my illness. While I have every respect for you as a woman of independent means and extraordinary natural resources, I cannot pretend to admire your morals, which I find distasteful in the extreme. Thankfully, the children are not informed of the full state of your relationship with their father. I would, however, urge you to look to your conscience. I counsel you to cease, if you have not already, your liaison with Igor, and thus allow him to discharge his proper duties as both a father and a husband.

Of course, he is to blame just as much as you for this regrettable affair. Probably more so, I admit. But you seem just now to be in a position to exercise an uncommon degree of control over his feelings. If you can find it in your heart to perform one last benevolent act in addition to those for which I have already thanked you, then please give him up. It might

surprise you that I do still care for him. We have been together
many years.

   The children need their father. I am dying by half inches
and need him more than you ever could. You will appreciate,
too, that Igor requires time and tranquillity in order to
compose.

   Many thanks for your consideration in this matter. The
children—Ludmilla in particular—send their love.

Respectfully yours,
Catherine S

Coco folds the letter carefully and returns it to its envelope.
She holds it with both hands for a moment as though absorb-
ing its contents. Then, slipping it into her pocket, she stares
blankly ahead.

After a strained and bibulous lunch, during which Igor eats
little and hardly says a word, he asks to speak to Coco in private. She looks at Dmitri, who shrugs imperiously, nodding
his assent. With gruff courtesy shading into regal disregard,
he says he needs anyway to clean his gun before hunting in
the woods.

   So Coco and Igor stroll about the garden, Coco with her
arms folded over her wool coat and Igor with his hands
planted stiffly in his pockets. It is bitterly cold outside.

   "So, what is it you want to talk to me about?"

   He volunteers, "I think you're making a mistake." His
words contain a hidden plea.

"What makes you say that?"

"I think we have something together we shouldn't give up."

"What's that?"

"I don't know. It's a feeling. Call it love."

"As romantic as ever, I see."

"You know what I mean."

"I have to protect myself." Coco's voice is planed of tenderness.

"We work well together. We fit . . ."

"Igor, tell me something."

"What?"

"Would you have left Catherine?"

"She appears to have left *me*."

"Would you ever divorce her, though?"

"That's unfair. She's extremely ill at the moment, and . . ."

"I don't want to hear any more excuses. You'll never give her up, even though you don't love her." Igor begins to protest. She raises her hand to stop him. "Now, I'm prepared to believe you love me. But that simply isn't enough. I can't stand having to pussyfoot like a strumpet around my own house. I'm thirty-seven. I'm rich. I deserve better than that."

Coco begins to move away. Igor catches her arm. Unyielding, she looks back at the house with her arms stiffly folded, locking him out.

"I know I've been selfish. I've been unfair . . . Things will be different."

"I'd like to believe you, Igor. And yes, you *are* selfish."

Then, pulling herself away from his arm: "Well, so am I." Her words are flung like stones in his face. "The trouble is, you want me to subjugate my life to your work. Well, I just won't do it. I'm not like Catherine. I have my own work. I'm ambitious, too."

"If you're so ambitious, then why waste time with that imbecile Dmitri?"

"I'm not going to be drawn into a stupid argument."

"He's eleven years younger than you. He's just a boy, for God's sake! I don't understand how you can be serious about him."

"Who said I was serious? Maybe I want some fun." As an afterthought: "Is that allowed?"

His voice contracts to a whisper. With his lips barely parted, the words emerge thanks only to the elasticity of his mouth. "Can't you see he just wants your money?"

Losing patience: "He's good to me. He pays me more attention than you ever would—more than you're probably capable of. And I like that. I want to be cared for. I like someone to be silly over me. Someone for whom I don't come a poor third after his piano and his wife." Indignant, Coco stamps her foot. With a sharp movement of her hand, she wipes away the beginnings of a tear. "And you're wrong about the money."

There is a charged silence between them. In the distance, a dog barks. A huntsman's rifle sounds damply in the air. An ash tree releases in a shiver the bright spear points of purple leaves.

A new toughness informs Igor's voice. "Now Catherine

has left, the sense of challenge has diminished for you, hasn't it?"

Coco makes as if to retaliate. Then in a tone all the more cruel for being neutral, she allows, "Perhaps you're right. Maybe you *are* less of a challenge now."

He feels as though an opponent in a tug-of-war has just let go, sending him crashing backward to the ground. "You can't play with people's lives like this. You've torn a family apart . . ."

"And I suppose you had nothing to do with that, did you?"

"I'm asking you," Igor says with renewed urgency, emphasizing each word with a kind of mad clarity, "to reconsider." His skin tightens visibly; his whole frame braces. His eyes shine with a desperate demand. "Diaghilev says the ballet is off to Spain. Why don't we go with them?"

"Dmitri wants to go to Monte Carlo."

"With you?"

"Yes."

"Are you going?"

"I haven't decided yet."

"Don't you want to be with me?"

Almost imperceptibly, she shakes her head. He can't believe it is ending like this, so casually. Desperate, he seeks for the one thread he might pull to make things whole again. "What do you want? Is it marriage, children?"

She remembers his shocked response to the news that she might be pregnant. Then, with greater contempt than she intended: "You're not exactly the father I'd choose for *my* children."

It's as though a spring within him snaps. "You know the trouble with you?"

"What? Do tell!"

"You're all surface."

Coco looks at him, hurt for a moment. Then her features relax into a smile.

"You're all surface," he says again, quieter this time, but with more needling conviction.

Her smile graduates into a mischievous grin. Adopting a roguish tone, she says, "What else is there?"

At this instant, Dmitri emerges from the house. He shouts, "Coco, are you coming?"

Ready for his walk, he has his shotgun with him. He always does when he goes into the woods. The rifle is bent at an angle over his elbow. His presence in the garden communicates power. Remaining at a distance from the two of them, he casually loads the gun.

"What else *is* there?" Igor goes on urgently, ignoring him. But the moment is lost. He continues to stare at Coco. An unflattering wildness glimmers in his eyes.

Suddenly there is a disturbance in the trees. They turn to see the source of the commotion. Following an impulse, Dmitri snaps the rifle straight and levels it. His body moves as one with the gun. Raising it high, he fires into the topmost branches. Two shots go off in quick succession. Each time his arm rears fiercely. Blue puffs of smoke escape from the barrel, and a wood pigeon with a white halter in a band around its neck drops like a stone onto the lawn. Instantly a fan of birds rises darkly, banking steeply across the tops of the trees. Dmitri whistles in triumph. The spent cartridges lie hot on the ground. The flat crack of each shot still rings around the garden.

Igor looks on in disbelief. The noise reverberates in his ears. As the acrid smell of the bullets hits him, his indignation spills over. His face becomes blurry. He is beside himself with rage.

"Must you destroy everything you come into contact with?" He starts toward Dmitri, breaking into a run. Arms flailing, he launches himself, fists battering blindly, at the other man's chest.

"What are you doing?"

Dmitri staggers back. The gun is knocked from his hands. More surprised than anything else, he absorbs a flurry of ineffectual blows. Then he turns and, with instinctive efficiency, hits Igor with a single blow smack against the nose.

Startled, Igor falls to the ground. He is hurt. His glasses have been knocked askew. Tears well in his eyes behind them. A fracture spiders across one of the lenses, splintering his vision. His nose feels out of joint. Gingerly his fingertips seek the point of impact. They come away sticky and darkened with blood. He looks to Coco, his request for love diminished now to a thin need for pity.

Dmitri watches for her response. He shrugs apologetically. About to say something, he changes his mind.

"Pick them up!" she barks sharply.

She directs Dmitri toward the two discharged cartridges lying on the ground. She shakes her head, exasperated by his insensitivity, yet unmoved by Igor's mute appeal. Then she turns and walks off.

Dmitri lingers sheepishly for an instant then trails after

her. Igor sits alone on the damp grass. He can see his breath in front of him. He can feel the blood thicken under his nose. It is as if all his fears have congealed in the cold.

He removes his glasses awkwardly and examines the crack.

CHAPTER THIRTY

Catherine and the children have been gone for over a week now. Joseph and Marie are still on holiday, Piotr has been given the day off, and Coco and Dmitri are out riding—again. Igor feels abandoned in this big house.

He has just heard that his mother has been granted a visa. He ought to be pleased, but the news fills him with dread. She says in her telegram that she's heard from Catherine and needs to know whether to travel to Biarritz or Garches. From her note, he doesn't think she knows much—just that they're not together. Catherine would not have said anything about their separation. He knows her well enough to be sure of that. But what is *he* going to say? How will he explain it? He folds the message into a small square, as if with this action he might shrink his difficulties into a manageable space.

The silence bristles around him. He smarts as he looks at his mother's photograph. He can't escape feeling intensely foolish. And, like a child who has done something naughty, he is fearful of rebuke.

He knows he has miscalculated, and now ponders the cost. His thoughts wander to Catherine and how she is coping with the children alone. An image comes to him of her laughing, enjoying a joke with some friends at his expense. And it strikes him that maybe she's relishing her time away from him. Maybe it has liberated her. In thinking this, he realizes how formless for the moment his own existence is.

Painstakingly he retunes the piano. The tuning fork pings like a dead electric bulb. He adjusts each note minutely: all eighty-eight in turn. Finished, he celebrates by dragging his hands in unhurried runs across the keys. Hard brilliant sonorities flow like water over stone.

Then he plays.

He plays with an elegiac tenderness and self-lacerating calm. His fingers touch the keys and lift from them gently. He closes his eyes and reaches deep into himself. The notes rise from beneath his spaced hands. Relaxing, he allows his mind to be drawn by the emotional impulse of the music. Chords mount to an expression of ecstasy, then blend into regret.

He continues for many hours, his fingers generating their own momentum. In playing, Igor is transfigured, seeming to enter into conversation with the piano.

At lunch he doesn't feel hungry but plays straight through. He doesn't even hear Coco and Dmitri come back, giggling sillily, from their ride.

He works hard to create tensions and postponements—to slow down the symphony in the final few bars before the passionate climax. He wants the harmonies to thicken and the dissonances at the last to resolve in a perfect concord. At the close, he wants a surprising stillness: the impression of silence stained.

———

That night, Igor sits alone in his study and drinks himself into a stupor.

He drinks two bottles of wine, followed by a half dozen shots of vodka. He drinks quickly until he is almost blind. Beside him, the ashtray brims with cigarette ends. Smoke leaks from between his teeth. He senses an emptiness enlarge within him. He pours in the alcohol to plug a gaping hole.

When he can no longer see well enough to light another cigarette, and when the vodka bottle shakes in a kind of prism before his eyes, Igor staggers up from his chair. Stumbling across the room, he knocks the metronome clatteringly off the top of the piano. The noise makes the shape of an explosion inside his mind. Clumsily he makes his way to the door. Beneath him the carpet takes on an elastic life of its own. As he leaves, he flicks off all the lights. Noticing a glow still behind him, he realizes he's forgotten one of them. But he can't be bothered with that now.

Slowly, on all fours, he negotiates his way upstairs.

It is two o'clock in the morning. His face is ash gray and his spectacles askew. The fracture in the lens from his spat with Dmitri merges into the generalized blur of his vision. A fine sweat appears on his forehead and spreads itself across his chest.

Coco and Dmitri, having retired to their shared bed much earlier, wake as they hear him scrabbling up the stairs. By the time they are conscious, though, he has reached his room and closed the door behind him.

Violently Igor rips open his shirt, and the buttons fly

everywhere. He kicks off his shoes in drunken frustration and falls crosswise upon the bed. He can feel his heart pound loudly. He's breathing quickly now. From above, the light shoots splinters into his eyes. Then abruptly he feels something rise within him. Possessing just enough presence of mind, he rushes to the bathroom. Some dim civilizing impulse prompts him to place his head over the toilet bowl.

Unpreventably he feels his stomach churn. A gorge of nausea ripples hotly up his throat. His eyes fill with tears. A burning rush of vomit breaks in straggly beards from his mouth. Bits splash from the toilet bowl back onto his clothes.

Gasping, he stands to see himself through tear-thickened lashes in the mirror. Though he feels hot, his face looks bluish gray. A numbness spreads to his hands and makes his fingertips tingle. He runs the tap until the water is freezing cold. Taking deep breaths, he cups the water in his hands and splashes his face. For a moment his palms rest like a mask against his skin. Then he drinks, squeezing the water with his cheeks around his rank and stinking palate. His teeth throb, the water is so cold.

Looking down, he sees a scaly mess move in the shallows of the toilet bowl, rising and falling, rising and falling like the body of a dead fish. The smell appalls him. Ribbons of sick harden around the enamel. A few slivers remain on the wall and on his clothes.

Aside from flushing, there is little he can do. He makes a mental note to clean up in the morning. The electric light in the bathroom is harsh and hurts his eyes. He feels the vomit still lingering in his throat and in his nose. He returns to the bedroom. Without undressing, he collapses onto the bed.

———

In her sleeplessness, Coco hears Igor's snores erupt unevenly through the night. She rises early and opens wide the windows in his study. It stinks of drink and cigarettes. Lifting the ashtray wincingly with her fingertips, she carries it at arm's length to the bin.

Midmorning, she decides to check that Igor is all right.

He stirs a little, his eyes opening slowly as she enters the room.

"Come on," she says.

She opens the curtains and he shrinks from the light.

"I feel sick again." With drunken clumsiness, he scrambles to his feet. Then he runs to the bathroom, where he vomits two or three times. Coco's reproachful tone is superseded by reassuring noises. She wipes his mouth with a damp washcloth. Soothingly she strokes the top of his head. Then, telling him to undress, she runs a hot bath. He hesitates, but sees she means business. Shyly he removes his clothes. Stepping in, his limbs appear warped in the water. She washes him like a child as he sprawls awkwardly in the tub.

"I'm sorry," he manages. "I feel ashamed." Like an instrument thrown out of tune by humidity, his voice has risen a semitone.

"That's all right."

"I've missed my morning's work."

"I think you have."

She bathes his face and squeezes a sponge over his head. The water trickles healingly across his scalp and down his cheeks.

"You're very kind," he says. "Honestly."

She smooths the lines of his eyebrows. "How are you feeling now?"

"A little better."

But he feels terrible. He hates her seeing him like this. It's humiliating. Not for the first time, he feels unworthy. Climbing out, he ties a towel chastely around his waist. Dried, he goes over to Coco. Affectionately they embrace. Surrendering to a childish impulse, their foreheads touch together. Their fingers intertwine. Still damp from the bath, he feels his hands adhere to hers.

He says, "You have every right to hate me."

"I could never hate you."

She is glad, she finds, to be with him at this moment. They indulge each other with the tenderness of lovers reconciled to loss.

"You know something?" he says. "I never told you. You smell marvelous."

They squeeze hands, then slowly allow their fingers to slide apart and let go.

"Don't think I regret it. Any of it," he says.

Gratefully Igor lies back upon the bed. Coco waves goodbye with her fingers. She blows him a kiss before closing the door.

CHAPTER THIRTY-ONE

Baton in hand, Igor rises to the podium to rehearse a revival of *The Rite of Spring*. A handkerchief billows from his jacket pocket. A mustache fills his upper lip. His glasses have no arms, but stick fast to his face thanks to the adhesive pressure of nose pads.

He readies the orchestra. His eyes narrow and his mouth opens slightly. Then, counting with his left hand and beseeching with his right, he calls the music into being. Six desolate notes float from the bassoon. As though haunted, the other woodwinds stir. The first violins scratch in answer; the flutes twitter nervously. There's a blurt from the second horns, followed by abrupt ejaculations from the brass and strings.

Igor's fingers stiffen to signal a quickening rhythm, his hands filleting the air. Then they relax to command more tranquil harmonies. Picking out individual instruments, he achieves an accent here, a softness there. The way he seeks out the musicians with a look, and the way the players meet his eye, generates a sly competition for his attention. He is keen to exploit this rare attentiveness, while all the time seeking to weave the fragments into a whole.

Suddenly a frown stretches tight across his brow. Something is missing. Lowering his baton, he taps exasperatedly on the lectern and calls the orchestra to a halt. He turns to the timpanist, who smiles benignly from beneath the nest of his fair hair. He thunders, "The passage is supposed to be *fortissimo!*"

Solemnly he walks from the podium to the piano. The hall in which they rehearse is underheated and his steps ring loudly in the cold air. Choosing to stand, he plays a few bars in vigorous illustration. "You hear?"

Mortified, and with the beaters still in his hands, the man blushes.

Having regained the podium, Igor picks up the music a few bars before the offending passage. He nods with approval as the timpanist responds to the baton's emphatic strokes.

Then he closes his eyes and listens. No longer needing to consult the score, he conducts blindly, knowing the music by heart. He feels its stabs and gentlenesses, sees the colors the notes make in his mind. A scent of resin rises sharply from the strings. He hears the familiar E flat and F flat major chords slide against one another.

As he continues, the music conjures images of its revision. He pictures himself at the piano in Bel Respiro with his ink pens and manuscripts propped above the keys. Summoned, too, are the sunlight and birdsong flooding his study. And then, unbidden, comes the memory of Coco herself, her features tricked into being by the rhythms. Her wide mouth, her short dark hair and thick articulate eyebrows, her hands answering the accents of the piano. Her kisses. The way her eyes would darken when he entered her, and how she moved when they made love.

The vision pierces him.

He's shocked to discover how much the music moves him. Until now he's always seen music as an absolute, pure and authentic: an essence that represents nothing but itself. Having resisted the expressive quality of his work for so long, he finds himself overwhelmed with the images and the memories it evokes. The back of his throat aches. His legs are trembling. Hearing it now, he's puzzled by the impact the music has on him. And yet there's nothing sentimental about the experience, nothing fuzzy or obscure. The recollections are sharp and exact, and the sense of loss all the more poignant for it. He feels the sadness hang upon his heart like a weight.

The principal violinist is alone in witnessing it. Closest to Igor and keenest to catch his look, he sees a tear well in the conductor's eye.

Igor feels it brimming, forming a lens that focuses all the aches and longings, all the tendernesses and caresses of his time with Coco, distilling for an instant the months he spent in Garches. Then the tear, already distended, its droplet tensely stretched, breaks—and with it the memory of their relationship shatters into a thousand fragments. Unmendable. Abruptly the music bursts upon his consciousness. The percussion thuds, the strings tighten, and the brass arrives in orgiastic crashes. Great swerves of sound.

And as it breaks, the tear slips from his eye, quickening down the plane of his cheek, slowing in the channel at the side of his broad nose. It warps finally around his mouth where, drawn into its dark space, it melts upon his tongue.

CHAPTER THIRTY-TWO

On the last day of her life, a Sunday, Coco returned from a drive.

Dismissing her chauffeur, she pushed her way through the revolving doors of the Ritz Hotel in Paris. Still disturbed by what she had seen, she felt exhausted. Her body felt so heavy, every step she took seemed about to pull her down.

That morning, as announced in the newspapers, a cull of pigeons had taken place. Everywhere she looked, the boulevards were strewn with their bodies, the streets were thick with the litter of dead birds.

Shocked by the sight of this slaughter, Coco had been startled, too, by the sudden silence that obtained. Aside from the occasional hum of morning traffic there was, she noticed, no undersong to the city anymore. Its melody, a kind of liquefied cooing furnished by the birds, had disappeared. Now everything suddenly seemed so still. Mist clung to the trees, making ghosts of them. The city seemed bleached of color. An odor of decay rose to Coco's nostrils and almost made her faint.

Back inside her permanent suite at the Ritz, she rested in her single bed. She did not have to go to work again until the following morning. Around her, the walls were white, the vases dense with flowers, and the shelves filled with leather-bound books. But inside her a sense of emptiness swelled.

Lying there, she heard the church bells chime. The sound transported her for a moment back to her schooldays at the convent in Aubazine. She remembered prayers being whispered in the church by the altar, and candles glimmering over rows of dried flowers. And through the intervening years arose a penetrating whiff of incense lifting in clouds above the Madonna.

Next to her, she saw the triple icon Igor had given her as a gift after leaving Garches some fifty years before. She wondered, Was it really so long ago?

She smiled, reflecting how, out of the dense weave of the century, they had managed to snag in the developing threads of each other's lives. In her memory, their love affair made a vivid pattern, a small but perfect dance. They were each in their late thirties then. In retrospect, it occurred to her how young they both had seemed. Now she felt so decrepit, so old and alone. She pondered what might have been had they stayed together; how differently for each of them things might have turned out. She still had, in storage somewhere, his mechanical piano. He had never returned to pick it up.

Memories of the last half century mixed with the impression of the room's whiteness, making the space within her seem infinitely wide. Slowly, as the sound of the bells faded, and the sense of her own tiredness grew, she drifted off to sleep.

An hour later, she awoke abruptly. A bubble entered her stomach. Pain crowded her chest.

She screamed to her maid, Céline: "Open the window! I can't breathe! I can't breathe!" The noise seemed torn from her.

Seeing the icon on her bedside table, an impulse seized her. She crossed herself. A series of images flashed across her eye: that first night at the Théâtre des Champs-Élysées; the bunch of jonquils he brought her at the zoo; the nacreous button she sewed back on his shirt; the night of the storm when she fell into his arms; her hands trailing noiselessly across the keys of the piano; the sunlit walks they both took in the woods; the dancing on the tables at Le Boeuf sur le Toit; and the pistachio-colored parrot that drove them crazy squawking her name.

The images condensed with hallucinatory clarity. She thought she heard a distant music: the spasms of a piano, a shadowy harmony. She caught and followed the song along the communicating rooms of her senses. And in the phantasmagoria of sudden memory she recalled how he looked as he leaned to kiss her, remembered sharply his dark eyes.

The pain spread in bands across her chest, arrowing down her arms.

She heard Céline utter something reassuring and saw her reach for a syringe. Her head lifted effortfully from the pillow. Her body arched upward, then fell back heavily. She felt something tighten around her. The scent of lilies touched her nose. A single tear filled her eye, tense with iridescence.

Then everything went blank.

An ocean away, Igor was getting out of bed in New York. He experienced a pain, as if a rib of his had cried out. A dull throb lingered as he rose to his feet. He stretched his arms to take away the ache. Then, dressing, he unwrapped a new shirt from a crinkly cellophane packet. He felt a tiny thrill of static exercise the hairs on the back of his hands. Teasing out layers of tissue paper, he detached a blanched cardboard support and a clear plastic halter from inside the collar. He released pins from the shoulders and the back. The sleeves were pleached like a cinema curtain. One square pocket framed the left breast. Then, undoing two or three buttons at the throat, he pulled the shirt on over his head. After a moment of half panic in which he felt he was being smothered, his head emerged through the neck of the shirt. Whitely he raised his arms as though about to fly.

Back in Paris, the vacuum cleaner scythed in giant sweeps across the foyer. The revolving door of the hotel spun clockwise on its axis. Brushes at the top and bottom shirred against the floor and ceiling, keeping the cold air out.

A BRIEF CHRONOLOGY

1882   17 June. Birth of Igor Stravinsky in Oranienbaum near St. Petersburg, where his father is a leading singer in the Imperial Opera House. The family lives on the fringes of court society.

1883   19 August. Birth of Gabrielle Chanel at a hospice in Saumur. Her parents are unmarried. Her father, an itinerant peddler, is away at the time of her birth.

1895   Chanel's mother dies. With her sister, Gabrielle is taken by her father to an orphanage in Aubazine run by nuns.

1900   Igor becomes a law student at the University of St. Petersburg.

Gabrielle is admitted to a religious institution in Moulins. The convent is both a fee-paying school for young ladies and a free school for impoverished and needy young women. Gabrielle makes occasional visits to Varennes-sur-Allier where, under her aunt's tutelage, she learns how to sew and fashion pleats.

1903   Igor becomes a pupil of Rimsky-Korsakov.

Gabrielle distinguishes herself as a seamstress and, after taking a room independently, begins to keep the company of lieutenants in the Tenth Light Horse Brigade, among whom she enjoys her first lovers.

1904   Gabrielle makes her debut as a *poseuse* (one of a number of young women enlivening the stage behind the main acts) at La Rotonde. She gains the nickname "Coco" from two songs: "Ko Ko Ri Ko" and "Qui qu'a vu Coco dans l'Trocadéro?" The sobriquet sticks.

1905   Igor graduates successfully with a law degree.

Coco leaves for a season as a singer in Vichy. She begins to design and make her own hats and gowns. After failing auditions with her "voice like a crow," she is employed as a water giver at the municipal baths. In the winter, she returns to Moulins.

1906   Forbidden by a czarist decree to marry his first cousin, Catherine Nossenko, Igor finds a priest in a remote village outside St. Petersburg to perform the ceremony. No member of either family is present. Rimsky-Korsakov agrees to act as a witness. The couple set up home in Ustilug in southern Russia.

Coco's friend and sometime lover, Étienne Balsan, inherits money and purchases an estate at Royallieu, where he breeds racing horses. Coco goes with him as an "apprentice."

1907   Igor's *Symphony in E Flat* is performed by the court orchestra in St. Petersburg. His first son, Theodore, is born.

1907–8 Coco lazes around, taking advantage of château life. She impresses all as a horsewoman and fraternizes with stars of the turf. She makes occasional sorties to Paris.

1908   Coco meets Arthur Capel ("Boy"). Bored with leisure and equestrian life, she begins to make hats for friends.

The Stravinskys' first daughter, Ludmilla, is born.

1909   Set up by Étienne in an apartment in Paris, Coco begins business as a milliner and becomes an immediate success.

1910   Premiere of Stravinsky's *Firebird*—his first collaboration with Diaghilev's Ballets Russes. Igor sets two of Verlaine's poems, "La Lune Blanche" and "Un Grand Sommeil Noir," to music. A second son, Soulima, is born.

Coco begins an affair with Boy and moves premises to rue Cambon, number 21, where she is licensed as a milliner.

1911   Igor completes *Petrushka*. A critic describes the score as "Russian vodka with French perfumes." He meets Debussy and Ravel and dedicates his next piece, *King of the Stars*, to Debussy, who comments that it might receive performances on Aldebaran but "not on our modest Earth!"

1912   Coco makes hats for leading theater productions and encounters a wide circle of artists.

1913   *The Rite of Spring* is conducted by Pierre Monteux at the Théâtre des Champs-Élysées in Paris on 29 May. The music, together with Nijinsky's choreography for the Ballets Russes, causes a riot. Coco attends the opening performance. She opens her first shop in Deauville. On its white awning, her name is stenciled in black.

1914   Igor's *Nightingale* is premiered. Exempted from military service, he seeks refuge from the war, in Lausanne, Switzerland. Birth of his last child, Milène.

        Baroness Rothschild patronizes Chanel's shop. Coco enjoys her first success as a dress designer.

1915   Aristocratic ladies fleeing an advancing German army repair to Deauville and to Chanel's to restock their lost wardrobes. Chanel turns out nurses' uniforms for those who volunteer help in hospitals and makes chaste bathing costumes for highborn ladies. She opens a shop in Biarritz across from the casino. Her total workforce now numbers sixty.

1916   Coco gains complete financial independence. With most male designers co-opted into the war effort, she is left clear to mop up the fashion market. Her workforce expands rapidly to three hundred.

1917   Following the Revolution, Igor is forced into permanent exile from Russia.

1918   Igor's *Soldier's Tale* is premiered in Lausanne.

1919   Boy dies in an automobile accident. Heartbroken, Coco has
her bedroom decorated all in black, including black curtains
and bedsheets. She goes to Venice with her friend Misia Sert
to recover. There she meets Diaghilev.

Igor's *Five Easy Pieces* is performed in Lausanne.

1920   Igor rearranges the music of Pergolesi for his ballet *Pulcinella*
and finishes his *Symphonies of Wind Instruments*. He also revises *The Rite of Spring*.

Coco moves from number 21 to number 31 rue Cambon, registering for the first time as a couturiere. Diaghilev—whose
name W. H. Auden will use as a slant rhyme for "love"—
introduces her to Stravinsky. Igor is invited to stay, along with
his family, at her newly purchased villa in Garches. The two
become lovers. Coco meets Grand Duke Dmitri, with whom
she later has an affair. In the same year, Chanel No. 5 is born.

1921   Following the death of her maid, Marie, from Spanish flu,
Coco sells the villa in Garches and takes an apartment in the
Faubourg. A piano is the first piece of furniture installed. Stravinsky and Diaghilev are among those who regularly visit and
play. Chanel meets Picasso and the poet Pierre Reverdy, whom
she takes as a lover. No. 5 is launched commercially.

Igor composes *The Five Fingers* and enjoys a successful revival
of *The Rite of Spring*, sponsored by Coco Chanel. He meets
Vera Sudeikina, who will eventually become his second wife.

1922   Igor divides his time between the family home and Vera's.
Thanks to Catherine's tact, his mother—who is reunited with
the family in Biarritz—remains oblivious of her son's affair, as
she will until her death seventeen years later.

Coco designs costumes for Cocteau's *Antigone*, so beginning a
long professional association.

1923   Igor's *Les Noces* (*The Village Wedding*) is completed.

1925   Igor comes to prominence as a virtuoso pianist and undertakes his first tour of the United States.

The year of the little black dress. Its funereal chic scandalizes and captivates Parisian society. Like the Model T Ford, it will become a design icon. Reverdy leaves Paris. Coco meets Winston Churchill and is courted by his best friend, the Duke of Westminster. The affair lasts for five years, and there is much speculation in the British press about marriage. During this time she tries desperately, but unsuccessfully, to have a child.

1926   Coco designs the costumes for Cocteau's *Orphée*. She begins a fashion for wearing mismatched earrings, sporting a black pearl in one ear and a white pearl in the other.

1927   Igor collaborates with Cocteau on a production of *Oedipe Roi*. Coco designs and makes the costumes. Struggling to keep up with demand, she grants sole right to manufacture and sell Chanel No. 5 to the Wertheimer brothers. Over the years, she is to have many battles with the family, who regularly block her attempts to launch or promote new scents.

1928   Igor writes the music for George Balanchine's *Apollon Musagète*, calling it a "white" ballet—a ballet based, in other words, entirely upon abstract choreography, devoid of any narrative or expressive interest, and performed in monochrome. Again, Coco provides the costumes.

1929   Both Igor and Coco visit Diaghilev on his deathbed. Coco organizes and pays for his funeral and burial on the mortuary island of San Michele near Venice.

1930   Igor composes *The Symphony of Psalms*.

The Duke of Westminster, tired of Coco devoting so much time to *couture* in Paris, finally elects to marry a fellow aristocrat (Miss Loelia Ponsonby). Coco's reaction is typically combative: "There have been several duchesses of Westminster. There is only one Gabrielle Chanel!"

1931   Coco is inveigled to Hollywood by Samuel Goldwyn and con-
       tracted, for one million dollars, to costume the stars exclu-
       sively, both on-screen and off. She goes with Misia, and the
       studio supplies a special train from New York decked out in
       white. Though she is fêted like royalty, and supposed to visit
       twice a year, her stay is brief and she never returns. She is
       suspicious of Hollywood, which she sees as controlled by Jews.
       She designs costumes for three films only, including *Tonight
       or Never* with Gloria Swanson.

1932   Coco has a liaison with designer and cartoonist Paul Iribar-
       negaray ("Paul Iribe"). She sponsors the ultranationalist and
       anti-Semitic newspaper *Le Témoin*, for which he is an illustra-
       tor. She allows her face to be used in drawings to represent the
       French republic against the threat of "aliens." The Fascists, it
       is claimed, learn from Chanel the power of the color black.
       The same year, Coco hosts a private exhibition of diamonds
       designed by herself—an apparent volte-face for a woman who,
       until now, has done much to democratize costume jewelry and
       ennoble fake gems.

1934   Coco moves to the Paris Ritz and leaves the Faubourg for La
       Pausa. As a result, Joseph, her butler, is dismissed. The two part
       on bad terms. He has worked for her loyally for seventeen years.
       Despite many lucrative offers from newspapers and biographers,
       he reveals nothing of the secrets of Chanel's household.

       Igor finishes *Persephone*. He becomes a French citizen.

1935   Igor performs, with his son Soulima, *Concerto for Two Solo
       Pianos* in Paris. After a second U.S. tour, he moves to Biarritz.

       Coco grieves after the sudden death of her lover Paul Iribe.

1936   The Chanel staff strike following Coco's refusal to implement
       a government directive reducing the working week to forty
       hours. She is refused entry to her own shop.

1937   Igor attends the opening of the Athénée in Paris. He seats him-
       self next to Coco in the audience. *Card Game* is premiered in

New York. He is invited to Hollywood as a guest of Charles Chaplin, himself an accomplished composer.

1938   Igor's daughter Ludmilla dies of tuberculosis. She had been working for Chanel.

Coco, in response to the constant strikes that have beset her shops, announces that Chanel is closing down.

1939   Following the death first of his wife and then his mother, and with Europe on the brink of war, Igor emigrates to the United States and sets up home in Beverly Hills, California. Arnold Schoenberg, Igor's chief rival, lives a ten-minute walk away. The two never meet. Igor does, though, meet Walt Disney, who, for a handsome fee, appropriates *The Rite* for his film *Fantasia*.

Coco designs the costumes for two French films, *The Marseillaise* and *La Règle du Jeu*.

1940   With Catherine now dead, Igor is free to marry his mistress of twenty years, Vera Sudeikina.

1941   Coco remains in Paris during the war. She takes a German lover, a high-ranking Nazi officer, von Dinklage, or "Spatz," who had terminated his first marriage some years earlier upon discovering that his wife was partly Jewish. Unusual for a French citizen, Coco is allowed to keep her suite at the Ritz. She attempts, unsuccessfully, to regain control of her perfume business from the Wertheimer brothers, citing Nazi laws that forbid Jews to control the manufacture or sale of goods.

While loathing the Nazis, Igor nevertheless flatters and courts Mussolini. When the Nazi press describes him as Jewish, Stravinsky is quick to deny it. The best part of his European income comes from Germany.

1942   Igor composes *Circus Polka* for a parade of elephants at the Ringling Bros. and Barnum & Bailey Circus. The elephants find the piece rhythmically difficult.

1943   Coco hatches a bizarre plan, dubbed "Operation Modellhut," for a peace settlement between England and Germany. She tries to contact Churchill and visits Berlin, where she conducts secret talks with senior Nazi officials, including Schellenberg.

1945   As the war ends and Hemingway downstairs "liberates" the Ritz with members of the Resistance, ordering seventy-three martinis in the bar, upstairs Coco is arrested upon suspicion of collaborating with the Fascists. The Duke of Westminster—and possibly even Churchill himself—intervenes. She is quickly released and leads the life of an émigrée, mostly in Lausanne, Switzerland, where her neighbor in time will be Charles Chaplin, on the run from Communist witch hunts.

Stravinsky becomes an American citizen. At his naturalization ceremony his chosen witness, the film star Edward G. Robinson, is discovered to have been an illegal immigrant for over forty years. With his *Ebony Concerto*, Igor attempts to mix the strategies of classical music and jazz.

1948   Igor meets Robert Craft, who will become his musical champion, chronicler, and confidant for the remainder of his life.

1949   Coco and Igor meet for lunch at Maria's in New York.

1950   Misia Sert dies. Chanel washes and perfumes her body, dressing her in white and festooning her bed with white flowers. She attends the funeral dressed in white, as she did for Diaghilev.

1951   First performance of Igor's opera *The Rake's Progress*, with libretto by W. H. Auden.

1953   Igor is a convert to the twelve-tone chromatic or serial system of composition, long championed by his recently deceased rival, Arnold Schoenberg.

After eight years of exile, and aged seventy, Coco decides to return to Paris and throw herself back into her work.

1954   5 February. Coco launches her fashion comeback in Paris. After an initially cool reception, she dominates the fashion scene until her death.

1955   Coco's aunt and friend Adrienne dies.

1957   Igor's *Agon* is first performed: another "white" ballet, for twelve dancers.

1961   Coco designs the costumes for Alain Resnais's *Last Year at Marienbad*.

1962   Igor visits Russia at the invitation of Soviet authorities. He composes *The Flood* for CBS television. He is a guest of John F. Kennedy at the White House.

1963   The assassination of JFK in Dallas. Next to the president, Jackie is wearing a pink wool Chanel suit, which is spattered with blood.

1964   Igor composes his *Elegy for JFK*.

1969   *Coco*, a musical version of Chanel's life, appears on Broadway with libretto by Alan Jay Lerner, music by André Previn, and costumes by Cecil Beaton. The septuagenarian Katharine Hepburn is engaged to play Chanel. Coco, in suggesting "Hepburn" for the role, had meant the much younger Audrey. Instead of covering, as promised, the 1920s and 1930s, the musical fashions a saccharine version of a seventy-year-old's comeback. Pandering to American audiences, the scenario suggests erroneously that it was an American designer who helped her make the crucial decision to return to work. With a budget of nine hundred thousand dollars and a mirrored set, the show is the most expensive in Broadway history. Coco hates it. The reviews are lukewarm. Plans for a film by Paramount are shelved.

       Largely for medical reasons, Igor moves to New York.

1970   Chanel No. 19 is launched, the number reflecting the date of Coco's birth.

1971   Coco dies in her bedroom at the Ritz on Sunday, 10 January. On her bedside table is an icon given to her by Igor in 1925. At her funeral service in the Madeleine, the church is filled with her favorite white lilies. She is buried in the main cemetery in Lausanne, Switzerland. On her headstone are five marmoreal lions.

       Igor dies on 6 April in New York at the age of eighty-eight— one year for every key on the piano. His funeral procession in black gondolas along the Venetian canals is accorded the same pomp and ceremony usually reserved for a head of state. He is buried on the mortuary island of San Michele, Venice, close by the grave of Diaghilev, who was laid to rest there by Coco forty-two years before.

1984   A new perfume, Coco, is launched.

1989   Karl Lagerfeld, the new Chanel fashion impresario, launches a new collection for the 1990s at the Théâtre des Champs-Élysées. The pageant opens to the music of Stravinsky's *Rite of Spring*.

ACKNOWLEDGMENTS

I would very much like to thank Susan Shaw, Charlotte Rawlinson, and Chris Fletcher for their many helpful suggestions. Heartfelt gratitude to my agents Caroline Davidson and Kathy Anderson, and to Sarah McGrath and Sarah Stein at Riverhead, for their exemplary professionalism and kindness. And thanks above all to my wife, Ruth, for her generosity and unfailing support.

Chief among the books I consulted on Chanel were Edmonde Charles-Roux's *Coco Chanel*; Axel Madsen's *Coco Chanel: A Biography*; Frances Kennett's *Coco: The Life and Loves of Gabrielle Chanel*; Amy de la Haye and Shelley Tobin's *Chanel: The Couturiere at Work*; and Janet Wallach's *Chanel: Her Style and Her Life*. On Stravinsky, biographies by Stephen Walsh and Michael Oliver proved especially useful, as did the collaborative volumes written with Stravinsky and edited by Robert Craft, most notably *Conversations with Stravinsky*; *Expositions and Developments*; and *Memories and Commentaries*.